ELIXIR PROJECT

Also by Kary Oberbrunner

Day Job to Dream Job
Your Secret Name
The Deeper Path
The Fine Line
Called
The Journey Towards Relevance

ELIXIR
PROJECT

KARY OBERBRUNNER

Copyright © 2016 by Kary Oberbrunner.
All rights reserved.
Printed in the United States of America

Published by Author Academy Elite
P.O. Box 43, Powell, OH 43065
www.AuthorAcademyElite.com

Library of Congress Cataloging-in-Publication Data
is available upon request.

Softcover: ISBN 978-1-943526-15-4
Hardcover: ISBN 978-1-943526-17-8

Also available in hardcover, softcover, e-book, and audiobook.

To Author Academy Elite and the Igniting Souls Tribe
for collectively creating a better way and a better world.

To Peter Pavarini for inserting the idea of fiction
into my brain over a decade ago.
A new world opened, and for that I am indebted.

I KNOW WHY THEY DID IT—WE ALL DO NOW.

AS I LOOK BACK, IT MAKES SENSE.

BUT NONE OF US SAW IT COMING.

IF WE HAD, WE WOULD HAVE STOPPED THEM—

AT ANY COST.

CHAPTER ONE

"STRIP SEARCH 'EM," barks the senior TSA officer to his junior. Then he lowers his voice. "After last week's events, I'm not taking any chances."

The younger officer snaps up from his stool. "You heard him. You two, follow me!" he says, scowling at an attractive couple in their mid-twenties.

Both look innocent enough. What set the agents off? I'm not sure if the junior officer's abrupt tone is meant to impress his superior or intimidate those of us waiting in line. Judging by our expressions, I don't think either strategy is working well for Mr. Mall Cop.

"You can't be serious," the woman says. "I'm not going with you. And I'm *definitely* not getting naked."

Her travel companion jumps in. "We're just tech professionals on our way to meet with a private client in London. Why the search?"

They argue back and forth. Their growing resistance and escalating voices cause other officers to stop their check-in process. Pens freeze midway through verifying a long line of travelers anxious to get through security and one step closer to their anticipated destinations.

The other officers place their paperwork down and shuffle closer to the couple. Easygoing chitchat among the passengers dissipates. Like a thin metal wire stretched taut, the patience in the room is dangerously close to snapping.

"I think there's going to be a problem here," Nick whispers to me, Darren, and Chloe.

"Yeah," Chloe says. "This is starting to feel a little weird."

The senior officer towers directly over the couple in front of us. He looks crusty and weathered, like old leather left out in the afternoon sun too long. His eyes bug out slightly, but oddly they don't blink. He's close enough to smell—a musty odor, a mixture of cheap aftershave and wet dog. I read the lettering on his narrow tan name tag:

Officer McNultey

"Don't give us that 'tech professional' spiel," the irritable officer hisses. "We know exactly *who you are*. We can either discuss details here or privately back in our control room."

At the words *control room*, I catch a glimmer in his eye. Maybe even a wink?

The woman's eyebrows narrow. "I said, I'm not going anywhere with you." Her speech drips of a strength that I envy.

Her associate maintains his poise, too, but I'm near enough to see his fingers twitch nervously. I'm sure he's capable, but the officers outnumber him half a dozen to one.

I want to look at my three friends instead. Maybe they know something I don't? But that would require turning from McNultey, and I'm not sure that's a good idea.

"We have passports and papers," the young business-man says, reaching in his pocket.

"*Stop!* And keep your hands where we can see them. We know you're linked with a SWARM sleeper cell here in the States."

Time stumbles and spins as I process his accusation. *SWARM? Here? Now?* A bead of perspiration trickles slowly down McNultey's face.

"Did you say SWARM?" a deep voice growls directly behind me.

Something hard smacks my back. I turn to see a large, balding man shaking with rage. His face twists and contorts, seizure-like. Bright shades of red streak from the tops of his ears all the way down to his wide neck and the gold chain encircling it. Tufts of dark chest hair sprout out from his button-down Hawaiian shirt.

He struggles to speak, as if someone has kidnapped his tongue. *"Filthy pigs. Y-you murdered my wife!"*

He lunges forward, flailing his arms and nearly knocking me over. The close quarters in this crowded line don't offer me much space, but Darren still has the presence of mind to react quickly. His arms catch me, gripping the small of my back, wrapping around my waist, and stopping me from a nasty fall on an unforgiving floor.

Before I can gather my thoughts or my balance, another voice screams from behind us. *"Hackers from hell! You ruined my family,"* a petite soccer mom yells. "You stole my identity, our money, and our dreams!"

Several others shout, voicing their disdain. Our once organized line pushes forward, mimicking a Black Friday crowd overly amped about doorbusters waiting on the other side.

"Quit pushing," an older man with a cane yells, trying to maintain his balance.

"Let security do their job," pleads a woman to my left.

Without space to stop the force welling up behind us, bodies begin toppling forward like bowling pins smacked by a heavy ball. Anger mounts, the cane falls, and fists begin to fly, in this supercharged, unforeseen escapade.

Scrunching down as low as we can, Darren, Chloe,

Nick, and I crawl to the right, hoping to avoid getting caught in the fray.

I catch a glimpse of the large balding man. Using his weight, he knocks over several more bystanders and army-crawls toward the young businessman, who must have fallen during the commotion. The balding man sits on the chest of the alleged SWARM member and pummels his face, bouncing his skull off the tile floor with each blow.

His arms pinned under the large man's weight, the businessman's only response is a series of high-pitched squawks. This barbaric scene rivals any mixed martial arts competition.

I want to run for help. As much as I hate SWARM, he should be tried in court, not beaten to a pulp. Before I can move, a red dot appears on the balding man's back, and a second later I hear a loud crackling and clacking noise. Blue bolts of lightning dance between the two electrodes at the tip of the senior officer's gun. I watch as thousands of volts of current shoot through his body. The balding man screams and shakes and then goes stiff.

Officer McNultey bellows in a deep voice, "Freeze! Everyone!" Even the other officers stop trying to break up the fights all around them.

The order finds its mark, and silence soon replaces pandemonium. The crowd sheepishly settles down, like elementary school kids caught misbehaving on the playground.

"Get an ambulance for Gramps here," he says.

Two other officers spring into action, helping the older man to his feet. Another recovers his cane, which got knocked away during the scuffle.

"What about the guy with the bloody face...and his blond friend?" the junior officer asks. "Better get them an ambulance, too?"

"Not a chance," the older officer says, putting his gun back in its holster. His tone is emotionless.

The junior officer doesn't pick up on the cues. "Yeah, but we're not even sure they're associated with the hacktivists."

The weight of the moment closes in on my chest. It looks like McNultey is going to turn his stun gun on his junior officer next. But instead, he tightens his lips and cranes his neck at an awkward angle. "Take them anywhere other than our control room and you can kiss your job good-bye." He whips around and storms away, huffing as he marches.

Heat flushes into the junior officer's cheeks. He straightens his belt, then issues a command of his own. "You heard him. Call an ambulance for the old guy." Then his voice drops. "And take those two suspects into the control room."

"What should I do with them there?" a middle-aged

female officer whispers. My friends and I are still close enough to hear her.

"You know what to do," he mutters. "Dispose of them."

CHAPTER TWO

NONE OF US speak until we get through airport security and to our gate. From our seats, we can still see the officers, but at least they can't listen in.

Darren breaks the silence. "Did he say 'dispose of them'?"

I didn't think much of Darren until we did a group project last semester. The girls in my dorm studied him more than the exams for their gen ed courses, often commenting about his wavy ash-brown hair. He is easy on the eyes, but I would never admit it to them—or him.

Darren listens unlike anyone I've ever met. On the surface, some might chalk it up as shyness. While others bumble on about their opinions, Darren stops to ask for mine. After a couple of conversations, I discovered what's truly behind those brilliant brown eyes: sincerity.

"I know," Chloe replies. "Think he was joking?"

"Hope not," Nick says. "They have what's coming to them."

Although it was a callous comment, he does have a point. Most everybody I know has suffered at the hands of SWARM.

"Cai warned us about the potential for high alert during our trip," I point out.

"Should we still board our flight or head back to campus?" Nick asks.

He doesn't sound scared, just a little concerned. Nick isn't the type to get alarmed by officers in the airport or by opponents on the football field. He can thank his running back frame for that extra shot of confidence—muscles bulging out from all directions of his dark mahogany skin. I bet Officer McNultey wouldn't last ten seconds against him—if he didn't have his stun gun to help him.

"It *only* counts as a whole semester's worth of credits," Chloe reminds us. "Besides, don't you think we owe it to Sienna's uncle after all the strings he pulled to get us this opportunity?"

Nick, Darren, and Chloe stare at me, waiting for my response.

"Sienna?" Chloe says.

"What?" I clear my throat before continuing. "He insisted on hooking us up."

"I'd say," Nick says, nodding. "The plane tickets, hotels, and meals..."

"Don't forget the details between the registrar and the Center for Global Engagement," Darren adds. "First quantum mechanics majors spending the summer abroad in Greece. Can't beat that."

The longer we talk, the better I feel. Conversation creates distance between the incident and us. Still, I wonder about the blond woman. *Did they succeed in transporting her to their control room? If so, she might be dead by now.*

"You boys pick your perks," Chloe teases. "But I've enjoyed our smart-rings the most."

I have to agree. Our smart-rings are the coolest invention I've ever worn or seen. I can't live without mine now, but last October was a different matter. I've never enjoyed receiving gifts. I get anxious thinking about what reaction I'm supposed to have when I untie the bow. Most years I forget about my birthday until the day it arrives. But this year Uncle Cai wouldn't let me. Between those reminders, he dropped hints about an extra special gift he'd selected for my eighteenth birthday. He insisted on giving me matching ones for my friends to help us prep for our trip to Greece. Though he never listens to my pleas of going cold turkey on his gift-giving addiction, I can't help but appreciate his thoughtfulness. For as long as I can remember, Uncle Cai's been the steady presence in my life and the closest thing I have to a father—or mother, for that matter.

I glance around at the other gates. People stand relaxed, scrolling on their phones and sipping beverages. All signs of what happened only fifteen minutes ago are gone.

The junior officer still flexes his dominance, flitting about to various stations. From this distance, I can't make out what he's saying. His gestures seem overdone, like he enjoys playing the part of the main character in his own personal drama.

I scan the faces of passengers filling the gate area. That SWARM couple were going to be on our flight to London. I know Cai is probably busy this morning, but I should call him anyway. He'd want to know.

When I was a toddler, my parents were in an accident. My lone memory of our former life together is captured in a family photograph from my third birthday. Uncle Cai told me the picture had been taken days before my parents were removed from me and from this life.

Over the years, I've stared at the picture more than I care to admit. Guess I keep hoping to find the truth. Like, what really happened? The details surrounding their deaths have always felt conveniently cryptic in nature. Fifteen years later, unanswered questions still infiltrate my mind regularly.

Heaven knows I've coexisted with ambiguity for far too long. A couple of years ago, I launched my own amateur investigation about my parents' accident via the Internet. A junior in high school at the time, night after night, I followed every lead in a web of interrelated mouse clicks. But in the end, I failed to uncover an alternative besides the official pronouncement: "an unfortunate accident."

Don't get me wrong. I'm deeply indebted to Cai for adopting me. My father's kid brother wore his protector role well, given the circumstances. Inheriting a toddler overnight is a big responsibility for anyone, much less a single guy highly committed to his career.

Growing up, I viewed Cai more like an older brother than an uncle or legal guardian. Still, I can't shake the unsettling sensation I have deep in my gut. Something about my parents' accident screams *non-accidental.*

"What do you like best about the ring, Sienna?" Darren asks, interrupting my thoughts.

"Umm…the ability to talk on it," I announce, trying to look engaged in the moment. I don't want him to think I'm distracted. Chloe calls my habit daydreaming. I call it a part-time job, staying afloat in my deluge of thoughts.

"Agreed," Nick says. "That feature saved all our butts last semester. No thanks to you, Chloe." He gives Chloe a flirtatious jab with his elbow.

"The way I remember, you were the one getting distracted. Don't you know you can't watch a playoff game and ace quantum physics at the same time?"

"She's got a point," Darren says. "They say multitasking decreases your IQ—producing the same effect as being stoned."

Chloe grins at Darren. She looks stunning as usual, despite the fact that we're in an airport and barely managed to escape a brawl. She has so much to be thankful for. Nick, her boyfriend, adores her, and her mom and dad love her. In a weak moment, I could let jealousy spring up and choke out the kindness I feel toward her. Lucky for me, Chloe's loyalty melts any ill will I'm tempted to entertain.

Our friendship blossomed over the past couple of semesters. She was the first girl I met on campus, even before moving in—all thanks to the admissions office. They switched our welcome packets on accident. Feeling responsible, they gave me her phone number, and we ended up tracking each other down through text messages.

After straightening the debacle, we chatted in the campus café for the remainder of the afternoon, talking about whatever popped into our heads: class schedules, embarrassing moments from high school, and how to avoid the freshman fifteen. To our surprise, later that day admissions reassigned us as roommates—not a common gesture at our college, I'm told.

Cai had worked his magic at the admissions office. He'd waltzed into Ravenwood Hall and emerged fifteen minutes later with a spring in his step.

"Good news, ladies. Admissions owned its mistake and regrets the welcome packet mix-up. They've reassigned you as roommates *and* put you in an upperclassmen dorm."

"Wow, Mr. Lewis," Chloe remarked. "You've got some serious pull here."

"Please call me Cai," he corrected. "I'm just happy you've got each other now. Sienna could use a friend like you."

"Thanks, Uncle," I said. "You think of everything, even picking my friends." I winked. "Guess I'll keep you, roomie. That is, if you still want me?"

Nick gets up from his chair. "You guys hungry?" he asks. "I saw they had some protein bars over there."

"No thanks," I respond. "After that latte on the drive over, I'm good."

If only it were true—me feeling good? This knot in my stomach isn't going to loosen until I talk to Cai. He always knows what to say.

In the tech world, Cai became known as a phenom at a relatively young age. Selling your first start-up while still in college tends to have that effect. He turned the heads of all the major players in the industry. No need to climb the corporate ladder when you can take the elevator straight to the top. His key roles at ELIXIR and on the Senior Board of Clerics, the governing entity for the global organization, come with plenty of perks.

"Sienna, when was the last time you saw Cai?" Darren asks.

I love the way Darren says my name. I could listen to him say it over and over.

I try recalling his question, but I'm distracted again, focused more on his mouth than finding the correct answer.

"Umm…he's been pretty busy with ELIXIR stuff. I guess they're putting the finishing touches on a new project. But I think we chatted Tuesday…in prep for our trip."

"He's so lucky, striking the lottery by joining ELIXIR when he did," Nick says, still hovering since nobody else wanted any food. Guess he gave up on those protein bars.

"Yeah, I'd give my left arm to work there," Chloe says. "You know I'm counting on you getting me in there for my internship."

"Who said I could get you in?" I tease. "I'm on Cai all the time just to get my résumé in front of the right people."

"Well, don't forget about your friends when the opportunity comes."

Cai joined ELIXIR way back when it was still relatively unknown. About five years ago, it became more popular among those with a taste for technology and innovation. But with the release of their new SWARM-fighting technology and recent stamp of approval from the League of Nations, ELIXIR crashed into the mainstream—definitely claiming the spot as the cool kid on the block.

"Which is it for you, Chloe—revenge or career?" Darren asks.

"What do you mean?" she asks.

"Your motive for working at ELIXIR."

"Motive? What am I, on trial or something?" she replies with an icy edge.

"It was just a question," I say. "I don't think he meant anything by it."

She stares blankly ahead. Tears well up in her eyes and start rolling down her cheeks and off her chin. I know the source of her sorrow because, as roommates, we often confide in each other. I even know things Chloe hasn't told Nick.

"I'm sure your secret is safe with Darren and Nick," I tell Chloe, trying to make it easier for her.

"I'm sorry, guys," she says. "SWARM's a sore subject for me." No one speaks—because it doesn't feel like we're supposed to.

"You could say SWARM stole my high school best friend—Amy. Back then I didn't know how SWARM tricks girls into the human-trafficking industry. They go online and pretend to be a teenage guy. After establishing trust and chatting for a few days, they ask the girl to do something she'll regret—nothing too big, but still something embarrassing."

"That's horrible," Darren says.

"It gets worse. They record it by hacking the webcam and then use it as blackmail, threatening to send it to her parents and classmates unless she continues down the regretful path. Each day they apply more pressure—upping the ante and demanding more. After weeks of torture, guilt, and self-hatred, victims will do anything to end this toxic cyber cycle. SWARM then offers an ultimatum. If she agrees to meet in person, they'll destroy the videos. If she doesn't, then they'll go public."

"Sounds like hell," Nick says, putting his hand on her arm.

"Nobody knew Amy was stuck until she didn't return home one weekend," she says, her voice cracking. "After confiscating her computer, the authorities put together all the pieces. For all we know, SWARM is still using her in one of their trafficking rings in some dark corner of the world." Chloe wipes her tears with her hands. Nick leans in—giving her a comforting hug. "I'd do anything to take out SWARM," she says.

"Wouldn't we all," Darren mumbles under his breath.

Out of the corner of my eye, I spot the junior officer and his female colleague huddled around an electronic gadget, like a tablet or something. They both seem animated, maybe even upset.

I turn back to my friends and look down at the new text on my ring—an alert about boarding beginning in fifteen minutes.

I remember when I first opened Cai's gift, I wasn't exactly sure what it was, so I simply stared at the box instead.

"Come on, Sienna," he prodded. "You don't even know what it is—do you?"

"Well, no." I blushed. But then I went on the offensive. "It looks like a ring, but okay, Einstein. What is it?" I picked up the simple silver band and turned it over in my hands, appreciating the sleek design.

"Try it on."

I slipped the ring on my finger.

"Cortex, call Cai," he said.

His phone rang on command. "Hello, birthday girl," Cai's voice boomed through the ring with crystal clarity.

"Shut up! It's a *phone*, too?"

"More than that," Cai boasted with as much pride as a new dad showing off his baby's pictures. "Watch this. Cortex, play Sienna's favorite childhood movie."

The ring glowed softly and then more intensely. A bright flash ripped through the silver circle. Above us, recognizable images were projected onto the flat white ceiling. The surround sound in his home office sprang to life somehow integrated with the operating system.

Cai spent the rest of the afternoon educating me on

Cortex, the new smart-ring he and his ELIXIR team had developed.

The gift opened up my mind to possibilities I never knew existed. Of course, it contains all the expected features—unlimited access to all things digital, an internal projector with built-in GPS, and Internet of Things integration. IoT connects you to everyone and everything, including your bank, your mechanic, and even your doctor.

Think you might need to change a lightbulb or replace the filter in your refrigerator? Cortex does most of it for you, the knowing, the buying, and the shipping—all done by instant drone delivery.

"What's this?" I asked. "A text informing me to drink a glass of water outside?"

"Oh, that's Prompts technology," Cai replied. "Your current level of hydration is low and your cortisol is high—hence the text message. You could use some water and sunlight."

Only in its infancy stage, Prompts influences brain waves by suggesting new thought patterns. Beta testing found it extremely effective for overcoming addictions to substances such as heroin and nicotine. Parents sang its praises for aiding their children in replacing night terrors with sweet dreams.

"But isn't it a little...*dangerous*?" I asked, shifting my weight on Cai's dark brown leather sofa. I tucked both feet up under my legs to get into a comfortable position.

"Prompts? How so?" He rested his chin on his fist.

"Well...," I fumbled, trying to form an educated objection. "Thought-influencing technology sounds awfully similar to mind control. Isn't it risky?"

"Risky? Come on, Sienna. What news feed have you been scanning? Sure, we have skeptics and haters, but think of all the good it can do."

"Like what?"

"Well...in beta testing, Prompts increased academic scores, decreased anxiety, and raised our propensities for charitable giving. Plus there are privacy settings you can enable. I set yours extremely high, so you have nothing to worry about."

He sat back in his chair and folded his arms. His blue eyes searched for a smile on my face. We both knew he had me. And although Cai often proves his point, it's my job to make him work for it.

"Need more proof?"

"Prompts also decreased violence in hostile environments and helped athletes shatter records in nearly every sport. And..." Cai stretched out his next statement for emphasis. "We need any edge over SWARM we can get. They're playing for keeps, remember?"

I let silence have its place, filling the empty space between us.

"Okay, okay. You've proved your point," I said.

"Prompts might be a breakthrough, but sometimes I worry about all of you at ELIXIR. You seem so busy creating I wonder if you have time to evaluate what you're doing. There's a price for playing God, you know."

"Well, any time God wants to step in and stop SWARM he can," Cai replied. "In the meantime, we'll do our part."

"Sienna. Earth to Sienna," Chloe says, tapping my shoulder. "That's the third time I said your name. Someone's calling you."

I snap out of my daydream. Tiny orange letters encircle my ring, revealing the identity of the caller. *Why would Cai be calling me?*

"Sorry, guys. I need to take this." I excuse myself a few feet away and accept the call.

"I thought you were on assignment with ELIXIR in—" But before I even have a chance to finish, Cai interrupts me with unfamiliar urgency in his voice.

"Sienna, whatever you do, don't get on that plane to London."

CHAPTER THREE

"What's wrong, Cai?"

"No time to explain." Then he shoots off a series of directives. "Find a TV or use your ring. SWARM is in London. They did something to the royal family."

"What are you talking about? When?" A thousand other thoughts hijack my mind.

"They're dead—all of them." Then, in a somber tone, he warns, "This is the beginning, Sienna. Everything is about to change—forever."

I don't recognize this person on the other end of the line. Cai has never been one for melodrama. He's the complete opposite. Forever the eternal optimist, he downplays negativity, sensationalism, and fear-based media.

"You're scaring me, Cai." Anxiety creeps up from the pit of my stomach, making it hard to swallow. Then our call drops—and he's gone. I take the ring away from my mouth and close my eyes. Darren, Chloe, and Nick stare back at me.

"You okay, roomie?" Chloe notices the fear plastered all over my face. She reaches for my hand. I clasp it and walk forward, pulling her with me, not once taking my eyes off the adjacent wall.

We join a small group of travelers huddled around a public transparent projection screen. I gaze at shaky footage on the left side of the screen shot by a cameraman who appears to be running through a crowded street toward a river.

The right side of the screen shows video from what looks like a mobile phone. Several cars with tinted windows speed down a city street, striking people and breaking through barriers.

Chloe and I inch forward hand in hand. Nick and Darren press in behind us. A reporter speaks:

"A day that started out so perfectly will end tragically for billions across the planet. Historically, May 9 is known as Europe Day, a day dedicated to peace and unity.

"The queen's eight state limousines—two Bentleys, three Rolls-Royces, and three Daimlers—departed at eleven a.m. Eight veteran chauffeurs, each extremely loyal to the royal family, transported European dignitaries from more than two dozen countries. Supporters lined the streets, waving flags, cheering, and greeting one

another with shouts of peace in their native language.

"Around eleven thirty a.m., the lead car with the royal family suddenly accelerated. Shortly after, the other seven cars in the motorcade broke line and followed in reckless pursuit. Reaching speeds of more than ninety miles per hour, the vehicles plowed through bystanders and barriers, killing several people. The chase ended when the cars broke through a final barricade and drove straight into the River Thames.

"Calls made from the dignitaries in the vehicles are now being compiled by officials. Apparently, screams of being trapped in the cars and cries of doors and windows that wouldn't unlock pepper these voice mails.

"Witnesses say several dignitaries broke the windows, but because of high speeds, they were unable to jump out. The onboard cameras reveal chauffeurs who appear oblivious to the screaming and pleading of their passengers. Each driver looks physically present, but mentally absent—not even panicked or aware of danger.

"Rescue attempts are being made as we speak by the emergency workers behind me. As of now, no bodies have been recovered. At the same time as this tragic accident, several large European government websites were hacked. Each site went completely dark except for the word 'SWARM.'

"We're left with more questions than answers. Was SWARM's attack retaliation for London's recent support to resurrect the League of Nations?

"One thing is for sure. This current attack is by far the most devastating and perplexing. Experts wonder if we've witnessed the first hack upon the human mind. Were these chauffeurs key players in a suicide mission they knew nothing about?

"If these suspicions are confirmed, then hacktivism has crossed a new echelon of evil, one that could infect us all.

"An official at ELIXIR—the international organization dedicated to SWARM eradication—promised a formal response within the next forty-eight hours. Our correspondent believes ELIXIR may reveal some new technological advancement that will deliver a deathblow to SWARM.

"Apparently, ELIXIR officials have been testing this technology for some time. And according to its spokesperson, Ms. Tilda Tulane, the world can't wait any longer.

"This is Lori Wicker reporting on-site in London. Stay tuned for more updates, including coverage of ELIXIR's response."

A man to my right curses, and a lady to my left cries.

"This is bad," Nick says. "Really bad."

Chloe lets go of my hand. She turns to Nick, burying her head in his chest. He wraps his arms around her and holds her close.

My eyes catch Darren's. Must be nice—finding comfort in the arms of another. But relationships never come easy to me—the price you pay for losing a mother and father you can't even remember. I'm not willing to drop my guard ever again if it means the possibility of loving and losing.

Cai is the exception—probably because I was too young to know otherwise. A three-year-old orphan needs love and affection no matter who they are. Research proves it. In my freshman psychology class, I learned about a study of infant deaths on forty newborns. Despite getting all their physical needs met, over half died within the first four months. The single reason: not being touched.

"Think we should still leave the country?" I ask Darren, since Nick and Chloe seem a little preoccupied with each other.

"Well, I don't think we should stay here."

He's right. The entire airport feels like a giant tinderbox ready to explode. No wonder Cai sounded flustered. ELIXIR is probably scrambling over how to respond. Dignitaries from across Europe might be dead, including the royal family. And SWARM is probably celebrating with champagne bottles in hand.

All those lives, gone with one single hack. But if SWARM can hack our minds and not just our devices, then we're all in danger.

I want to run, but my feet feel heavy, like they're stuck in thick mud. My finger beeps again. "Sorry. Think we got disconnected," Cai says.

"I just saw the news. You okay? Was it SWARM?

What's ELIXIR going to do?" I fire off questions.

"They didn't report even half of it. Look, I can't have you board that plane." He sounds more relaxed this time, more like the Cai I know.

"I'm worried about SWARM and so I've made some arrangements for you and your friends to get out of the airport safely," Cai instructs. "In a couple minutes, a guy in a uniform is going to come get you. Go with him. He's on our side."

"Okay. We will. So I take it our summer in Greece is on hold. No connection flight to London means no—"

"Sienna, I need to run. We're making a big announcement in the next forty-eight hours."

"Sure, go," I say. "What's the name of the guy coming to get us?"

"Officer McNultey," he replies.

CHAPTER
FOUR

"Sɪᴇɴɴᴀ Lᴇᴡɪs!" a gruff voice behind us calls.

Chloe frowns. "Oh, it's you...Stun Gun himself. How can we help you today?"

"I'm the one asking the questions," he barks. "Unless you have a problem with that, Chloe?" The officer moves his right hand near the stun gun clipped to his belt.

"How do you know her name?" Nick asks.

"Nicolas Logan Elliott. Highly recruited football player from Columbus. Quantum physics major, 4.0 honors student. Want me to keep going?" McNultey says with a sparkle in his eyes.

Although taken aback, Nick isn't one to step down. "Try me."

"Favorite restaurant? Hot Wings and Things. Childhood friend? Cardale Smith. Fear of snakes and fear of failure," the senior officer says. He unloads his words the same way a soldier in a firing squad unloads bullets. But I think McNultey, unlike a soldier, enjoys inflicting pain. "I got more where that came from, Nick, but that might just embarrass you in front of your friends. Want me to talk about who you dated before Chloe? Your deceased older brother? Or the organization you contacted at age sixteen?"

I wait for a comeback from this all-American running back, but instead I hear nothing.

McNultey looks him over with a condescending smirk. "Didn't think so. Hey, next time how about you keep your mouth shut?"

Then he turns in my direction, like a predator in pursuit of his next meal. "Ah, yes, of course, Ms. Sienna. You're even more stunning in person. Me and Kiran enjoyed reviewing some footage we found on your Cortex," he says, wiping his mouth. "You know, it's amazing what these new smart-rings capture when you're not even expecting it. Next time you might want to take it off before you freshen up after your morning run."

"You're bluffing," Chloe argues. "Don't listen to him."

Darren tenses up, but I grab his wrist before he shifts his weight forward.

"Not now," I whisper under my breath. He stops and puts his foot back down. "We need you."

Darren turns his head and fixes onto my gaze. The

energy between us ignites a spark deep within my chest. But I don't give myself permission to unpack those feelings. Even if I cared for him in that way, I'm not about to let him know. In the long run, it's far less painful to keep on pretending.

"Your uncle instructed us to take you," McNultey says.

"And if we don't go?" Chloe asks with an undercurrent of defiance. "Will we miss out on our summer abroad?"

"Young lady, SWARM just murdered European dignitaries from more than two dozen countries," the officer says. "A summer abroad doesn't even matter at a time like this. How about you grow up for a second? ELIXIR is the only one with a potential answer, and Sienna's uncle is on the Senior Board. I'd shut up, if I were you, and do whatever he says."

She flushes with embarrassment.

"I'll go," I burst out, surprised by my own voice. My friends stare, their expressions convincing me they think I'm insane. I swallow hard before speaking. "I don't like the idea, either, but Cai told us to go with McNultey, and my uncle hasn't led us the wrong way yet." Nobody moves a muscle or speaks a word. And the longer they wait, the more my stomach turns.

"She's got a point," Darren says, breaking the silence. "Nobody's landing in London until they get this mess sorted out anyway." I lock onto his brown eyes and push the corners of my lips upward, acknowledging his support.

"All right," Nick responds, still looking shell-shocked from the verbal spar with the senior officer.

We all stare at Chloe. She shrugs. "Okay, fine."

"Follow me," McNultey says. Then he takes off in the direction of the security line.

"Where are we going?" Nick asks.

He halts and turns his right shoulder in our direction. Beaming back at us, he says, "To the control room, of course."

CHAPTER
FIVE

THE CONTROL ROOM IS underground. We traveled by a six-seater electric cart from the terminal and out to the tarmac. After driving into an airplane hangar, McNultey led us to an elevator, where we descended to level five. After a series of security checks, we arrived at a dimly lit hallway. On a desk a few feet behind me, I see what looks like a blond wig with a dark red streak on it.

"Still think we should have listened to Cai?" Chloe whispers to me.

Her question stings because, on the drive over, I had a similar thought. Why would Cai associate with the likes of McNultey?

"Guess we'll find out soon," I say as relaxed as possible.

"Drink this," McNultey orders. His eyebrows squish together at the top of his forehead just below his hair. Streaks of silver give away his age. He points to four vials of orange liquid on a high-top table in front of us. The clear glass cylinders rest on a simple glass tray.

"What is it?" Nick holds one vial between his right index finger and thumb. He lifts it up to the single lightbulb overhead, trying to identify the contents.

"An elixir, you might say," a high voice says from beyond the shadows down the hall. "Created by none other than ELIXIR."

"Oh, I didn't see you," Nick says, cupping his left hand above his eyes, squinting into the darkness.

"I've been overlooked my entire life." A short man surfaces from a corner. "Standing less than four feet tall has that effect, you know," he giggles, finding humor in his own comment. More humor than the comment deserved.

"Forgive me." He clears his throat. "I'm Kiran, and I've been following you all for quite some time. It's an honor to finally meet you face-to-face." With jerky movements, he extends his hand up. But rather than shaking our hands, he bows dramatically, as if he's greeting somebody important.

I glance at Chloe. His comment about following us makes me feel more anxious than I already do.

"Ready to verify them? What'd you call it...3FA?" McNultey says, interrupting Kiran's pageantry.

"Is that similar to 2FA?" Nick butts in.

"Same thing as two-factor authentication, except

we use three sources to confirm your identity," Kiran replies. "When you drink your vial, you'll already have two identities confirmed. But I'm not answering any more questions until you swallow the elixir."

Darren fidgets with his sleeve—folding it one more time, up toward his elbow. None of us knows what to do, so we don't do anything. I'm certainly not a fan of drinking anything they recommend.

"Chloe, don't you want to see your best friend from high school again?" Kiran winks. "Amy is her name, I believe?"

"How do you know her?" Chloe says, surprised.

"And you, Sienna. Wouldn't you like to know more details about a certain couple who died years ago?"

"Come on, people," the senior officer growls, tapping his foot on the hard floor. "We have to move." He places his hands on his hips, one hand near his stun gun.

For all we know, Kiran is manipulating our emotions, baiting us to drink the vial. But his cruel methods create anger and resentment, not trust and belief. As much as I want to resist his directives, I need to discover the truth.

I reach for one of the vials. Chloe follows suit.

"Ah, gentlemen, there's a reason you two may want to follow orders, too," McNultey says. "Something about your past. Hmm...?"

Reluctantly, Nick and Darren each grab a vial, too. Although I try to give Darren an encouraging smile, he looks down at the floor instead of at me.

Together, all four of us drink the orange liquid. The sugary aftertaste reminds me of summer evenings by the fire pit in the backyard. I sipped more drink boxes than I can count sitting next to Cai on those white Adirondack chairs. He told adventurous stories, and I licked gooey marshmallow that'd leaked out onto my fingers when I'd squished the chocolate and graham crackers together.

"Perfect," Kiran says, wringing his hands.

"Now for the explanation?" I ask.

Kiran reaches into a pocket inside his jacket and pulls out a clear pane of glass just a tad bigger than a smartphone.

"For the past seven months, you've each been *wearing* the first identification credential. You know it as your smart-ring. We refer to it as a luxury wearable. As for the second identification—ingestibles—you just drank it. Each vial contained tiny microchips. I'm verifying your identity and monitoring your vitals here on my tablet."

"That's only two," Darren says.

"Oh, of course, dearies, I almost forgot," Kiran admits with vigor in his voice. "Injectables." Then he raises both hands in the air and announces, "McNultey, fire at will."

Perplexed, I turn in McNultey's direction. But instead of seeing a crusty old man, I stare straight down the barrel of a pistol. I hear four loud pops, and then Kiran cheers with glee. Cotton fills my ears and the space just above my eyes. Sounds muffle and then fade. My world grows dim and then swarthy dark.

I am no more.

CHAPTER SIX

MY MIND STIRS before my eyes open. I hear muffled sounds, and I'm not sure if I'm awake or asleep—or somewhere in between. I want to lift my eyelids, but they feel frozen shut.

My head spins. I remember waking up in a similar semiconscious state sometime in my past. I strain, trying to access the memory, something about a dentist's office and wisdom teeth.

The first injection of local anesthesia didn't faze me, so he settled for a double dose instead. A few minutes later, when I still tasted the sensation of chewing broken glass, he resorted to general anesthesia.

I woke up in my bed a day later, with Uncle Cai in the adjacent room on his laptop—catching up on work for ELIXIR, I'm sure. The instant I stirred, he pushed the footrest on his recliner down and sauntered over to my bedside, trying his best to cloak any concern for my condition.

"Morning, bright eyes," he said, putting the back of his hand on my forehead.

"Morning," I moaned, using my arms to prop myself up. The toasty flannel sheets clung to my body.

"What happened?"

"Well...the dentist said he couldn't put you under, despite his best attempts and strongest medicine." Cai chuckled. "He warned me his next option was a baseball bat."

"You sure he didn't use that bat?" I said, rubbing the back of my neck.

"Evidently, you have quite an immunity to pain medication. His exact words were 'a freakish resistance.' Is there something you're not telling me?" Cai said, folding his arms across his white T-shirt.

He hadn't shaved in a day or two, but his kind eyes softened his appearance. Up until a few years ago, Cai took his impeccable health for granted. But then, at a routine physical, his doctor discovered an irregular heartbeat that scared us both.

Around that same time, his colleague at ELIXIR had been working on an advanced digital implant designed to regulate the heart. Always an early adopter, Cai volunteered to test this new technology inside his chest. Since then, he's been a poster child for perfect health.

"Morning, bright eyes," says an unfamiliar voice this time. The greeting jolts me out of my ride down memory lane, even if that road was about wisdom teeth removal.

"How about I fill in some blanks, dearie? I'm sure your journey into Neverland has you flying higher than usual."

"S-sure." I yawn. The slumber clings to the corners of my mind, trying to pull me back into the dream world.

Bright sunlight soaks into my face. I open my eyes slowly and notice dense, tinted windows. Nick is zonked out in the seat behind me—his neck cranked at an awkward angle. His body swallows up the thin black seat belt.

The mental fog lifts—but at a sluggish pace, like a steamy morning mist burned off by the rising sun. Chloe is next to me, leaning against the right window. At least her seat belt fits her better, keeping her somewhat erect.

A pang of panic sets in. *Where's Darren?* I turn and see a crumpled-up combination of plaid and denim lying facedown on the dark leather seat behind me.

Maybe the haze dulls my inhibitions or maybe with all the recent events, I just need *someone* to hold on to. My fingers extend confidently—dancing in and out of his thick brown hair.

My breathing quickens, as does my pulse. A jolt of fire travels up through my arm and into my shoulder. I'm wide awake now. My lips curl up, content to be connected to a person I've only admired from afar. And as long as he sleeps, I don't need to waste time worrying about being rejected.

But then a speck of guilt grows from somewhere deep inside. Is it right to enjoy a connection with someone who's unconscious of the experience? I push away the thought, knowing now isn't the time or place to wrestle with complicated issues. For all the incongruence I feel around me—with Cai, SWARM, and ELIXIR—the world is right, even if in this single moment.

"Hey, did you call me bright eyes?" I ask. The stranger's odd greeting took a minute to sink in. *Is he reading my thoughts or accessing past memories, or perhaps it was just a lucky guess?*

"My bad, dearie," says the voice. The stranger turns and I see what looks like a small boy gleefully rocking in the front passenger seat—Kiran, of course. "I figured using a familiar greeting would help you acclimate easier."

I snatch my hand away from Darren's head and move it near my chest. *Am I dreaming?* I press three of my fingers around my sternum, mining for broken bones from getting shot in the chest. Rather than finding fractured ribs, I locate a heart full of angst. A flood of emotions rips through me.

My uncle, my one source of stability, put me up to this. I want to believe he knows what he's doing. He's always protected me from pain. *But now he's the one allowing it.* He's either culpable or ignorant. But when has Cai been ignorant of anything? His work at ELIXIR demands meticulous precision. A civil war commences between my heart and my head. And the one logical explanation leads me to a lonely place—one without Cai. But if I don't have him, then who else do I have?

My friends and I followed Cai's prompts with unquestioning obedience. I glance down and see Cortex—my smart-ring—wrapped around my finger. *Prompts?*

Speculations spin around like the saucer ride at the annual carnival. Faster and faster. I feel my body beginning to detach.

How much of the last seven months has been the result of my own volition? And how much has arisen from the Prompts and Thought Influencing Technology pulsating into my brain through the metal band bestowed to me as a gift? Was it even a gift? Or simply a digital leash designed to monitor my friends and me?

My mind can't stop racing. I'm not quite sure how much of my life is actually *my* life. What events have been manipulated or manufactured simply because I'm part of a larger experiment? Am I some kind of lab rat, the plaything of irrational ELIXIR scientists?

Anxiety rises within me. I want to rip this ring off my finger. I want to jump out of this vehicle. I want to get back home. But right now I'm not so sure who to trust.

Right now I'm not sure of anything.

Right now I feel like the orphan I truly am.

I put my hand around the ring, intending to remove it. I don't like being monitored. But before I can, a voice interrupts.

"Congratulations, Sienna," Kiran announces, scanning his device. "Confirmed. Genetically speaking, we had to make sure it was really you."

Confirmed? A haunting thought hits me. "Unplugging" from Cortex isn't even an option. They would know if I removed it because I'm not alone anymore. And I haven't been for quite some time. For how long? Who knows? Probably Cai—if he's willing to tell the truth.

"Glad to hear it works," the driver says mockingly. "Your department requires a big enough budget to fund all your little toys, especially this new wii initiative."

I tilt my head to get a better view of the speaker and see McNultey. *Why am I not surprised?* "Did you say wii?" I can't help asking. "ELIXIR created a *gaming* system?" At this point, any facts would help me feel grounded.

Kiran snickers and spits, doubling over in his seat from my comment.

He's wound tight—so tight his gestures are simply reflexes birthed out of the weird, internal world he occupies. I have a hunch his oddities originated from sitting glued to his computer screen for twenty-plus hours a day in somebody's basement—maybe his mom's—if he even has one.

"Not a gaming system, silly," Kiran laughs. "Try an initiative to take down SWARM. Wearables, ingestibles, and injectables? Get it? Wii? You and your friends were the very first civilian beta testers."

I hear every word Kiran says, but I'm far from understanding the connection.

"You going to play her Tilda's video?" McNultey asks.

"Ahh, yes, of course," Kiran responds. "But according to my monitor, the other three will be out cold for at least another twenty minutes. Sienna's resistance levels were much higher."

McNultey accelerates the vehicle, despite the road signs cautioning us of the upcoming curves. "Well then, genius, put the stupid thing on repeat and play it again when they wake up." He tilts the rearview mirror with his right hand.

"Hey, I thought you were a TSA officer. How do you know Cai?" I still can't believe Cai would put me in harm's way, sending us with these two kidnappers. Maybe I just don't want to believe it?

"*TSA?*" he sneers. "Those officers back at the airport are part of *my* team, not the other way around. I can be whomever I need to be to get the job done—TSA, FBI, CIA. But if you're asking who pays my salary, it's ELIXIR, just like the freak next to me in the front seat."

Kiran starts the video and bobbles in his seat. He reminds me of a tiny tot standing in line at the Ferris wheel. When the video begins, he cocks his head sharply and grins. "Welcome to your new destiny, Sienna. We've been waiting for you."

As if choreographed, the intro music cuts in. A yellowish-orange ELIXIR Project logo materializes and then fades away. The speed and angles of the cinematography remind me of Cai's drones we flew occasionally during my senior year of high school.

He taught me how to hover, steer, and even engage the onboard camera. One time we flew the drone over my teacher's house. When Cai spotted old Mr. Mackenzie's backyard, he grabbed the remote and broadcasted a warning through the speakers:

"Make the senior history final exam easier or suffer wrath from above!"

I slugged him and stole back the controls, and we both cracked up at the innocent prank. Lucky for me, Mr. Mackenzie never discovered who owned the drone.

But right now I'm not laughing, and I can't push away the rage I feel for anything to do with Cai.

A female voice narrates over the breathtaking cityscapes.

"Welcome to ELIXIR. My name is Tilda. I serve as spokesperson for the Senior Board of Clerics."

Hovering in midair, the drone drops abruptly with

dizzying speed. The earth pushes up, threatening to swallow it. A second before crashing, it hovers again, this time above one particular skyscraper.

In theatrical flair, layers of dark, dystopian, electronic music rise. The camera zooms in, projecting the outline of a woman's back. Her thin arms stretch out on the railing in front of her as she watches over the city. She rotates to face the camera. Cheekbones protrude from her thin face, and her sandy-colored hair flows high above her forehead. Hints of unkind years infect the corners of her eyes.

But then I find them—or maybe they find me.

Unmistakably blue, ignited by a bottomless fire. Her gaze pierces me, unwrapping every fiber and undressing every mask. Then she speaks again, her voice a blend of seduction and mystery, dripping with hypnotic intonation:

"Please let me offer an apology and congratulations. First the apology. Although I'm unsure of the exact measures administered to bring you to ELIXIR, I'm assuming they were somewhat extreme. Understand, our current campaign against SWARM demands we adhere to the highest levels of security. We could not jeopardize our Project at this time by providing details about your relocation to you or your families. In the future, you will know the whole truth.

"And now for the congratulations. Unbeknownst to you, we've been monitoring you for quite some time. We'll share

more on this topic when you arrive. You are one of twelve clerics we have recruited from all corners of the world to assist in the overthrow of SWARM. Soon you will become household names.

"I'm sure you have questions. But rest assured, ELIXIR has the answers—and in time you will, too. Breathe deeply. I know the angst you taste. I was once recruited by ELIXIR, too. I chose to accept the call for my country, my family, and myself. Today my life is forever changed.

"I look forward to meeting you very soon. Remember, fear no one but truth."

CHAPTER
SEVEN

"How LONG TILL we get some food?" Nick says, yawning from the backseat. "I'm starving."

"That's how you feel when you go without food the entire night," Kiran says.

"Yeah, I guess getting knocked unconscious works up a significant appetite," Nick replies.

Kiran checks his tablet, then announces something about the other three being confirmed thanks to the nanotechnology from the injectable.

"I think I got Tilda's whole over-the-top video, but would either of you care to explain why you had to drug us?" Chloe asks. "Walking out the front entrance of the airport would have been a little less...traumatic."

"Couldn't," McNultey replies. "We received confirmed reports of more SWARM agents at the airport. And the board gave us strict orders about transporting all twelve clerics safely."

"And we're supposed to believe you?" Chloe asks. "I've already snapped photos of you with my ring. Who says we're not going to turn both of you in to the authorities on charges of kidnapping?"

"*Authorities*," McNultey laughs. "Did you hear that, Kiran? Young lady, you're going to find out real quickly something you'd better never forget. We are the authorities. And someday you'll look back and thank us for 'kidnapping' you. SWARM knows you twelve clerics are valuable, and that's why they're after you."

"Where are we going?" Darren says, sitting up in his seat. He moves gingerly like the rest of us.

"Don't these rolling hills look even a little familiar to you?" Kiran replies.

"Should they?" Chloe sputters back. Though she is still groggy, her sharp tongue never sleeps. "McNultey shot us in the chest, remember? We're still a little out of it."

After a few more minutes and even more twists, we turn onto Route 1318 toward our college campus. "I recognize it now," Darren says, stretching his arms above his shoulders. "Wow, you must have used some potent stuff, to mess us up like that."

"Only the best," McNultey mutters.

We turn right onto Liberty Street and head up the hilltop. It doesn't look like the same serene campus we left yesterday morning. "Who are all those people?" I ask, looking at the young men and women across the lawn, sparring with each other. Dressed in dark attire, they resemble a special ops militia in some kind of elite training.

Kiran pounces to answer. "We've commandeered the campus, and the people you see in black are ELIXIR—proxies, we call them."

Outside the campus café, I notice a black tent with the word *ELIXIR* printed on the side. I bet they're not playing cards and drinking coffee in there.

McNultey takes a right and heads down a narrow road. After a minute we close in on Radcliffe Hall with its characteristic daunting stone tower. As we pull up to the curb, I spot someone I'm not sure I want to see. Without time to prepare, I can't decide whether to hug him or hit him—or which he deserves more.

CHAPTER
EIGHT

"Thank God, you're safe," Cai says, opening the door to our vehicle. He reaches out a hand to help me out.

"Safe?" I snarl, avoiding his hand. I step out of the vehicle. "You call getting kidnapped *safe*?"

Unfazed by my comment, he raises his arms and offers a hug. I block his embrace and use all my force to push off his chest. The last thing I want to do is reciprocate affection with a caregiver who put me in harm's way. But my small frame is no match for his strong arms. He catches my wrists and draws me in close.

"Not now," he whispers through his clenched teeth. "They're watching us. Things aren't always what they seem." Then he smiles and kisses me on the cheek, switching back to the good-natured-uncle gig. "Welcome back to campus."

What does he mean? *Who's watching us?* Does he

think a couple of phrases can erase the sting of betrayal inhabiting every cell of my body?

"Got a feisty niece there, Soter," McNultey says,

"*Soter?*" Nick asks. "Who's that?"

"Cai. Who else, idiot?" McNultey taunts.

Cai cringes at McNultey's name-calling and goes on to explain further. "At ELIXIR, we each pick a new name that reflects something true about us. Because of my public role, I'm often called by both names."

"So what does *Soter* mean?" Chloe asks, adjusting her hair in the reflection of our vehicle

"Soter was the spirit of safety and deliverance from harm," I say. I am still fresh off a final exam meant to prepare us for our summer abroad. Whether I like it or not Greek mythology still dominates my short-term memory.

I try using the tinted window to straighten the collar on my shirt, but it's no use. After getting shot with an injectable and then thrown into the vehicle, I'll bet this shirt has seen its day. "But I'm not so sure that name fits you any longer, Uncle," I say, glaring at him.

Cai winces. I pause and consider the unlikely. *Maybe he's protecting me, even now?*

"College kids." McNultey shakes his head. "You'll get your new names soon enough."

"Tonight, at the Name Change ceremony," Kiran replies. "Of course, you're going to need some work before you make your grand entrance to the worldwide audience."

"Excuse me?" Chloe says. "Did you say *world?*"

"Why, yes. London is in shambles and humans have now been hacked. ELIXIR must respond with swift action or the whole planet will be thrown into chaos," Kiran explains. "Why else would we go through all this trouble—kidnapping as you call it?"

I still don't understand what Kiran is saying.

"What's ELIXIR's strategy, McNultey?" Darren asks. "Got some kind of secret weapon you've been hiding here on campus?"

"Wise guy, hey?" McNultey replies. "Of course we have a secret weapon."

"What is it? A rocket? Supercomputer? Nuclear weapon?" Nick asks.

"More powerful than all those combined," Kiran replies.

"What could be more powerful than a nuclear weapon?" Chloe asks.

"Why, that's simple, dearie—you. *You're* the secret weapon."

May 10

I'm not going to lie. It's quite a bit to take in. I feel so violated that my entire past seven months was hacked. At least I've got my journal. Where would I be without it? The one safe place where I can work out my thoughts and feelings. At least they can't hack that...whoever "they" are.

I've always found pen and paper my preferred style of processing, probably because Cai gave me my first journal for my ninth birthday. I've been filling journals ever since. But this past semester, Chloe helped me talk out some of my past reservations about trusting others. Maybe she knows the idea of being with Darren is starting to work its way into my heart, or that I need to learn to trust if I ever hope to love.

I still haven't had a chance to clear things up with Cai. And what he said was so strange. But we were around other people, so we couldn't really talk. I need to get him alone so he can come clean with whatever he needs to tell me.

Where to start? The past forty-eight hours have scrambled my plans, to say the least.

Sure, I'm bummed about the trip to Greece being canceled—who wouldn't be? All the prep we did with passports and plans, not to mention the extra class on Greek mythology.

But McNultey was right. Our summer abroad seems petty considering SWARM's attack on London. Hacking humans—seriously? What does this mean for life going forward? I sure don't know.

We're hours away from something Kiran called the "Name Change," and I hate not knowing how to prepare. At least I have Chloe, Nick, and Darren with me. Sounds like we might get our wish of working for ELIXIR somehow. More on that to come. They didn't give us any time to chat, either. The guys were escorted to their dorm rooms, and we were taken to ours.

I want to take off my ring, but what's the point? ELIXIR would know immediately, and I'd probably get in trouble.

I want to go for help, but according to McNultey, they are the authorities. So who would I tell?

Chloe's in the shower now. I'm not sure what either of us is going to wear. How are you supposed to dress when the whole world is watching? It's not the world's opinion I care about as much as Darren's.

Gotta run. More later.

—Sienna

CHAPTER NINE

STANDING IN FRONT of my mirror, I brush my hair while wearing my favorite bathrobe—a white one Chloe got me last Christmas. She swore she'd never worn a softer one and insisted I add it to my shower routine.

I've always wondered what it feels like to have a mother brush your hair. If mine ever did, I was too young to remember.

When I'm overwhelmed, I wish I could bury my head in my parents' arms, even if I am eighteen. I lack childhood memories of snuggling with them in their bed at night during a frightening storm. And today I find myself in a storm of epic proportions.

With Cortex on our fingers, microchips in our elixir, and nanotechnology coursing through our bloodstream, I guess the board trusts us enough to get ready in our rooms without someone here watching us. I bet this wii initiative gives them a digital leash long enough to ease any anxiety they might have of us running away.

I'm not completely alone, though. Chloe stands next to me, brushing her teeth in front of the sink. She wears the same bathrobe except hers is pink. Uncle Cai pulled some strings so we could leave our dorm room as is during our summer abroad. We should be touring Athens right now, not preparing for some ceremony.

"So let me get this straight, Sienna…," she says, rinsing her toothbrush and putting it back in the holder.

I sit down slowly at the foot of the bed. "Listening," I say.

"Oh, I can't do this," Chloe confesses. "My mind feels like mush, and we're supposed to meet the world in a couple hours. If it were up to me, I'd run away. But where would we go, Sienna? And why is SWARM after us? What do they want to do—hack our minds, too?"

"*Stop!*" I raise my hand. Then I soften my voice. "Chloe, you're one of the strongest women I know. And we're in this thing together. Now, just like you always do, tell me what you're thinking, roomie, one thought at a time. Besides, nobody's running anywhere. With SWARM out there, staying here on campus with ELIXIR is probably the safest place we can be."

She looks down at the duvet, tucks her hair behind her ears, and continues. "Well, based upon what the reporter said yesterday and what Tilda told us in the video today, SWARM stepped up its hacktivism these past several years…and they have no intention of slowing down their threats. ELIXIR saw this coming and took strategic steps to fight back. They developed the wii initiative, a state-of-the-art worldwide monitoring system."

Chloe relays her interpretation with as much calm as she can muster. Then she asks a difficult question, one I can't answer. "But why exactly are *we* here? And what does ELIXIR plan to do with the twelve of us—clerics, they called us?"

Before I can respond, a loud knock on the door startles us. I lift my right index finger up to my lips. Chloe nods. We both know danger might be behind this door.

"Who is it?" Chloe says, trying her best to sound casual.

"ELIXIR," responds a female voice from behind the door. "I insisted you both needed help preparing for the Unveiling."

The Unveiling? I mouth to Chloe, hoping she can read my lips.

"You didn't think you'd have to do it all by yourself," the voice from behind our door says. "We have a small army equipped with dresses, makeup, and shoes."

"Did somebody say *shoes?*" Chloe says. "Now you're speaking my language. Come on in." Before she opens the door, she turns to me. "Like you said, it's not like we're going anywhere. Might as well make the most of it and enjoy ourselves."

With the slightest crack in the door, half a dozen women pour through, arms piled high with boxes of various shapes and sizes. They set them down and exit only to return with a second load of boxes minutes later.

One thing's for sure: Makeup and dresses will distract both of us long enough to block out the stress of all these unknowns. I want answers as much as anybody else, but I also know we're not going to get closer to the truth by sitting cooped up in our dorm room.

"Good evening, ladies. My name is Phoebe, and my number one goal is to make you both look stunning," the woman says. Scanning us up and down, she continues, "Which won't be difficult at all because you've already provided us with a great start."

I glance at Chloe. She looks as surprised as I feel. If we're going to meet the world, we might as well do it in style. "Well...," I say, rubbing my hands together. "When do we begin?"

Over the next two hours, I come to appreciate Phoebe. Clearly, she has a high degree of fashion intuition. But I discover other sides to this multifaceted matriarch, too.

Probably in her mid-forties, she seems to be a walking enigma. Toned muscles, yet graceful poise. Strikingly beautiful, yet uncommonly intuitive. Phoebe exudes a variety of characteristics I admire and hope to emulate someday.

Phoebe doesn't stop telling stories. But I like it. The more she talks, the more my internal knot unravels. And for as much angst as I feel about ELIXIR, getting kidnapped, and the events that await us, Phoebe's demeanor puts me at ease.

Her team mainly focuses on Chloe, pulling and twisting, brushing and braiding. Every so often I catch a glimpse of my friend and the transformation taking place. But then my mind drifts back to Phoebe.

She insists on working on me—though I'm not sure why. And yet I'm caught up in it all. She asks me how I feel and if I'm nervous about the Name Change or Unveiling. I find myself telling her more than I typically would share with a stranger. But for some reason, she doesn't seem like one.

When we near the end of our beautification process, she asks, "May I?"

"May you what?"

"Brush your hair."

What…? Does she know what I'm thinking, too?

Part of me wishes to let her engage in this simple but symbolic act. But part of me wants to run and hide. I'm sure for thousands of years mothers brushed their daughters' hair.

"Yes," I say with mixed emotion.

I close my eyes and imagine it's my mother brushing my hair as I prepare for some important event—prom perhaps? I wonder if Phoebe, probably my mother's age, has any children. I want to ask about her family, but I know better than asking strangers these types of questions.

I refrain from speaking and keep my eyes closed instead, savoring every swipe—hoping to cram eighteen years of hair-brushing depravation into one single experience.

"You know something, Sienna? I once had a daughter, a long time ago"—Phoebe's voice cracks—"but life thought it best to take her from me." She swallows hard. "Our little girl had your same hair color."

A small bubble of warmth grows inside me with each detail she shares.

"What was her name?"

"Kale. But she passed when she was just a small girl, three years old to be exact."

I've always loved that name—Kale—the same name as my neighbor down the street. She and her brother, Kevin, often played in our backyard.

"You named her after one of the daughters of Zeus?" I ask.

"Yes." She hesitates. "Her name meant 'beauty' and that's exactly what André and I thought the first time we saw her in the delivery room." She looks out the window, like she's stolen away to some far-off place, perhaps somewhere in her painful past. Then after a few seconds, she looks down at me again, never once pausing the swipes of her brush. Her lips stretch into a thin smile.

"You know, she'd probably be about your age…," Phoebe speculates with a twinge of sorrow. "If she were still with us."

Then I do something uncharacteristic. I stand up and give her a hug. I'm not sure why, but my gut said it was the right thing to do.

She returns my embrace and we hold each other for an extended moment. Our action seems to heal a certain internal ache—Phoebe, a mother without a daughter, and me, a daughter without a mother.

"This one…is done," one of Phoebe's team interrupts. I sit back down and give my full attention to my roommate.

Chloe spins around in her sophisticated white evening gown. Her brown hair falls all around her bare shoulders. She stands taller than usual thanks to her heels, which add three more inches.

"You look gorgeous," I say. Chloe always looks amazing, but tonight she is perfect.

"You think so?" Chloe asks.

Phoebe rushes in to remove any doubt. "Chloe, if looks could kill, then SWARM doesn't have a chance of survival."

An alert on Phoebe's smartwatch sounds: *"Three hours until the Unveiling."*

"My heavens," Phoebe squawks. "You ladies still need your Name Change. Come on, Sienna, your turn."

With all of Phoebe's talk about Kale and my thoughts of a mother I never knew, I forgot about the makeover being done to me the past two hours. Sure, I noticed the styling of my hair, the application of my makeup, and the fitting of my dress. But at the same time, I didn't *truly* notice it.

"Stand up, girl," Phoebe says. "If you're late for the Unveiling, I'll suffer the board's wrath, and trust me, I don't want any of that nonsense." I rise to my feet, and a collective gasp erupts throughout the room. I shiver, uncomfortable with all the attention.

"Look," she says, pointing to the mirror behind me.

I marvel at the young woman staring back at me. She looks like me, but older. Most days on campus I feel like a little girl homesick for a place I've never been. But what Phoebe performed on me is nothing less than a miracle.

She selected a forest-green tulle gown with a knot-tied waist and an elegant neckline. My eyes follow my figure up to my shoulders and to my face. I wrinkle my nose when I see my mouth. I never would have chosen such a prominent lip shade. The color reminds me of burning embers found in our fire pit back home.

"Do you think it's too much?" I ponder aloud. "All of it?"

"Too much?" Phoebe asks, as if my comment doesn't register. "I calculated every detail to draw out your natural beauty. Sienna, the world won't know what hit it."

Her heartfelt approval sinks in, and for the first time since I arrived, I might be ready for whatever awaits me.

"What's that noise?" Chloe asks, referencing the loud sound in front of our dorm.

"Transportation," Phoebe says, checking her smartwatch. "Yep, right on time. Ladies, your chariot awaits."

She points to the single window in front of my desk. Sometimes, when I can't sleep at night, I sit there and write in my leather journal by the light of an enclosed candle. In those dark moments, while breathing in the scent, I fumble over words in an effort to articulate the pain I feel inside.

Sometimes my words befriend me, leading me to a place of escape. But other times my words betray me, leading me into more angst. In those moments, when the night looks bright compared to the darkness I feel inside my soul, I seek out a stronger way of communicating my pain. A time or two, my pain danced dangerously close to the edge of a knife. But thankfully, the dawn always came before the blade.

Chloe and I rush to the windowsill and observe a sleek black craft touch down on the grass.

"What is it?" I wonder.

"Some kind of hovercraft?" Chloe guesses.

"Actually, we call it the Xcraft," Phoebe clarifies. "This carbon fiber transport tops out at ninety-five miles per hour and flies much higher than most traditional hovercrafts. You'll float over in style to the Name Change ceremony."

Phoebe's team snaps into action and starts packing up their supplies. "Follow me outside, ladies," Phoebe says. "You'll be joining the other ten clerics at St. Paul's for your Name Change. And then afterward, you'll all walk over to Radcliffe Hall with Tilda for the Unveiling."

We both nod.

I move down the stairwell, making sure not to trip on my gown. Outside, Phoebe opens the Xcraft door and flips down a small step. I half climb, half crawl up the vehicle, trying my best to be ladylike. Clearly, the Xcraft designers didn't have two college girls decked out in formal wear in mind.

"How many people can fit in this thing?" Chloe asks.

"Four, comfortably."

I sink into the cushy seats and notice the touchscreen cockpit display and refrigerated personal drink wells. Phoebe reaches over me and punches in some random keys, causing the engine to roar.

"Kiran put a security code on it," she explains. "Said he doesn't want a couple million dollars floating away from his budget because someone figured out how to hotwire it. Don't blame him, though. Enter an incorrect code twice in a row, and the entire vehicle shifts over to safe mode. Won't start then until he manually unlocks it."

"That's pressure," I say.

"Got that right," Phoebe says. "But once I punch in your destination, it's self-driving. You can just relax."

She turns on the surround sound, and our favorite song comes on. I look at Phoebe, who is grinning in admiration, pleased by the wonder in our eyes. We ascend gently, a few inches off the ground, floating on a pillow of air.

"Hey," Chloe says. "How did you know we like this song?"

"We know everything about you." Phoebe winks.

Although I'm sure Phoebe's statement was meant to be comforting, I find it more concerning than anything—a little creepy, actually. Before I have time to think further, we lift up a couple of feet higher and then take off toward the church—clueless about what awaits us.

CHAPTER
TEN

DARREN AND NICK ARE leaning up against a couple of trees outside the old church. Our Xcraft descends, and the boys stop their chat and stroll over to Chloe and me.

"Nice ride, ladies," Nick says. He assists Chloe out of the vehicle. "Wow! You look amazing."

"And you are handsome as always," she says, looking him over. "Hey, your white pocket square and vest match my gown."

My eyes find Darren's. He smiles back and steps closer, helping me exit the Xcraft. I release my grip the moment my foot touches the ground and search for something intelligent to say.

Darren starts, "Sienna, you are...I mean, you look..."

"Fantastic?" Chloe interrupts.

Darren's face brightens a couple shades of red. "You could say that. I was going to say beautiful."

"You look great, too," I say. "And your suit fits perfectly. It's like they knew your size or something."

"Yeah, it's all a bit unsettling, if you ask me—the monitoring, the kidnapping, and especially the wii initiative," Darren says.

"Not to mention how Kiran knew about my best friend from high school," Chloe adds. "I'm resenting the day I started wearing this ring...and it's not like removing it solves the issue, either."

I don't disagree, and although I'm sure Chloe wasn't directing her comment at me, I feel responsible. Cai gave me the rings, and I passed them onto my friends.

I notice Darren's pocket square—forest green, the same color as my dress. ELIXIR picked that out, too? But if ELIXIR knows about Darren dominating my thoughts, then maybe I'm dominating his thoughts, too? That possibility makes me feel both excited and anxious.

"I think we'll find some answers in there," Nick says.

Just then, our rings light up with an orange glow. The words *Front Entrance* scroll across our metal bands. Without speaking, we gather with who must be the other eight clerics near the heavy wooden doors at the front of the church. Although each wears a dress or suit similar to ours, the posh clothes can't hide the apprehension behind their nervous smiles. At least we all share an emotion in common—angst.

The bells ring, and then, a few seconds later, the

doors open. Music from an old pipe organ spills from the church, overtaking the cricket chirps outside.

Though I've walked past this building many times, I never found the time nor the desire to go inside. Like anybody else, I appreciate the craftsmanship, but something about sitting in an old, quiet church with just my thoughts never appealed to me.

Nick, Chloe, Darren, and I hang toward the back of the group. When it's our turn, we file in through a narrow aisle. Four long decorative benches face the aisle on both sides. Bright stained glass windows create a beautiful contrast to the plain walls, each glass mosaic featuring a different word in the center.

A large soldier dressed in black—a proxy, I think Kiran called them—closes the large wooden doors behind us. Shaved head and chiseled jaw, he stands guard at the back entrance, expressionless and arms at his side. *Is he trying to keep us in or others out?*

Poking my head around Darren, I spot a raised altar on the far side. Twelve young adults in formal wear, standing single file in a several-hundred-year-old Gothic church, awaiting a Name Change ceremony we know nothing about. Who said ignorance is bliss?

"Attention!" says a familiar female voice. Her command causes the organist to stop playing in the middle of his song. I look up and see a blond woman dressed in a formfitting business suit. She's even more intimidating in person than on video.

"On behalf of ELIXIR, welcome. My name is Tilda. We've already divided you into one of three groups—soma, amrita, or ichor. Please check your ring now and sit with your respective cohort. A proxy in your section will verify your text message."

A small flurry erupts as the twelve of us look down at our rings for the orange text. "Members of soma cohort sit on the left, amrita on the right, and, finally, those in ichor down in front," Tilda instructs.

"I'm ichor," Chloe says.

"Ditto," Nick echoes.

"Me too," Darren says. "What about you, Sienna?"

I check my ring again for the fourth time—spinning it deliberately, making sure the scrolling feature still works.

"I got nothing."

The other eight clerics self-sort into their respective cohorts on the left and right. The proxy assigned to each section verifies their orange text. Worry slowly creeps from my stomach, into my throat. So far in my life, I've been able to blend into the crowd. But in this moment, I know exactly how a cockroach must feel when someone flips on a light switch—exposed. Obviously, I'm with my other three friends, but I never got a text, so the proxy can't verify me.

Tilda leans on her lectern to the left of the altar,

tapping her fingernail, agonizing over every wasted second. It's painful to watch her wait for the other eleven clerics to find their seat.

"Sienna," she snaps, catching me out of the corner of her eye. "Why aren't you sitting with your cohort?"

"Um…I never got a text."

"You're Cai's niece," she says. "You should have received one."

When she mentions my relationship to Cai, I hear clerics in the other two cohorts murmur, making me even more self-conscious. Before I can melt into the reddish-orange carpet, Cai emerges from a back door just to the right of the altar. He walks toward Tilda at a brisk pace. She hunches down over the lectern to listen. Though I'm not sure what he whispers, Tilda lightens her tone.

"Sienna, please join ichor down in front."

"Thank you," I sigh, dashing to the front pew with as much poise as possible. Darren and Chloe split apart to clear a small space, and I plop down between them. My cheeks probably match the color of my hair. Good thing *this* ceremony isn't being broadcast.

Before Tilda speaks again, I scan the room for Cai, hoping to thank him for putting me with my friends. But in the commotion, I didn't see where he went.

"Why a Name Change?" Tilda asks, the question we're all wondering.

The candle on the altar to her right flickers high

above its glass cylinder. "Let me ask you, clerics. How many of you have suffered harm—directly or indirectly—from SWARM?"

One hand goes up—then another and another. Soon, we all extend our hands into the air.

"Enough!" Tilda laments. Then she makes a fist with her left hand and puts it up to her mouth, biting down on her knuckle. "Enough," she says again, with anguish in her voice.

She descends from the lectern and onto the main floor. Taking her time, she paces in front of us, pausing to make eye contact with each of us clerics.

Hawklike, I fixate on every move she makes, unsure when she'll break the silence. But she pauses for so long I don't know *if* she'll break the silence.

After a few more seconds pass, she begins again, much quieter. "It's time I tell my story," she says. "And honestly, I've never publicly shared it."

She breathes deeply before continuing. Maybe Tilda's story will help me find answers to some of my own questions—like why my friends and I were chosen. On the verge of hearing the truth, I can't stop my hands from shaking.

Why do I feel so afraid?

CHAPTER
ELEVEN

"FIVE YEARS AGO, my life was very different," Tilda explains. "I served as CEO of the trillion-dollar technology company Arete. We earned a reputation for penetrating the dark web and demanding radical reform. Before our efforts, criminals enjoyed unregulated access and engaged in the vilest of crimes with few repercussions."

I glance at my fellow clerics. They look spellbound, transfixed by every word flowing from Tilda's mouth.

"Years ago, I thought the dark web was an isolated digital 'back alley' somewhere on the Internet where people exchanged pirated movies and music. But then one day my team came to me with the truth, packaged in an executive summary. That summary shifted my vision from making Arete profitable to making it a catalyst for global reform.

"In the summary, my team revealed the size and scope of the dark web through a common search engine we probably all use. Like many people, I tried staying oblivious to the dark web, but as a mother and a CEO of a technology company, I couldn't claim ignorance any longer. As expected, the summary highlighted pirated content and illegal drugs. Counterfeit currency and stolen luxury goods came next in line. But then the summary moved into more significant crimes such as identify theft, purchasing false documents, and even buying weapons, ammunition, and explosives.

"At this point, I told myself I'm only one woman. How can I take on the dark web? But when I read the next page, something inside me changed forever. To be honest, much of me wished I never saw that page. It forced me to confront a new depth of depravity—one I didn't think humankind was capable of.

"While I sat sipping tea, somewhere in the world adults were being killed for their kidneys and livers and children were being sold for pleasure.

"The next morning I commissioned my senior team to create what would be known as the Arete Report—a strategic initiative to shed light on the dark web and SWARM's potential link to it. My personal mission was to recruit other influential CEOs to read the Arete Report and then join forces to institute dark web reform."

I move my head to see Chloe. Although she's holding Nick's arm, she stares ahead at Tilda. Everyone in the room is engrossed, too—in body, soul, and spirit.

"Yet one thing mattered more to me than any title or salary, or even the Arete Report," Tilda says. "My heart revolved around my five-year-old son—William.

"He was the sunshine in my life and the only living memory I had of his father, who died protecting our country two years prior. William and I were inseparable. On weekends, we'd leave town and head to our ranch out in the country. For two straight days, we'd ride horses and make memories. I called him my Cowboy Will and he'd call me his Cowgirl Mama."

I don't like the way Tilda uses the past tense when referencing her son.

He was. William and I were. We'd leave.

Past tense is how I've been forced to refer to my parents throughout my formative years. For those who've loved and lost, the past is cruel and bitter. It haunts the living with the fading memory of what might have been. It chokes out the present and kills the future, leaving an unpleasant aftertaste in the minds of all who survive.

Tilda continues her story.

"One Friday afternoon I left work to pick William up at school. When I arrived, they told me he never came in that day. I called my younger sister, Anne. She dropped off William on Fridays so I could start early and end early. My heart sank when she didn't pick up my call after more than half a dozen attempts. I knew something terrible had happened. I just didn't know what."

Mechanically, Tilda sits on a nearby stool and wipes a tear.

Unrest rises within me the longer I hear her story, like a dam about to burst from too much pressure behind it.

"You okay?" Darren whispers.

I measure the space between his mouth and my ear. The warmth of his breath sends a shiver through my entire body. Beginning at my neck, flowing down my torso and legs, and surging out through the tips of my toes. I ache, longing to bridge *that* space.

I want to tell Darren I'm not okay and that I need him to hold me. I want to tell him to run away with me, from SWARM, from ELIXIR, and from the ghosts of the parents I never knew. *But I can't.*

"Yeah. I'm fine."

He nods, but I know he sees through the thin mask I hide behind. Times like this, I wish Darren weren't so intuitive.

CHAPTER
TWELVE

TILDA BLOWS HER nose into a tissue before continuing. "In the midst of trying to locate William, I received a call from a number I didn't recognize. I heard William screaming for me in the background. They hacked my phone and inserted a live video feed. Through my tiny screen, I saw my little Cowboy Will writhing in pain. A group of men in masks surrounded him, laughing and poking him. I begged them to stop.

"Fury filled my lungs and rage hijacked my brain. To this day I'm unable to erase his screams. I wished I could reach through that phone and strangle each of his attackers. A computerized voice spoke off camera, identifying itself as SWARM. The voice cursed the Arete Report and me for threatening their enterprise. Then it told me...it set up—"

Midsentence, Tilda nearly falls from her stool. Several

ELIXIR proxies rush to her side to steady her. She shoves their hands away. "Let me finish," she shouts. "These clerics must learn why they're here and why SWARM must be stopped!"

Although she stands back up unassisted, Tilda looks dangerously close to toppling over. She breathes deeply, searching for words.

"The digitized hacker's voice pronounced a death sentence upon my little Cowboy Will. They set up a live murder and started taking orders from a pay-per-view audience. Using Bitcoin, the preferred currency of the dark web, viewers purchased abusive acts that SWARM performed upon William in real time. I don't have the strength or stomach to tell you what happened for the next sixty minutes. I wanted to hang up and run, but I couldn't abandon my son or his screams. Despite all my power, all my connections, and all my wealth, I stood there impotent.

"Moments before ending William's life, they offered a solemn ultimatum. I could either press ahead with the Arete Report or I could resign my post as CEO. If the report continued, then every day SWARM would hack my phone and I'd witness another child's abuse and death in real time.

"I couldn't continue knowing my actions would cause the death of another innocent child. My name Felicity meant 'happiness,' but Felicity Tulane died that day along with William and my sister, Anne."

I can feel Darren's shoulders shaking next to me. "You okay?" I whisper. He stares off into nowhere, his eyes downcast and glassy.

He shakes his head before the words come out of his mouth. "No...I'm not."

"Can I help?" I say.

"*Is there a problem?*" Tilda asks. Clerics and proxies alike twist their heads toward us. Their stares cause my heart to race. I try to avoid making eye contact with Tilda. "Sienna, would you like to tell the group about your private discussion with Darren? Or maybe you find my traumatic tale too boring for your tastes?"

I join Darren staring at the floor, controlling my breathing. I shake my head. Although now isn't the time to talk, I touch Darren's hand, letting him know I'm here to listen.

"Then I'll continue," Tilda says. "Authorities covered up SWARM's crime. They released a story about my son dying suddenly when a drunk driver struck him on his bicycle. They told the public that the grief initiated a nervous breakdown, and Arete had let me go so I could recover. Of course, to save face, Arete gave me a generous severance package.

"Only a few people knew the real reason for my departure. Authorities told me—off the record—that any type of exposé would simply exacerbate SWARM's rage and unleash a bloodthirsty attack on a global level. The world wasn't ready to deal with a hacktivist group so powerful. And so out of fear they looked the other way, oblivious to the truth—that every day SWARM grew in size and strength."

I swallow hard. Up until this point, I had no concept of SWARM's capacity for terrorism. Naively, I thought they were just a loosely organized group of criminals, not a superpower poised for world domination.

Tilda glances down before continuing. "So here we are five years later. Twenty-four hours ago SWARM initiated its most strategic attack to date, hacking humans and killing dignitaries from more than two dozen countries worldwide. If the human mind can be hacked, then there is no end to the evil SWARM can unleash.

"Thankfully, not everybody just sat around these past five years waiting for SWARM to swell. One visionary did something to fight back.

"While grieving William's death, I received a call from the renowned philanthropist André Saradon. He invited me to join him and his wife, Phoebe, at their estate to chat about a new project. As a jobless widow who recently buried her only child, naturally I refused. I didn't need more money, nor did I need more relationships. I still had an influential network of true friends.

"I was about to hang up when he said one word that forced me to reconsider. *ELIXIR*. André told me he knew the truth about William, the dark web, and SWARM's uprising. He and Phoebe recently invested their personal fortune—billions and billions—into the independent research and technology company ELIXIR. Their goal was to infiltrate the dark web, initiate reform, and ultimately eradicate SWARM. He assured me that with ELIXIR's talent and his funding, they'd pick up where the Arete Report left off and they wouldn't let up until they accomplished the mission.

"ELIXIR's board believed I brought the needed charisma, clarity, and clout to spearhead what he referred to as ELIXIR Project. They needed me to leverage my corporate connections and persuade them to join forces with ELIXIR. So, fueled by passion from William's passing and a desire to personally contribute to SWARM's downfall, I accepted the role as spokesperson for ELIXIR."

The light in the church is too dim to tell for sure, but Tilda's lips seem to curve upward at the ends. "And so this brings us to tonight. These past five years we've been preparing for the Unveiling, and for you twelve clerics."

Three proxies move to the front of the church. Each holds a small velvet bag. Tilda reaches her hand in one proxy's bag and pulls out a small dark object.

Then she nods, and the three proxies pass their respective bags to each cohort. Before the velvet bag comes to me, I wipe my hands on my dress. I am still warm and sweaty from Tilda's rebuke only a few minutes ago. What had upset Darren so much? Was it something about SWARM or maybe William's death?

The velvet bag reaches me, and I pull out a dense, dark, heavy stone. I smell strong incense when I bring the stone close to my face.

Another proxy brings Tilda a gold platter. She places it on the altar in the center of the cruciform. Tilda raises her dark stone in the air. "Clerics, there comes a time when we lose ourselves so collectively we can find a new way forward. A time to forget our past so we can embrace our future. Tonight I invite you. Let your old self die and let your new self be reborn. We memorialize this commitment through the Name Change ceremony."

Another proxy stands at the front of the altar holding a metal censer suspended from chains. Tilda places her dark stone inside. Gray smoke slithers out of the slits like a famished serpent in search of prey.

"Felicity, meaning 'happiness,' buried in death," Tilda announces. Then she picks up a white stone off the altar and lifts it in the air. "Tilda, meaning 'strong in war,' raised to new life." She places her stone on the gold platter.

"Clerics, ELIXIR has chosen you twelve to usher in this era—one where SWARM no longer exists. Together we'll accomplish this mission even if we need to go through the gates of hell to do it. This thurible will lead our procession to the great room, where the entire world will join us for the Unveiling.

"If you accept your role with ELIXIR, I invite you to come forward, one at a time, and receive your new name. At the Unveiling, you'll discover why we chose you twelve to join one of the greatest innovations ever created, ELIXIR Project."

Certain parts of Tilda's story sound preposterous—the live-stream murder and the Arete Report cover-up for starters. Still, in my heart I know she's telling the truth. Her words burrow their way deep into my being. Isn't this what I've wanted? To begin again? To forget the past and the pain of losing a mother and a father?

"We'll start with soma, then amrita, and finally ichor."

But her invitation is confusing. *Do I even have a choice?* Nothing about ELIXIR seems optional—from us drinking the vial back in the control room to being shot with an injectable. I scan the church one more time, hoping to see Cai. He'd know what to do. Although I don't see him, his warning from earlier today still haunts me.

They're watching us. Things aren't always what they seem. Who was he referring to? SWARM? ELIXIR?

Clerics from soma step forward one by one, depositing their dark stones into the censer. They declare death to their old names and then place their white stones on the platter.

Part of me wants to join them, but what am I saying yes to? Working for ELXIR? I've always respected them, but the past two days have caused me to question some of their actions.

"What are you going to do?" I whisper to Chloe. I imagine her choice will influence Nick. He won't let her go into the Unveiling by herself.

"I'm doing it. I've heard enough tonight to convince me there's a whole different world out there. Plus I wouldn't mind a new name." She smiles.

I kind of like my name, Sienna. I'm told it means "little redhead." Cai helped me with my research in elementary school during an assignment on our family trees. I was named after a city in Italy. I guess I could make do with a new name if it means finding answers about my parents.

The amrita clerics form a line in front of the altar.

"I'm in," Nick says in a hushed tone. "We're too far into this already, and I'm worried what happens if we *don't* go. Tilda is amped up about this Project, and I'm sure SWARM knows something about it. They wouldn't have had agents in the airport otherwise. Besides, I'd rather be under ELIXIR's protection then out on my own."

I want to shake them. Am I the only one who feels this Name Change ceremony is a little weird? How can we trust Tilda or ELIXIR, for that matter? How can we trust anyone?

I turn to Darren, scanning his face for some clue into what he's thinking. Maybe he's the only sane one left. But rather than speaking, he just shrugs, like he hasn't made up his mind yet.

"What's your new name going to be?" I whisper to Chloe.

"Check your ring," she says. "They picked a Greek one for me and it even has a cool meaning. Maybe they feel bad for taking away our trip."

I look at my ring, but just like before, there's no text.

"You both got one, too?" I ask Darren and Nick. They nod. Maybe mine's the only one broken?

"Ichor, your turn," Tilda says abruptly.

Chloe walks forward and places her dark stone into the censer. "Chloe, meaning 'green shoot,' buried in death." Then she picks a white stone off the altar. "Karme, meaning 'harvest,' raised to new life." She places her stone on the golden platter.

Nick follows her lead, placing his dark stone into the censer. "Nick, meaning 'victory,' buried in death." Then he picks a white stone off the altar. "Phoenix, meaning 'immortal,' raised to new life."

Two more stones. Two more spaces. One for Darren. One for me. Darren looks like a startled animal caught in a cage with no way to escape.

"I'm out," Darren announces.

"*You're out?*" Tilda repeats, shocked by his answer. "Do you know what this means?"

"No, I don't, and that's exactly why I'm not doing it," Darren says plainly.

"But this is your chance to clear your name, to forget your past, to start over," Tilda coaxes. "Are you sure you don't want those things?"

Darren hesitates. Tilda spots an angle and seeks to exploit it.

"Please weigh your decision carefully," Tilda warns. "Remember, any information we have stored on you could naturally be hacked by SWARM. Imagine them using that information to hurt you or the ones you love."

He stares at the ground for a few seconds, appearing to let her admonition sink in. With a reluctant gait, he walks forward and places his dark stone into the censer. "Darren, meaning 'gift,' buried in death." Then he picks a white stone off the altar. "Damon, meaning 'to tame,' raised to new life." He places his stone on the platter.

Before I have time to decipher Darren's actions, Tilda addresses me. "Sienna, only one spot remains."

What's the meaning behind Tilda's warning to Darren? A thousand thoughts flood my mind. I worry about SWARM and Darren and the Unveiling. I think of William and the dark web. I hear McNultey's laugh and Kiran's snickering. I long for more time with Phoebe and the memory of a mother I never knew.

The whole experience is overwhelming. I wish Cai could help me navigate this murky path. Despite his recent behavior, I know I can still trust him. "Yeah…" I start in with my rationale for declining her offer. "Um, I just don't think…"

I notice the orange glow encircling my finger and use my left hand to shield the message: *Choose Aryedne.*

I turn my torso and scan the pews. Cai is the only person who knows the significance of that name. In tenth grade, I tried writing my first novel. Unsure of what to name the heroine, I asked Cai for his advice. He suggested researching Greek mythology. I stumbled upon a story about Ariadne that captured my attention.

Ariadne—meaning "holy"—was the daughter of King Minos of Crete. She fell in love with Theseus and gave him a ball of thread. After killing the Minotaur, Theseus used the ball of thread to find his way out and escape the Minotaur's labyrinth.

Although I loved the story of Ariadne, I wanted to give my novel a unique twist, so I changed the spelling to Aryedne. Maybe this text is a clue from Cai? Maybe he's telling me to continue down the path before me? Maybe I'll be led out of this labyrinth of questions, too?

"Sienna," Tilda says, interrupting my thoughts. "We're waiting for your answer."

Chloe, Nick, and Darren lock onto me. At best, joining ELIXIR might be a calculated step into unknown risks or unrealized rewards. For all I know, maybe both.

But what other option do I have? I could go back to

my predictable past. At least it's clear and familiar. Or do I run toward my uncertain future?

My feet shuffle toward the censer. Sometimes we need to step forward in spite of our fears. Sometimes we need to mentally check out so we can emotionally jump in. I resist thinking at all. And so, on autopilot, with the orange glow imprinted in my memory, I place my dark stone into the censer.

"Sienna, meaning 'little redhead,' buried in death." Then I reach onto the altar and pick up a white stone. "Aryedne, meaning 'holy,' raised to new life." I place my stone on the golden platter and complete the circle of twelve.

CHAPTER
THIRTEEN

WE MAKE OUR way down the path to the great room inside Radcliffe Hall. The cold air slices across my bare arms and legs.

We enter through a door cut into the massive stone tower. Tilda keeps marching us forward. We journey down the hall into a dramatic, glass-ceilinged atrium. Metallic fixtures hang above us, infusing a splash of progress in this otherwise stone-relic gathering space.

Although the atrium contains several windows, the darkness from the night sky ensures a dim ambience. Only the window in the southwest corner permits moonlight to leak across the floor.

A dozen or so ELIXIR proxies gather in small groups around screens—probably here to monitor the Unveiling. Others outline the perimeter, touting a variety of futuristic-looking gadgets.

Over the years, Cai brought some of these ELIXIR devices home, presenting them in a high-tech version of show-and-tell. Like most teens, I occasionally played video games and even engaged in a little virtual reality. Rarely with Cai, though. He was too good, and I hated losing to him. Cai says I must have the competitive gene he and my father shared.

Once he surprised me with an electroencephalography headset. Sure, it took a little getting used to—the thought of an electronic device connected to your brain—but nothing compared to moving your avatar with your mind rather than your controller.

We shuffle toward a glass case about the same size as a clothes dryer. Its shelves are lit with a variety of neon colors—yellow, blue, and green. Four pairs of glasses rest on each of the three shelves.

Tilda greets an older Hispanic proxy guarding the case. Although his tattooed body, facial hair, and size might intimidate most people, there's something about his mannerisms that reminds me of a gentle giant. "Edge, would you mind educating our clerics on iris technology?"

"My pleasure, Tilda," he says, pulling out the bottom tray and laying it on top of the case. "Soma cohort," he announces, "please take one of these with the neon-yellow accent."

"Neon-yellow sunglasses?" a female voice scoffs. Her thick disdain mixes with her Spanish accent. "Why would I want to wear something that clashes with my dress so poorly?"

Unfazed by the criticism, Edge doesn't skip a beat. "Um, sorry. But I didn't catch your name. Biographical data is Tilda's department, not mine."

"Lyric," she says. "Or do you prefer my given name instead?"

"Lyric works. Given names died at the Name Change," Edge replies. "But trust me, *little lady*. You'll want to wear iris—regardless if you think it clashes with your dress or not. And one other tip—if you want to shine at the Unveiling, you might want to swallow a little pill called humility."

Lyric's jaw drops. Based on her reaction, she's probably not used to being referred to as a little lady or called out publicly for her pride. She towers over every other female cleric even without heels.

Uncomfortable with Edge's remark, she spins toward me, her jet-black hair twirling with her. She raises her finger and points at me. "Give your juvenile little sunglasses to her. Anyone can see she needs all the help she can get. Besides, she looks like a ten-year-old. Have you even had your first period yet—*little lady*?"

Her words sting—like getting beaned by an ice ball on the school playground in the winter. *Why is she talking to me? What did I do to her?*

Without a mother growing up, I've already battled

serious doubts about my appearance. But to be called out in front of my friends—especially Darren—and on the topic of my menstrual cycle, I'm not even sure how to respond. Heat rises within me—a messy concoction of sweat and fury.

Lyric smiles smugly at my inability or my unwillingness to make a comeback. She turns her backside to me—mission accomplished—deflecting Edge's comment by shifting the focus toward me.

"Okay, clerics, since Lyric feels she's above iris, she can go without them," Tilda says, interrupting. "The rest of you—the teachable ones—might want to wear your pair. Your survival could depend on it."

Her admonition injects a flash of apprehension into the room—and judging by her face—into Lyric, too. "Give me one good reason why I need iris?" Lyric shoots back.

"How about three? Clarity, competence, and confidence," Edge answers. "And trust me, at the Unveiling you'll need all of them. Everyone is looking to you because you twelve clerics are ELIXIR's answer to SWARM's most recent attack. In a real sense, you're the hope of the world. So tell me, are you ready to address the world?" Edge asks.

"Um...no," Chloe says, brave enough to verbalize what we probably all feel inside.

"Exactly," Edge agrees. "Think of iris as another set

of eyes. Whereas Cortex knows where you are, iris sees what you see. And because we see the world through your eyes, we can guide you on what to say and whom to say it to. Each pair of iris contains a discreet microphone and earpiece to ensure crystal-clear communication between you and ELIXIR."

"Don't overthink it," McNultey adds. "Two simple questions—that's all! Where you're from and your motive for joining ELIXIR Project. If you freeze up in there iris will do the rest."

"If you think we're just stupid kids, then why are we here in the first place?" the cleric with the dreadlocks says. I notice Lyric's hands intertwined in his.

"Name?" Edge asks.

"Pallas," the soma cleric replies.

"*Dumb?* Hardly. *Ignorant?* Absolutely," Edge says. "Tilda, care to enlighten them?"

Tilda straightens her navy jacket. She pauses before scanning each of our faces—intentionally making eye contact. Some clerics look down. But when she turns to me, this time I stare straight back. And like the blond back in the airport confronting Officer McNultey, this time I don't back down. Tilda steps closer to me and begins speaking to everyone, but still staring only at me.

"Clerics, when André and Phoebe recruited me to ELIXIR after my dismissal from Arete five years ago, we understood the magnitude of our mission. Although we knew a global mandate for wearables, ingestibles, and injectables would do wonders for monitoring SWARM and eventually eradicating it, we also knew the initiative was grossly underfunded. Equipping billions of people with monitoring technology isn't cheap. And operating all that equipment posed some problems, too.

"But those issues were minor compared with the main hurdle. Wii technology still needed private verification and public validation. Society would dismiss mandating this type of worldwide surveillance unless it understood the ticking time bomb of SWARM.

"The League of Nations gave us access to classified reports of global SWARM threats on a daily basis. With the league's permission, we instituted a selective monitoring campaign conducted through a common smartphone app and began with a small sampling of the general public—"

"Hold on a minute," Lyric butts in. "My dad is a high-ranking government official in my country. He's been grooming me to be the first female president someday. If I told him you hacked smartphones so you could spy on people, you'd be shut down by morning."

Several clerics in the other cohorts roll their eyes. Nonetheless, the room stays quiet, anticipating a response from ELIXIR.

"We do much more than spying, dearie," a voice from behind us bellows.

"Clerics, if you haven't met our chief technology officer, I introduce to you Mr. Kiran Sheyer." Kiran stands proudly and as tall as possible—which is still shorter than every cleric.

"You spied on us through our phones, too?" Pallas says incredulously.

"How else could we find you, clerics?" Kiran asks. If he intended humor, none of us are amused. "What other device do you eat with, sleep with, run with, and"—he clears his throat—"and...*ahem*... take to the restroom?

"Sure, taking over a phone's operating system allows us to identify SWARM sleeper cell activity worldwide. But it also allows us to track much more. Smartphones serve as hotbeds for biometric data. Before globally instituting the wii initiative, we needed to make sure we did our due diligence and worked out all the bugs."

"What kind of bugs?" Nick asks.

"Well...," Kiran says, thinking. "For starters, we realized the population self-selects into three groups quite naturally. The majority of the population, about seventy-five percent, has a resistance level of one. This means that to monitor them effectively, all we need to use is a wearable. About twenty-two percent of the population has a resistance level twice as high. They require a wearable and an ingestible..."

"And the other three percent require a wearable, ingestible, and injectable," Darren says.

Kiran dances over to Darren, grabs his hand, and raises it above his own head—which isn't too high. "I told you he was one of my favorites," Kiran announces. "Didn't I tell you, Tilda?"

"About a hundred times," she responds.

"Wonderful deductive reasoning skills, my good man," Kiran says. "But then tell me, which resistance level group are you twelve clerics: R1s, R2s, or R3s?"

We turn to Darren, hoping he has the answer.

"Ha," Kiran says mockingly. "Stumped, are you? That's okay, Mr. Damon. We were, too—at least at first. But the answer is quite simple—none of them!"

CHAPTER
FOURTEEN

KIRAN'S ANNOUNCEMENT ABOUT us not being like the rest of the world smacks me hard—shaking my stability. It certainly confirms a number of hunches I've had. My vision spins and my pulse quickens, like someone pumped a pound of espresso beans into my bloodstream.

Tilda must sense my growing unrest. "I know it's a lot to process," she says sympathetically. "You've chosen new names. You've been taken from your families and—"

"And some of us have been *betrayed* by our families," I say. "I want answers!"

"Put yourself in our place for a second," Chloe demands. "We *deserve* answers."

Kiran looks at Tilda and then at Edge. All three of them stare at one another, as though they are unsure what to say.

Finally, Tilda breaks the silence. "We began monitoring

ourselves about two years ago in a beta phase. All our ELIXIR team members worldwide installed the app on their smartphones and submitted themselves to biometric analysis. Even on our team, we saw the normal spread of resistance levels. But the data also surprised us, too. Our whole Senior Board—André, Phoebe, Chevon, Cai, Kiran, and I—came in as R3s."

Tilda checks her watch and then resumes her explanation.

"When we were still in our ELIXIR team–monitoring phase, an unidentified civilian borrowed a team member's smartphone to make a quick call. When we retrieved the biometric data for that smartphone, the complete wii initiative was temporarily called into question.

"At first we thought it was a glitch. This user's data didn't fit into any of the three categories. Although wii technology could still identify and monitor this particular user, the results were conclusive. This user possessed some form of internal immunity. Wearables, ingestibles, and injectables could not perform their intended function on this person."

"And that function was…?" asks Chloe.

"Hacking the brain," replies Tilda, as if it were an activity on par with brushing teeth or sweeping floors.

ELIXIR's wii initiative was designed to hack human brains? At this point, no news seems too far-fetched.

In a world where nothing is certain, everything is up for grabs. But if this technology is so dangerous for SWARM, then why did ELIXIR create it?

"Isn't ELXIR supposed to be stopping SWARM from doing this very thing—brain hacking?" Darren asks.

"Simple answer—really," Kiran explains. "Hacking the human mind—made possible through the wii initiative—provides us with a perfect defense. Through mandatory global monitoring, we will identify SWARM's next move *before* they make it. With everybody on the grid, nothing can slip by us. And those who refuse to become wii compliant could then be identified and eliminated immediately. Ask any athlete—a good defense is the best offense. Right, Phoenix?"

All eyes turn toward the gigantic running back. Although he gives a slight nod, I don't think he appreciates being referenced in the same conversation as brain hacking.

"Why does this one particular user pose such a threat to ELIXIR?" I ask.

"ELIXIR isn't threatened by this outlier or anyone else," Kiran boasts. "We simply labeled this particular user as an EP. Knowing other EPs could exist, we instituted worldwide use of the new smartphone app so we could locate them."

I wonder what he means by EP.

"But what about all the people without smartphones?"

asked a cleric from the amrita cohort. "There's probably a whole bunch of them out there."

"Not a problem," Kiran says. "We found a suitable alternative. Since our brains use electrical impulses, with a little creativity, we cobbled together a patch using satellite technology.

"Any other questions?" he asks, not even bothering to look up from his glass tablet.

"If ELIXIR Project is so important and SWARM is so powerful, then why broadcast us live to the world?" Pallas asks. "Seems to me you'd want to hide us until after we achieve our mission."

"Hide from SWARM?" McNultey chuckles. "Impossible. You don't beat SWARM by hiding. You beat them by winning."

"Tonight's Unveiling will send a clear signal to SWARM," Tilda explains. "Besides, they already know you twelve clerics exist—a recent leak confirms this. So instead we're leveraging that knowledge and uniting the world by showing them we're not afraid. Just the opposite, actually. We want to strike fear in their hearts. Because when they're afraid, they make mistakes. We'll capitalize on those mistakes beginning tonight."

"I hope you have some tight security," Nick says.

"Only the best," McNultey says. "All civilians and media within a two-mile radius of the campus were evacuated earlier this morning. Any non-ELIXIR personnel found within this two-mile radius are assumed to be potential SWARM members or allies and will be eliminated on sight."

"Anybody have other questions?" Kiran asks.

"Yeah, how does all this tie into eradicating SWARM?" Chloe frowns.

"I'll take this one," Tilda replies. "EPs are important for several reasons. Remember, hacking is a two-way street. Anyone who can be hacked by ELIXIR can also be hacked by SWARM."

"And…anyone who *can't* be hacked by ELIXIR *can't* be hacked by SWARM, either," Darren guesses.

"Exactly!" Tilda smiles. "Immunity to ELIXIR's wii initiative also means immunity to SWARM itself. That's why we needed to gather the twelve of you together."

"Us twelve?" Lyric wonders aloud.

"Come on, Lyric. Don't you get it?" Chloe says. "EPs? Elixir Project? You're an EP like the rest of us clerics. Does that make sense to you, *little lady*? Or haven't you had your period yet?"

"Ouch!" I say, without even thinking. Leave it to Chloe's loyalty to stand up for her friend.

From the corner of my eye, I spot Lyric's muscular arms coming toward my chest. Without time to prepare, she shoves me hard. I am no match for her size and strength. Her force causes my stationary sandals to slip on the slick tile floor. I fall backward and smack my cheekbone against the glass case on my way down.

I've never been knocked down in a fight. Come to think of it, I've never *been* in a fight—at least not one involving physical violence. The room spins all around me and my chest aches with sharp pain.

"What's your problem?" Chloe screams.

Pallas grabs Lyric around the shoulders. Edge steps between us, preventing Lyric from doing any more damage.

A shrill whistle prevents another verbal retaliation. "Stop it!" Kiran warns. "You'll get your chance to fight each other soon enough, all of you."

Lyric brushes herself off. She stands up and adjusts her dress coolly, as if someone else caused the brawl.

Nick and Darren help me to my feet, and Chloe leaves to find some ice. With the Unveiling only minutes away, I'd prefer not to have the world see me with a swollen purple cheek.

Edge hands me a bottle of water. "Here, drink this," he says kindly. "Don't pay attention to that arrogant brat. But try to stay out of her way next time. Okay?"

I take a sip. "Thanks for the water…and the advice." My brain feels cloudy from the fall.

"You know, your uncle Cai is an amazing man."

"I think so. I take it you know him?"

"We met a few years ago, when I first came to ELIXIR. He always found a way to make me look good in front of the decision makers. And thanks to him, I kept rising through the ranks."

"I'm sure it had something to do with you, too," I say, now aware of my wobbly legs. "He's kind, but he also has a knack for spotting talent."

Edge smiles back at me. "I'll keep an eye out for you during your time here. And if you need anything, just let me know."

"A stool would be nice. Got one of those?" He slides me one from behind the glass case.

Tilda's and Kiran's comments sounded so confusing. I want to ask them my other questions, but the room is still spinning. If my neck weren't attached to my skull, I swear I'd be a stranger in my own head.

"Tilda, I understand almost everything you said…," I moan.

Nick interrupts me. "Sienna, why don't you just take a moment and—"

"I'm fine."

"Leave her alone, Phoenix. What were you about to say, Aryedne?" Tilda asks.

It takes a moment for me to realize Tilda is talking to Nick and me. This whole name-change thing is difficult enough with a clear mind, but when you're suffering from a blow to the head, it's nearly impossible.

I appreciate Nick's concern for me. But I need to get these questions out before I forget them. "I get the different resistance classifications, the smartphone app, and even the twelve clerics—EPs as you call them. But four of us EPs have been friends for almost a year now. What are the chances that out of only twelve EPs in the entire world, four of us would meet at the same college, choose to be friends, and even book a trip to Greece for a semester abroad?"

Tilda winks at me and then the other clerics. Then she starts clapping, in a placating kind of way. "Bravo, Aryedne. Bra-vo! What are those odds? Well, if *you* chose your college and your friends, then yes it would be impossible. But what if someone else chose your college and your friends for you?"

"W-what are you talking about?" I stammer. "Uncle Cai helped me choose my college."

"I'm sure he did," Tilda laughs. "And Uncle Cai also chose your roommate at the admissions office before you moved in. Remember? ELIXIR also recruited Phoenix onto the football team with a full scholarship and Damon on academic scholarship. And…if SWARM hadn't attacked the royal family yesterday, you and your three friends would all be in Greece right about now. All bought and paid for by ELIXIR, of course.

"But as we know, things don't always go as planned. Sometimes we don't choose our future. Sometimes our future chooses us."

"I don't believe you," I shout back. "I don't believe any

of this." I never realized how one simple statement could undo everything you ever thought was true. But Tilda planted so much doubt inside my mind I don't know anything any longer. I'm not even sure if my roommate is my friend or an ELIXIR proxy monitoring me.

"Why did you do this to us?" Chloe yells.

"Do what?" Kiran replies. "We're trying to help you so you can help the rest of the world. Besides, if you want to 'blame' someone, start with your roommate. If Aryedne hadn't borrowed her uncle's phone during the beta phase of the app, you twelve might have simply slipped through the cracks. Thanks to her biometric data, we knew exactly how to find the rest of you."

I stare at the ground and wish I could sink into it.

The hot stares from the other clerics bore a hole straight into my skull. I want to run, but to where? Even standing in the midst of other people, I feel completely alone.

"Look on the bright side, clerics," Edge cuts in, trying to make the moment feel lighter. "At the Unveiling tonight the world is going to love you. You're their hope and salvation from SWARM itself. You're never alone because you have each other. And if you're humble enough to wear it, you also have iris, too."

Edge waves a yellow pair of neon sunglasses in the air. Lyric breaks free from Pallas and pushes her way to the case ahead of anyone else.

"On second thought I'll take a pair," Lyric admits.

"Brilliant choice, *little lady*." Edge smiles.

"Me too," another cleric from amrita says.

We all crowd around the glass case. Edge passes the yellow pairs to soma, blue to amrita, and green to us in ichor. I'm sure we look ridiculous, but I'm not about to go to the Unveiling without coaching from ELIXIR. Although I don't like the thought of someone telling me what to do, I like the thought of me all alone even less.

CHAPTER
FIFTEEN

"TEN MINUTES UNTIL showtime!" McNultey screams. "Fall in line!" We prep in the atrium, the holding space before we enter the great room for the Unveiling. The board members and the rest of the world wait for us on the other side of those doors.

I clutch a plastic bag of ice with my right hand. Half melted now, the cool water leaks from a small hole in one of the corners of the bag. I scan the room for a trash can, hoping to avoid any more embarrassment. Don't need a wet dress in addition to an already swollen cheek.

"Here, let me take that for you," Chloe offers. She must have seen the water dripping down my hand and onto the floor.

"Thanks, friend."

As roommates, we've grown close. I'm now able to finish her sentences and guess what she's thinking.

Although she's intuitive, too, it's harder for her to read me. Most times I don't even know what I'm thinking—or feeling. Makes her figuring me out nearly impossible.

"Ready to make a good impression in there, beautiful?" McNultey says, goading Chloe on her way to the trash can. She walks past him without saying a word. Then, after discarding the bag, she heads back to join the rest of us in line.

In a flash, he grabs her wrist. His movement is surprisingly fast. "Didn't you hear me, Karme?" McNultey snaps. "When I speak, I expect a reply."

"Let go of me," she says.

"After you acknowledge me, maybe. You know, I can make or break you in there. Haven't you heard about respecting your elders?"

"Ouch! Stop it."

McNultey pulls her closer.

Nick spins and sees Chloe caught up in McNultey's grasp. He tightens his fists, and in less than a second, he closes half the distance between him and McNultey.

"Freeze, Phoenix!" the officer says, reaching for his stun gun with his free hand. "It's time you learn the pecking order around here. I make the rules. And you obey them!"

I see the airport encounter all over again. I envision McNultey sending fifty thousand volts through Nick's chest. Or Nick tearing the old man in half. Or maybe both?

This standoff isn't going to end well. McNultey won't budge. He's defending what's most important to him—ego. And Nick won't budge, either. He's defending what's most important to him—Chloe.

"*Tell McNultey 'Aletheia,*'" a computerized voice whispers.

Where did that come from?

"*Tell McNultey 'Aletheia,*'" again, this time louder.

Iris! The voice came through my earpiece connected to my glasses frame.

"*Tell McNultey 'Aletheia'!*"

Nick takes another step toward Chloe. McNultey responds by drawing his gun.

"*Aletheia!*" I shout.

All eyes turn toward me, and I don't know why.

"What did you say?" McNultey asks, visibly shaken. I hear a slight tremor in his voice. What about these four simple syllables makes them so powerful?

"Aletheia," I repeat, this time more confidently.

He sizes me up. I glare back at him, not allowing myself to blink or to breathe. He makes a nervous snort, then looks away, shoulders slumping.

Chloe runs to Nick, who swallows her up with a bear hug. McNultey straightens his hat, returns his gun to its holster, and walks to the other side of the room.

Darren turns to me. "Where did that come from?"

"Iris told me. Besides, I didn't have many other options."

"Nice work. That was courageous," he says.

I didn't intend to be courageous. I needed to intervene—when no one else would. Maybe there's something to this iris thing. Or maybe it just gave me permission to act.

"Okay, clerics, five minutes until doors open," Edge says. "Hope you're ready."

If I knew what to expect, maybe I could prepare myself.

"Hey, why don't we watch the preshow on my ring?" a boy from amrita suggests. "They're live-streaming right now."

"Great idea," Darren says.

"I'm sorry, we haven't met," he says, extending his hand. "My name is...or, I mean, my *new* name is Ares. Guess we're all still getting used to this name thing, mate." His accent gives away his Australian roots.

A striking girl with golden-blond hair butts in. "Ares means 'god of war and bloodshed.' But at least I'm in his cohort, so I can't cross him." She smiles, her straight white teeth beaming. "Not that my name is any kinder— Erida means 'goddess of hate.' Tilda told me on the way over that, according to legend, I was appeased only when blood was spilled."

Darren and I shake their hands.

"Nice to meet you," we say.

An awkward pause transpires. I'm not sure if these other clerics are enemies or allies. Kiran's comment about fighting each other sounded strange, so I'm chalking it up as a warning to keep on my guard.

Erida bumps Ares. "Um, yeah, we don't have much time. Let me fire it up." His ring glows soft and then more intense. A bright flash of orange light rips through the silver circle. An image projects above us, and a familiar voice surrounds us.

"Turn down the volume," Erida scolds. "They're shooting live in there, idiot. We don't want the world to know we're listening to the preshow. Makes us look... desperate."

Erida's got spunk for sure. I like her energy and I'm sure we'd get along well together.

"Yeah, yeah, give me a sec," Ares says defensively.

"This is Lori Wicker reporting about May 9, a day that will now go down in history as 'Dark Day,' the world's most significant terrorist attack to date. Top leaders from more than two dozen countries were murdered yesterday in a single plot designed by top-level SWARM masterminds.

"Since yesterday, the world advisory security system has issued a code red. The League of Nations has granted ELIXIR 'autonomous status' empowering them to use whatever force necessary to eradicate SWARM.

"Our channel has been granted exclusive media coverage for this worldwide event. The entire broadcast will provide commercial-free, nonstop coverage.

"Conservative estimates project that ninety percent of

the worldwide population will tune in to the Unveiling beginning in sixty seconds."

When I was ten years old, I had a sleepover with one of my friends. We stayed up most of the night watching one of those long fantasy movie trilogies. In one scene, a group of horrific creatures surrounded a defenseless castle. The creatures chanted, beating their axes and swords against their shields and breastplates. Townspeople hid in the castle, cowering behind a large wooden door, intimidated and afraid. They covered their ears, hoping to shut out the evil awaiting them on the other side.

Each night for a week after I saw that movie, I snuck into Cai's room and slept on the floor at the foot of his bed. Knowing he was next to me made the night terrors fade. Eventually, they stopped and I found comfort in my own room again.

Tonight I wish I could crawl back into his room and forget this bad dream. But Cai isn't here to protect me any longer, and I'm not about to lean on anyone else.

"Here we go," Darren says, putting his hands on my shoulders. He twists me so I face the door to the Unveiling like a soldier ready to confront whatever creatures await. I'm sure he's trying to distract me from the fear inhabiting every atom in my body. The warmth of his hands lingers on my exposed shoulders. I wish he didn't take his hands away so quickly.

"Doors opening, clerics," Edge informs us. "In three, two, one…"

Bright light spills onto the dim atrium floor, casting long, ominous shadows behind us. With iris snug against my head, I follow Erida, shuffling forward on the hard floor.

Half a minute later, it's my turn to straddle the threshold that connects the atrium with the great room. In a real way, these four inches serve as the gateway to my new future.

I have a strong hunch in this new world that I'm going to have to make trusting my gut a habit. And at the present moment, my gut tells me Cai's right—not everything is as it seems.

CHAPTER SIXTEEN

THE GREAT ROOM is longer than it is wide. Rich wood-paneled walls fill in the space between the massive stone pillars and stunningly crafted stained glass. The decorative windows on my right tell stories of classic works from American and British literature.

Large exposed wood rafters hold up the immense weight of the roof bearing down on our global Unveiling. Half a dozen or more chandeliers hang from the large arched ceilings above.

ELIXIR proxies dressed in black encircle the entire room. They stand at attention, each holding at their sides a long, intimidating stick pulsating orange. I'm relieved I don't have to discover what type of pain this weapon inflicts.

Ornate wooden chairs surround a daunting rectangular table.

"Welcome, clerics, and welcome, world!"

I gaze up and notice Tilda perched on a small balcony at the north end of the great room. She stands confidently, hands gripping the dark iron rod railing in front of her. I can't read her expression from this distance.

But then four transparent screens—one on each wall—flicker to life, projecting a close-up of Tilda's face. I peer into every crack and crease. She looks worn, like she's been through a war. I guess in many ways she has. I overlook her gruffness and feel a shred of sorrow for her loss.

WHOOSH!

A camera attached to a thick wire above my head zips through the air. The combined budget of this broadcasting gear must cost a small fortune. I suppose it's nonnegotiable when the entire planet is glued to their screens.

Fear creates one thing for sure: a captive audience. No wonder SWARM thrives on injecting a regular diet of fear into the social psyche. Now they've raised the stakes—hacking the human mind. No doubt ELIXIR plans on flexing some serious muscle tonight. If they fail to recapture the faith of the world, all hell might break loose.

"Step forward."

I obey the familiar voice in my earpiece.

"Stand behind the second chair from the left on the south end of the table."

The other clerics file to their chairs on each side of me. I'd hate to think what happens if one of us doesn't oblige.

"Sit down on the count of three. One, two, three."

We all sit down in unison.

"Look, Sienna." Chloe bumps my right arm with her elbow.

A familiar face enters through a doorway on the north end, directly beneath the balcony. Camera tripods throughout the room spin to capture Cai, projecting him to every corner of the globe.

Even if I still feel a little hurt and confused, his smile melts much of my apprehension—it always has. It reminds me of the time I clipped the driver's side mirror backing out of the garage. Fresh off receiving my driver's license, I waited for him to scold me for being too careless. But to my surprise, his anger never surfaced. Instead, he squeezed his arm around my shoulders and mentioned a new type of epoxy that would do the trick.

No matter what mess I got myself into, my larger-than-life uncle always shielded me from whatever storms swirled around me.

I underestimated how reassuring it would feel to see my uncle. He looks so content tonight, and he should be. He's invested every ounce of energy in ELIXIR, researching, creating, and testing. And now, because of

SWARM's terrorist tactics, the world needs Cai and ELIXIR more than ever.

I hear his wisdom reverberating in my mind: *When you prepare for the moment, the moment is prepared for you.* And Cai has prepared for this moment his entire life.

"My name is Tilda Tulane, and it's my honor to serve as emcee for tonight's Unveiling. I wish our inaugural global gathering had been for reasons of peace, not war. And yet, as I speak, a pandemic threatens our survival as a species. If this threat were simply an infectious disease or biological pathogen, rest assured our brightest minds would have already isolated and obliterated this evil.

"But this enemy is much more subversive. The filth of SWARM stains us all. We've suffered—directly or indirectly—financially, emotionally, and even relationally. This digitized cancer knows no bounds—infiltrating our government, school systems, and places of worship. SWARM continues to ravish our lives until it hacks the 'final frontier'—our minds."

She pauses. Maybe she's reliving William's last moments of hell on earth. It must eat her alive every single day. Mission accomplished for SWARM—inflicting endless mental anguish upon those who survive. But then she snaps out of her trance.

"You're experiencing tonight's broadcast in your own native language thanks to our chief technology officer, Kiran Sheyer, and his ELIXIR interpretation app.

"Your viewing device functions as a receiver and a transmitter. You receive our signal and then, through revolutionary technology, our computers identify your language of choice and broadcast in the most popular language found in that radius."

The room erupts in applause. Kiran soaks in the praise like a dry sponge. His face is always unattractive, but projected onto a large screen with high-density pixels, it reminds me of a frightening cartoon character.

"Next please give a warm welcome to our director of strategic implementation, someone the tech world knows as Mr. Cai Lewis," Tilda announces. Cai gives a genuine wave and a nod to the camera. The room full of ELIXIR proxies erupts into another thunderous applause.

"Give him a standing ovation—NOW!"

All twelve of us clerics rise to our feet. We clap and cheer. Whoever is speaking for iris seems bent on influencing the pageantry tonight. Rather than calming me, its constant commands stress me out.

"Let the Unveiling begin."

CHAPTER SEVENTEEN

"Yesterday SWARM changed the rules of engagement forever," Cai explains. "Their disregard for human life spoke loud and clear. And tonight we respond with one voice, united."

Cai turns from the cameras to the main screen. With that cue, the lights dim, and Cai's voice narrates this prerecorded footage.

"At tonight's Unveiling, we find ourselves weeks if not days away from a new class of instability—one of apocalyptic proportions. If SWARM succeeds in its single mission—hacking the collective mind of the human race—it can then wield this global consciousness in whatever way it deems suitable. Overthrow of governments, mass murders, and national slavery are just the beginning.

"If the dark web is a minuscule reflection of what's

possible with unrestrained access to evil, imagine what horrors will be unleashed upon an entire world deadened to its moral filter thanks to mass mind control. Billions and billions of minds will be pawns in a game where only one wins: SWARM.

"Our state of affairs would be much different tonight if philanthropists André and Phoebe Saradon hadn't stepped up several years ago. Thanks to these angel investors and their billions of dollars in funding, ELIXIR secured the necessary talent and resources to defend against SWARM and also launch our own counterattack.

"We call it the wii initiative, and it's a sophisticated defensive strategy. Although it's not the long-term solution, it buys us the time we need to develop a deathblow to SWARM.

"Counterintelligence suggests that SWARM is now less than thirty days away from instituting its global hacking strategy. But thanks to ELIXIR's wearables, ingestibles, and injectables, humanity will experience immunity from SWARM's future attempts at human hacking.

"We want to thank the League of Nations for its cooperation in our efforts to fight back against SWARM. Global law has granted ELIXIR autonomous status, empowering us to use whatever force necessary. Even developing countries understand their vulnerability and have requested ELIXIR's protection.

"At the conclusion of tonight's Unveiling, ELIXIR outposts will begin implementing the wii initiative worldwide. Humanity will then be 'hack-free' for the short term. Our permanent solution will be established through ELIXIR Project. Then no one will have to fear anything except truth itself."

At the conclusion of the filmed segment, three proxies dressed in sleek black attire enter the great room through the north entrance. Cai points to the ELIXIR threesome. "I give you wii technology."

A voice crackles through my mind. *Give them a standing ovation—NOW!*

All twelve of us clerics, adorned with our neon irises, stand and clap. Tilda, Kiran, and Cai join in the applause, and the room erupts with fanfare.

Cai motions for us to sit back down. He then starts to demonstrate on each proxy how simple and noninvasive wii technology is. The blond woman goes first, showcasing Cortex on her finger. A two-minute promo video playing in the background explains some of the unique features and benefits.

The male proxy goes next. He holds up an orange vial for the camera to see. After swallowing the liquid, Cai explains the purpose of the microchips the proxy just ingested. Besides tracking vital signs, the microchips create an internal defense system, protecting him from a SWARM hack.

The thin brunette woman goes last. Wisely, ELIXIR refrains from shooting her with an injectable via a gun, like McNultey did to us back in the control room.

This version looks more like an auto injector, similar to those used by people allergic to bee stings. The proxy rolls up her sleeve and presses the pen to her forearm. Cai explains how with one simple push, the injectable served its role, pumping nanotechnology into her bloodstream and protection from SWARM.

"Thank you, Cai," Tilda says. The three proxies bow one more time before exiting promptly through the north entrance.

"A strong defense like the wii initiative is essential," Tilda says. "Dark Day proved that truth for all the doubters. And yet SWARM will continue to thrive unless we deliver a deathblow. If we want global peace, we must go on the offense and launch our own attack."

"Start pounding the table in front of you."

As odd as it sounds, I obey the orders, and in unison we begin pounding the table. The water in our glasses nearly spills from all of the banging. Tilda allows the chaos to carry on for about ten seconds before she interrupts.

"I give you ELIXIR Project."

CHAPTER
EIGHTEEN

THE FOUR SCREENS spark to life again. In rapid succession, each of our pictures flashes across the screen with our new name underneath.

"We've designed a Project to systematically dismantle SWARM."

The proxies outlining the perimeter of the room start tapping their long weapons against the tile floor. One hundred-plus weapons clang in unison, their chant echoing off the stone walls encircling the great room. The loud vibrations travel through my sandals, up through my toes, and into my legs, jarring my bones—and my confidence.

"Naturally, the strategy surrounding the Project is highly classified." The clanging trails off as Tilda speaks again. "Our mission might be secret, but we don't want our clerics to be. These modern-day superheroes serve as our global hope. It's time to get to know them. Soma cohort…rise."

The four clerics to my left stand up. The neon yellow light from iris illuminates their faces, casting a haunting glow. They look like four frightened children, especially Lyric.

"After your name is announced, state your continent of origin and then share with us why you chose to embrace your role in ELIXIR Project. Lyric, we'll start with you."

"South America," she says. For someone who seems to crave the limelight, she appears mighty anxious to step out of it. She swallows hard before continuing. "A few months back, my sister was taken. We received a package in the mail shortly after she went missing. Inside we found a plastic bag containing her light yellow shirt. The letters S-W-A-R-M were spelled out in human blood across the front."

Sympathetic gasps fill the room. For a moment, I feel a pang of emotion, too. *Maybe Lyric is human after all?* But then I remember the impression she left on my cheekbone thanks to her shove. I press two fingers up to my face—still puffy, still stinging. My empathy for Lyric subsides as quickly as it came.

"Pallas," Tilda says.

He steps forward—he's nearly as wide as he is tall. Long dark dreadlocks spill out from his head.

"South America," he says with an accent. "My kid brother dreamed of playing pro ball. One day a group of men showed up at his practice. They said if he wanted to go big, he needed help. They got him hooked on their drugs, and he quit playing ball. I've had no brother since. Got a postcard in the mail months later of what you call a soccer ball here in the States. No return address. Only one word—*SWARM*."

Sounds of disgust rise from clerics and proxies alike.

"Lelantos, you're next," Tilda says, expressionless.

My hatred for SWARM grows with each tragic tale. I keep listening for the common thread in all these SWARM attacks, but for the life of me it all feels so random. Different genders. Different regions. Different crimes. I only see one common denominator—evil.

I thought the Unveiling would bring worldwide unity by bonding us together. Instead, all I hear is pain. I glance down at the silverware in front of me and notice the grooves in the serrated knife. But maybe this is the point? Maybe—in a peculiar way—pain unites us more than joy ever could?

"Europe," says the tall, thin cleric named Lelantos. The board selected a sharkskin notched-lapel wool suit to go with his chestnut-brown hair. He's the youngest-looking male cleric of the bunch.

"Two years ago my bloke and I created a computer program in my parents' garage. It garnered so much attention that we received several buyout offers from large corporations in America and China. The financial packages and stock options alone would take care of our families for generations to come.

"The day before the deal was finalized, we discovered the aftermath of a sophisticated hacker's carnage. Someone or *something* worked its way into our program and infected it from the inside out.

"Whoever corrupted our program knew exactly what they were doing. They stole all our coding and files. News of our attack leaked out, and the corporation withdrew its offer immediately. Twenty-four hours later, we received an anonymous e-mail announcing that nearly all our digital assets were now uploaded to the dark web in an open-source format. Whoever wanted to access our program could do so at no charge. Corporate secrets free for the taking, or—more accurately put—for the stealing.

"Twelve months of our life, flushed down the drain, in a matter of minutes. The e-mail concluded with: 'Cheers, SWARM.'"

"That sucks," Chloe says under her breath.

Everybody in the room would agree. Seems like SWARM enjoys robbing *and* killing. Doesn't matter who you are or where you live, if you have something valuable—with SWARM around—you're vulnerable.

"Styx, you're next," Tilda says.

"Asia," she says. Her dark hair is pulled back into a tight bun high on her head. Her flowing sleeves move up and down as her hands fill in the gaps of her story.

Before she spoke, I wondered why her name is now Styx—after the goddess of the underworld river, a literal personification of hatred. She seems benevolent enough. But after hearing her SWARM story, I can understand the source of her anger.

Her grandmother was found in a dumpster barely breathing and missing her only healthy kidney a little over two weeks ago. It took her six days just to get out of the ICU. When she did, she received several bouquets of flowers delivered to her room. Each bouquet contained a small card with a message of mockery: *Get well soon. —SWARM.*

According to Tilda, SWARM sold her kidney on the black market, a crime increasing in popularity because of high profit margins. Because SWARM can hack into global databases, it matches donor-recipient pairs ahead of time to increase efficiency. When a wealthy patron needs an organ, the dark web simply alerts a middleman, who informs SWARM to dispatch personnel to remove the organ.

Soon drones will do the dirty work through aerial assaults. Unsuspecting victims will be tranquilized from above. Onboard AI will extract the organ and pack it in ice, and drones will fly it back to a SWARM sleeper cell, where an on-site surgeon will perform the transplant.

With billions of potential donors in the world today, SWARM will automate the process just to keep up with the demand.

According to Styx, her grandmother is dying slowly from the failing kidney they left inside her.

"Let's give the soma cohort a big hand for their courage," Tilda says, clapping. "Thank you, Lyric, Pallas, Lelantos, and Styx. We share your pain and we honor your bravery."

The four clerics nod.

"We'll hear from the four amrita clerics now. And after that we'll take a sixty-minute intermission. Then we'll reconvene so you can meet your final four clerics in ichor."

I should be nervous when Tilda mentions I'm up soon. I should obsess about my response to her questions. But instead my mind drifts to a world where drones commit crimes from the sky and hackers drain financial empires with the click of a mouse. That mental image drowns out the voices of amrita's stories.

Tilda's announcement snaps me out of my daydream. "Before we break, let's show amrita our support."

This time we don't need any prompting to give our applause. Who knows what we're all about to encounter? Death? Maybe. But if robots are ripping out kidneys, livers, and hearts from the sky, then maybe death doesn't seem so bad after all.

"Thank you, Ares, Erida, Metis, and Ophion." The cameras zoom on each of their faces, lit up with the neon-blue hue from their irises. Metis—the goddess of craftiness—looks sweet enough, but her smirk tells me something else. It screams of mischief, like she's up to something—planning and plotting.

And Ophion—the serpent god, cast down—at least that name fits with the large snake tattoo on the back of his shaved head. Better block off a week if you plan on counting the other ones spread over his body. With all his ink and piercings, he looks like he belongs on a motorcycle, cruising down some deserted road. I hope we end up fighting *with* each other, not against.

I have to find Cai—if he can sneak away from the cameras long enough to chat. I need answers. My finger vibrates.

Meet me on the top of the tower at break.

Looks like Cai read my mind. Then again, should I be surprised? He probably did.

CHAPTER NINETEEN

"YOU GUYS WANT to get some fresh air?" Darren asks.

"If I don't get some, I might pass out," Chloe says, pushing her chair back and standing up slowly. I'm sure those heels don't favor sudden movements.

"I'll go with you," Nick chimes in.

"You coming, too, Sienna?" Darren asks.

"I got a text from Cai, and I need to talk with him before we four have to address the world, you know?"

"Got it," he says. "See you after the break."

I push my chair in and turn to go find Cai.

"Aryedne," someone says. "Wait a second, please."

I keep walking until I realize she's talking to me. My new name still takes some getting used to. I turn to see Tilda breaking away from a conversation with McNultey. She gives him one last instruction and then dashes over to me.

"I guess this is our official introduction. Welcome," she says, holding out her right hand as if I'm supposed to shake it.

I reach out and clasp my hand in hers. In all my life, I've never touched skin that made me want to pull away so quickly. It's as if her hand is on fire, not because of heat—but cold. I leave my hand clasping hers longer than tolerable. Pulling away feels like a bad idea, though I'm not sure why. "Nice to meet you."

"So, how do you like iris?" she asks.

I lift up both hands to touch the sides of my face. "I guess I forgot I had it on."

"The technology takes a little getting used to," Tilda says, chuckling. "But I hope it's giving you more confidence. Speaking to the world can be a little intimidating."

"Confidence is always a good thing," I reply, trying to fill in the uncomfortable space.

"Well, your cohort is up next. Just be sure to listen to iris and you'll be fine," she says, though it comes off more as a command. "Oh...have you seen Cai? I need to run over our script before we reconvene."

I must maintain eye contact. "Nope. I was just going to use the restroom before the break." I wonder if she knows about his text.

"Well..." She pauses for a few seconds. "If you *do* see him, tell him I need to talk before the cameras go live again?"

"Sure. No problem." I spin away before she tries to engage me any longer and then push through the large double doors that lead toward the restroom. Once they shut behind me, I take a quick left.

Reaching to steady myself on the wooden railing, I notice my pulse pounding from my chest all the way down to my fingertips. Something about that woman unnerves me, like she's sizing me up the same way a predator does before eating its prey.

I ascend the narrow stone staircase. Stained glass windowpanes on each level break up my journey toward to the tower roof.

At the top, I send Cai a text: *Here.* No need for long texts, in case I'm being monitored.

Though I've never been in this space before, I've heard plenty of rumors. During orientation week, some unruly seniors unloaded a bunch of paintballs on unsuspecting freshmen below.

The large door in front of me creaks open. "Sienna!" Cai says, giving me a giant bear hug. "You look amazing tonight."

"What are you talking about?" I say. "I look amazing *every* night."

He lets out one of his Cai laughs.

"Not yet, mister. I'm still mad at you, you know."

"Shh…" He holds a finger up to his lips. "Come on out here."

He grabs my hand and escorts me onto the tower roof. He shuts the door and pulls out a small, flat disk the size of a silver dollar—pushing the middle of the device. It vibrates briefly, and then a small pink light circles the perimeter of the disk. He sets it on the railing next to us.

"Now they won't be able to hear us." He smiles. "Something I created back in my lab called husheye. It has a dual purpose, depending on the mode. Records audio or jams any signal within a fifteen-foot radius. I put it on jamming mode so they can't listen in."

"Who's *they*? You keep saying 'they.'"

"Look, Sienna, I know you've been thrown into the deep end, and I want to explain everything. In time I will. But for now, you just have to follow directions and fall in line."

"'Fall in line'? Seriously, Cai? I'm not some proxy assigned to your jurisdiction. I'm your niece, remember? The one you've watched grow up the past fifteen years. The one you decided to raise after my parents died."

"Killed!" interrupts Cai. "Not *died*. Killed!"

"What are you talking about?"

"You *really* want answers, Sienna?" Cai barks. "Because if you do, then for starters *they* killed your parents. And God knows I'm leveraging everything I can to prevent the same thing from happening to you, too!"

Cai's voice breaks and he looks away, off into the distance. He sounds exasperated, like he's grasping for control but can't quite get it. Then his voice softens. "I'm sorry—for yelling. But if they take you from me, too, then I've got nothing left. Don't you see? All this is to protect you."

I pause before responding. I'm not familiar with this version of Cai—the desperate and vulnerable uncle. "All of what?" I speak slowly. I don't want to corner him any more than he already feels.

He begins again at a steady measured pace. "ELIXIR…clerics…the wii initiative—all of it. I don't know for sure. Sienna, at the moment I don't know anything for sure."

"You're on the Senior Board of Clerics, Cai. If you don't know what's going on, who does?"

"That's just it. I've always been the insider, the one managing classified information. But in the last twelve months, I've had my doubts. And in the past few weeks, these suspicions have grown.

"And?" I ask, hoping to yank something conclusive out of him.

"And…and things aren't always what they seem. They're watching us."

"I know. You already told me that this afternoon. Remember?" I say impatiently.

"I can't risk giving you wrong information, Sienna. When I figure something out, I'll get you what you need to know, okay?"

"Okay…but tell me this. Can they control my thoughts with my Cortex ring?"

"You? Nah. Tilda meant what she said. You're unhackable, and because of that, you need to be careful. For you EPs, all they can do is monitor your thoughts, not control them."

"That's reassuring. Hey, what's up with McNultey?" I ask. "That guy's a jerk."

"More like a creep," he says. "I hated sending you and your friends with him. But I had to. SWARM agents were crawling all over the airport, and we needed to get you back on campus after that London hack."

"What's McNultey's story?"

"I don't know all the details, but he came to ELIXIR with André and Phoebe when they invested their fortune. Guess he has tons of combat experience, and André insists that he head up security operations."

His watch flashes Tilda's name. "Why is she texting me now?"

"Oh, I forgot. She told me she wanted to see you," I say.

"Tilda? When? What else did she say to you?" he says, scanning her message on his watch. "I gotta go, Sienna," Cai blurts. "And we shouldn't be seen reentering the great room together."

"Oh, I see.…Call me up on the tower—only to leave me full of more doubt and questions. It's not fair, you know, bringing up my parents after all the years I've asked about them."

"Sienna, I only found that out yesterday. Trust me, I want to discover the truth, just as much as you." He lifts my chin up with his hand. "I'm sorry," he says tenderly. "It isn't fair. You're right."

"I'm right all the time," I say, putting my hand on his arm.

"Hey, when this is all over, I'm going to leave ELIXIR and set up shop in some remote fishing village down in Guerrero. Maybe I'll even let you visit me and we can go snorkeling in the ocean together," he says, chuckling.

"Not a chance," I tease. "You without round-the-clock, fast-paced drama? I'd like to see that. What are you going to do? Make friends with the villagers and become a fisherman?"

"Watch me," he says.

"So what should I tell my friends?"

"Nothing," Cai says. "You have to be careful—at least for now—careful of what you say and whom you say it to."

Based on his comment, I wonder if I've said too much to them already.

"Look, we have about thirty minutes before the Unveiling begins again, and I have to connect with Tilda," Cai says. "She's always making last-minute tweaks to the script. Just promise me one thing, Sienna?"

"Depends," I say playfully.

"Throughout the Project, remember: Don't believe what you think; believe what you know."

"There's a difference?"

"*Big* difference," he says emphatically.

"Okay. Thanks for the brilliant insight, Uncle," I say, unsure how to process his cryptic warning.

"And, Sienna…," he says, opening the door back to the stairwell. "Remember—I love you."

"I love you, too. Oh, hey, don't forget your little jamming thingy." I hold up the silver-dollar-size device.

"Keep it," he says. "Never know. Might need it sometime."

"Right," I say, tucking it down inside my dress—next to my heart.

The door shuts behind him, and I'm left alone.

Let's hope not.

CHAPTER TWENTY

"WELCOME BACK, CLERICS," Tilda says. "We'll go back to the live stream in about twenty minutes. I was told during intermission that several of you asked my ELIXIR colleagues an important question: details of your compensation for participating in the Project. Yes?"

I turn to see Metis and Ophion elbowing each other—no doubt the culprits in it for themselves.

"Although ancient Greeks crowned their victors with olive wreaths, we found something much better. Naturally, you'll have the chance of becoming a hero, but we have something else, too. We call it a Boon. Think of it as your deepest desire, your greatest ache, your truest longing."

"You gonna give me a billion dollars?" Lyric blurts out.

A few giggles emerge, but then the room goes silent.

Some might chalk it up as a joke, but Tilda doesn't let it go unchecked. No doubt she smells Lyric's unbelief and isn't going to let her get away with it, especially in front of the other clerics.

"Stand up, young lady!" Tilda orders. *"Now!"* The soma cleric complies and rises to her feet, posing defiantly.

Tilda composes herself before continuing. "I said your *deepest* desire, Lyric. It's more than money. I know who it is and so do you."

Lyric clenches her fist. "You can't bring her back. I held her bloody shirt in my hands. She's gone forever."

"Ah…but that's where you're wrong," Tilda says. "That's what SWARM wanted you to think. Our smart-satellites located her just last week. We dispatched several drones and verified her identity. Although she's being held hostage in a remote compound, she's still very much alive. Look for yourself."

All four screens project an aerial shot of an outpost building with infrared imaging. Dozens of bodies patrol the outside. Inside one particular room, a small body lies on a flat surface, perhaps a bed. Her arms and legs are sprawled out and appear restrained.

"Sofia!" Lyric's cry reverberates hollowly off the stone-cold walls. She buries her head in Pallas's arms.

"Sofia is captive but unharmed," Tilda says. "Not even your daddy's powerful government connections could have discovered that truth. Now do you see why your mission is so critical? Sure, your efforts will eradicate SWARM, but if you're successful, the winning cohort will also receive their Boon—safe and sound.

"Notice a theme in all the SWARM stories?" Tilda asks. "Think about it. All eight of you from soma and amrita told a story of loss. You'll hear the same melody in a moment from Aryedne, Karme, Damon, and Phoenix, too. SWARM took something from all of you: a dream, a business, or a loved one.

"Your Boon is the ability to get that something back unscathed," Tilda says.

Her announcement produces the same effect as when you visit a foreign country and hear a language other than your own. You catch the words, but they don't link with meaning. Seconds pass. And then finally her words do connect.

Disbelief spills across the great room. Tilda's tale is just that—a fantasy. There's no way she knows my Boon, and there's no way she can bring my parents back to me.

"*Unbelievable?*" Tilda questions. "Yes. But certainly not impossible. Styx—your Boon—a perfect kidney match for your grandmother. Lelantos—a financial fortune returned to you and your business partner. Pallas—a prodigal brother reunited with you, drug free."

Around the room Tilda goes. Each of the eight clerics she names clings to the claim she makes. And with each promise, a shred of hope flashes onto the screens. An infrared image of a loved one or a bank statement with more numbers than I can count.

She pauses and says to Nick, "Your Boon—a reputation protected." Then she turns to Damon. "Your Boon—a guilty conscience washed clean." Chloe and I look at Nick and Darren. Both stare down, unwilling to make eye contact with us.

"Karme," Tilda says. "Your Boon—a best friend returned. And yes, Aryedne, even you."

A photograph of my family appears on the next slide—the only image of them I've ever known. The one when I was just three years old, taken days before my parents were *killed*, according to what Cai told me on the roof. Tilda can't bring back the dead.

"W-where did…" My throat tightens, making my voice raspy and garbled. I try again. "Where did you get that?"

"Easy, young lady. From your uncle, of course."

I snap my head to look at him. His eyes never lie—at least not to me. He can fool others, but I know when he's telling the truth.

Yet when I look at him, I find nothing—not even a return glance. My own uncle, unwilling to grant me the respect I deserve. He'd rather look at the floor.

Tilda rushes ahead to fill in the awkward space.

"I wouldn't say so if it weren't true, Aryedne. ELIXIR Project will eradicate SWARM and its hold upon *all* our lives. We will *all* be repaid for the years SWARM has eaten—all but me, of course. DNA testing confirmed my little William's death. We buried his body, and nothing can bring him back to life." She closes her eyes.

I can't tolerate it any longer. "Sounds like a perfect little pitch, Tilda," I say. "Except for one small truth."

"And what's that?" she asks.

"I don't believe you, and nobody else should, either."

"Thank you, Aryedne, for that strong vote of confidence," Tilda says. "But things aren't always as they seem. If anybody should know that, it's you."

Did she hear Cai's warning through my ring? Maybe husheye didn't jam the signal after all.

"You have a choice, Aryedne, just like every other cleric," Tilda says. "You can believe what you think or believe what you know."

She definitely heard us talking on the roof.

"We can get you your Boon, but if you opt out of the Project, you'll never know the truth. Tough choice, isn't it?"

I don't give her the benefit of answering. If she is telling the truth, then winning my Boon would be worth any price, even participating in the Project. Honestly, though, I still have my doubts. ELIXIR might be powerful and even capable of miracles. But last time I checked, not even ELIXIR has discovered a way to bring the dead back to life again.

CHAPTER TWENTY-ONE

"Places, everybody," Edge shouts. "Five minutes until we go live."

I take a sip of water from the glass in front of me. A couple other clerics fix their hair.

It seems like Tilda can't suppress her intensity. She talks loud enough for us all to hear. "Before we go back on, how are we doing with our live-stream audience?" she asks Edge. "Have we received any comments from social media?"

"Yeah…tons," Edge replies. "A critique, too—in case you want to adjust. They're saying it's too scripted."

"What do you mean?" Tilda asks. "It's supposed to be scripted."

"Only repeating the comments, and it's a frequent one, too. People want authenticity, not perfection. They want to know what the clerics are thinking."

"What do you suggest, Edge—passing around a mic so we can all have sharing time? Forget it."

"Look, here's an easy tweak," he replies. "Why don't we have the tech team pick up some reactions from the clerics? Still stick to your script. We'll simply point mics at the table and let the clerics respond to the information."

"Why take a risk? We've been designing this Project for years."

"Because if you don't, then we may lose the audience and their trust," Cai says. "You said it back in our board meetings. It's a global response to SWARM's evil. If viewers feel like the Project is being done *to* them instead of *with* them and *for* them, then we risk a rebellion even with global law on our side."

Tilda mulls it over in her mind. "Fine. But, Edge, feed me some questions on my tablet, too. We'll mic the tables and integrate a little Q-and-A. If all this nonsense helps us take down SWARM faster, then I'm willing to try it. Happy with that, Cai?"

"Sounds like a plan," he replies. "Clerics, just make sure you add some commentary to Tilda's script. Be yourself. Shouldn't be too hard."

"But don't overdo it, either," Tilda warns. "I have a plan, and I don't want to deviate from it."

"And we are live in three, two, one...." Edge backs away from the large wooden table.

The camera above our heads springs to life again, closing in fast on Tilda's face before abruptly halting in midair.

I think I know why Tilda's presence demands undivided attention. It's her passion. One thing's for sure. Tilda will do what it takes to bring SWARM down. She's willing to suffer more than anyone I know because William's death caused her more pain than I'll ever understand.

Cai sits between Kiran and McNultey at the north end of the table. At least now he looks more relaxed.

"Before you meet your ichor clerics, I'll address the three key themes floating all over social media," Tilda explains, scanning her tablet. "First, the wii initiative. Naturally, many of you are wondering if you're an R1, R2, or R3. Thanks to ELIXIR's smart-satellites, your resistance level has already been identified.

"Following the Unveiling tonight, you'll be able to visit our brand-new website. From there you can create a username and password and see your personal profile. Simply click the Deliver button and an ELIXIR drone will be dispatched according to your coordinates with your customized wii components.

"If you delay registering for more than forty-eight hours after the Unveiling or if you don't have access to the website, an ELIXIR proxy will be dispatched and help you become wii compliant.

"If for some reason you resist, you'll be labeled a SWARM loyalist and dealt with accordingly. ELIXIR will not rest until SWARM is completely eradicated."

"Aryedne, you'll be the first ichor cleric to speak. Do so immediately after Tilda finishes addressing the questions from our live-stream audience."

Tilda wasn't joking. Iris does take some getting used to. And the longer I wear it, the less I like it.

"You also asked about our strategy for dismantling SWARM through ELIXIR Project. We're refraining from discussing specific strategies because we don't want to tip off SWARM.

"We'll save the strategy talk for tomorrow at five-thirty a.m. All twelve clerics will join me and the Senior Board. We'll meet in the $100 million, 263,000-square-foot athletic center—the perfect space for what we call the Abyss. The past couple of days, we've been transforming it into an experience where the twelve clerics will be pushed to the edge—physically, emotionally, and psychologically. They'll experience breathtaking heights and unpredictable depths—all in an effort to discover the truth."

Grunts reverberate from the clerics seated along the table. "Did she say five-thirty a.m.?" Chloe moans. "Somebody shoot me."

"Too right," Ares complains. "I'm still jet-lagged

and I won't be worth a zack in the morning."

"Who cares about sleep?" Erida scolds. "You missed the part about physical torture. Besides, I have a severe case of acrophobia and I don't remember signing any release forms."

"I'm not sure what a zack is, but I agree with Erida," Nick says, chuckling. "Sounds like serious pain to me."

I wonder how the clerics' commentary sounds on social media. Maybe Edge and Cai were right. Maybe the audience needs more authenticity. In any case, it's certainly getting a large dose of it.

"Enough questions," Tilda says, probably fed up with all the clerics' commentary. "This is a perfect transition for you to meet our third and final cohort." Tilda clears her throat. "I give you ichor."

"Stand up, Aryedne. You will speak first."

I obey iris. Darren, Chloe, and Nick stand with me.

After the applause from proxies and clerics dies down, Tilda turns her attention toward me. "Your two answers, Aryedne?"

"North America," I respond unemotionally.

"Reason for joining ELIXIR Project?" Tilda asks.

I pause, mouth open, fully intending to speak— though I'm not sure exactly what I'll say.

"Tell them SWARM took your parents from you at the age of three."

I shake my head at iris's directive. SWARM wasn't

even around back then—at least that I know of. Maybe it knows something I don't?

"Tell them SWARM took your parents from you at the age of three."

Should I just pretend like Cai does and suppress the truth? It might be safer until I find out more information.

"TELL THEM SWARM TOOK YOUR PARENTS FROM YOU AT THE AGE OF THREE!"

I set my jaw and my stance. I'm not about to play the part of somebody's puppet.

"The truth," I say shakily. A surge of adrenaline races through my body, injecting more strength into my speech.

"I joined Elixir Project to discover the truth."

Instinctively, I look for Cai. Maybe my confession crossed a line? My eyes find his. He shakes his head left to right. Is he disapproving? Most wouldn't pick up on his subtle gesture, but in this moment I feel dialed into a different frequency. Is he giving me some kind of warning? I sense evilness in the air.

"Truth?" Tilda says methodically. "Isn't that what we're all after, Aryedne?"

Before I have time to formulate a response, the four screens surrounding us go pitch black. A digitized voice booms across the speakers.

"Greetings, global citizens. We are SWARM."

CHAPTER
TWENTY-TWO

"Tsk-tsk, Tilda. Don't you know your manners? We heard about your little party, but we never got an invitation."

The screens cut in with the sole image of a dark hooded figure seated at some sort of desk. A purplish glow emanates from behind his hood. Although I don't know how, Tilda maintains perfect poise. I bet every cell in her body longs to make him suffer, the same way SWARM made William suffer.

"It's been years and time certainly hasn't been friendly to your face, Tilda. The last time I saw you it was minutes before exterminating your little cowboy. He *was* such a pretty little boy." The voice laughs wickedly.

"But tonight we've hacked your little global powwow. And if you were disgusted by what we did with William, you have no idea what we have planned."

My skin crawls. I've never heard the voice of evil this raw and palpable.

"Hear me loud and clear, clerics—SWARM can't be stopped."

Moments before, we gloried in hopes of Boon, reunions with loved ones and recovery of lost fortunes. But now every cleric looks disoriented, like the rest of the world, I'm sure.

"What a pitiful director of strategic implementation, Mr. Lewis," the digitized voice says mockingly. "What do they call you? Soter?"

Cai sits in silence, unshaken.

"Stand up, Cai," SWARM commands.

Cai breathes deeply, pushes his chair back, and starts to stand. Both Kiran and McNultey put their hands on his shoulders and hold him down. Cai clasps their hands and nods reassuringly. He stands up without speaking a word.

"In a world where everything is connected...," SWARM begins.

"Anything can be hacked," Cai finishes.

"Very good, Mr. Lewis. Too bad knowledge isn't power. You're vulnerable now, like the rest of the world. You're going to have to do better than your lame wii initiative. Maybe your pretty little niece has some words of wisdom for you. Aryedne—what a beautiful new name—look into your uncle's eyes," demands the digitized voice.

I rip iris off my face so Cai can see me clearly. Tears pool at the bottom of my eyes. I must stay strong for Cai's sake.

"Don't cry, sweetie," SWARM says mockingly. "Just do one little thing for us. Tell your uncle he's going to die."

I bite my lip and shake my head.

"Look into his eyes." The voice presses harder. "Tell him we hacked his digital heart implant. Tell him we're simulating a heart attack to punish him for failing. Tell him SWARM is god and we can hack anyone we want. *Tell him!*"

I cover my ears, hoping to drown out the foul voice.

"Tell your uncle he's going to die, and we'll make the heart attack quick and painless."

I breathe in slowly to compose myself. Cai grimaces. He grips his chest with one hand and braces with the other. This could be the last time I see him alive.

I give my uncle a forced smile—the man who raised me and taught me everything I know about living and loving. "Uncle," I say tenderly. He doesn't hear my voice, so I speak again. Hot tears stream down my cheeks. I can't lose him, too. "Cai, listen to me. You're *not* going to die."

He clutches his chest and falls straight onto the table, shattering glasses and knocking over pitchers of water.

He yells in pain, jerking violently. He slides across the broken glass, red blood spraying out from various places all over his body.

"Good-bye, Soter, the spirit of safety and deliverance from harm," SWARM says. "You've been hacked."

CHAPTER
TWENTY-THREE

I SIT ON A BLACK leather chair sipping my green tea latte. My eyes bounce from my phone screen to the entrance every time I hear the door chime. Unknown faces enter the café, each dressed in black and holding something in their hands.

Where is he?

A few people pass through a beaded curtain on my right into the adjacent room.

Finally, Cai opens the front door. After a quick hug, he sits down across from me in an identical black chair.

"You feeling okay?" I ask.

"Yeah, why wouldn't I?"

I search my mind for some clue, but I can't recall the source of my concern.

"Sienna, I asked you to meet me here for a reason." Then he scans the room to make sure no one can hear us. In a hushed tone, he says, "Whatever you do, don't let your cohort win in the Abyss."

I laugh. "And why not?"

"I'm serious, Sienna. If you do, your life—and the lives of your friends—will be in danger."

"For winning? But what about the Boon?"

"*What about it?* Haven't you been listening to what I've been telling you?" Cai shifts his posture gingerly. "Do you know what I had to do to get here tonight?"

"No, I don't. You never tell me anything, remember?"

"Well, I'm telling you this. Whoever wins dies!"

His warning tightens around my heart. I open my mouth to ask more questions, but I feel two hands pushing down heavily on my shoulders. They shake me.

"*Sienna!* Wake up, Sienna! We're going to be late," Chloe warns.

"Where am I? What time is it?" I say, fighting back a deep yawn.

"You're in bed and it's five fifteen. We need to be at the Abyss with the other clerics in fifteen minutes."

"Why didn't you get me up earlier?" I snap.

"I've been shaking you the past ten minutes," my roommate says defensively. "I was about to call the Board of Clerics and tell them the dose they gave you was too strong."

"What do you mean, *dose?*"

"Put on the outfit they left for you, and I'll tell you on the way."

Chloe helps me gather my things and splashes some water on my face. "Why do I feel like a truck hit me?" I ask.

"You collapsed after Cai's heart attack. They transported him to the Cleveland Clinic. On the way, they replaced his digital implant. Said they didn't want to take any more chances with SWARM hacking it again."

"He's alive?"

"Barely," Chloe sighs. "Sounds like the next seventy-two hours are critical. He's in a coma."

"Oh, poor Cai." My heart hurts for my uncle. "How did I get back to our room?"

"Tilda insisted on a high dose of meds—probably so they could peel you away from Cai. She said the Project needs all twelve of us if we have a shot at eradicating SWARM. The board is more motivated than ever after the stunt they pulled last night, hacking the Unveiling."

I slip my arms and legs into the formfitting black fabric. It's unlike any material I've ever felt against my skin. A small, thin band of greenish light around my wrists and ankles turns on automatically. It's the same color as my iris glasses the night before. I still feel groggy, but every detail Chloe shares wakes me up, igniting more anger inside.

"I can't believe SWARM hacked the Unveiling. What was the fallout from Cai's attempted murder? I'm sure with the global live-streaming, the public lost some faith in us and the whole wii initiative." I finish tying my shoes and then stand up. "Ready."

"Five twenty-five. We gotta hustle," Chloe warns.

I flip off the light and lock the door. Then we head down the stairs.

"Nothing," she continues. "Kiran secured the data breach just before SWARM hacked Cai's heart. The live stream went dead for about fifteen minutes. Once Cai was removed from the great room, Tilda resumed the Unveiling. She downplayed SWARM's hack and used her spokesperson charm to regain global trust."

"That's quite some charm," I say. The cool morning air pushes away the remaining cobwebs from my mind.

"So you ready to win the Boon?" Chloe asks. "God knows Amy needs to be saved, and it's been years since I've seen my best friend."

Thoughts from last night came flooding back, bringing a wave of anxiety with them. Even though Cai's warning came in a dream, something about it seemed so real. Still, I'm not about to throw the whole competition based on a dream, especially one I had while under the influence of potent meds.

I've never played to lose, and I'm not about to start. Besides, the stakes are too high, and my Boon is too big.

I turn to my roommate with fire in my eyes. "I'm

ready to win," I say. But deep in my gut I understand the weight of my words. If Cai was telling the truth, then I just pronounced a death sentence upon my three friends and upon myself. No Boon is worth that price.

CHAPTER TWENTY-FOUR

CHLOE USES THE flashlight on her Cortex ring to guide us along the wood-chip walkway. The path snakes down through the small, dense forest joining the older part of campus with the newly developed sports complex. Passing through the final trees outlining our path, I spot the massive structure.

This combination of steel and glass boasts the latest advances in kinesthetic and technological integration. It's a work of art to behold, comprised of soaring glass walls, a roof spanning more than four acres, and brilliant illumination made possible by more than fifty skylights.

On a normal day, I'd enter through these glass doors—accompanied by my newest playlist—expecting to work out. Sometimes I get so engrossed in exercise I lose sense of time and self. I've blown through half an audiobook—even clocking a personal record—completely unaware of fatigue until I finally stop or my smart-ring runs out of power. My internal critic shuts down, and I simply embrace the present moment.

But there's nothing normal about today. For all I know, my uncle's life teeters on a knife's edge, and the fate of the world rests upon twelve teenagers.

We walk over to the other clerics, congregated in the entranceway. They wear the same black outfits as us, except for the green light encircling our wrists and ankles. Soma clerics sport yellow lights, and amrita, blue.

"Feeling any better?" Darren asks me.

"Still waking up. Tough night, you know."

"I'm surprised you didn't tear off Tilda's head," he says. "I was kind of hoping you would."

"We would've had your back if you did," Chloe says.

"For sure," Darren says. "You think she was telling the truth about the Boon?"

"If not, the conspiracy was quite convincing," I say. "The way they researched our Boons and then strung together those pictures and videos. I know I was impressed."

"Me too," Chloe admits. "But some Boons seemed more cryptic than others—like yours, for example." She stares at Nick and Darren, but neither says a word. Sensing Darren's uneasiness, I try changing the subject.

"How did Cai look when they wheeled him out of the room?"

"Not good," Nick says. "I've seen plenty of injuries

on the football field, but he was in an entirely different category."

"Nick!" Chloe elbows him. "Be a little more sensitive."

"It's all right," I say. "I'd rather have honesty than deception any day of the week." Darren looks off into the distance. Something must be bugging him. "You okay, Darren?"

"Yeah." He turns back to us. "I guess I'm just not ready for the Abyss. That's all."

"With you on that one," Nick agrees. "We got here early and walked around a bit. You should see what they've done to the place. Put it this way: It's no longer up to safety standards."

"That bad, eh?" Chloe asks.

"Worse," a voice behind us says. I turn to see Tilda towering in white heels and an elegant two-button crepe skirt suit.

The other clerics begin gathering around our no-longer-private foursome. Darren squeezes my hand. "Thanks," he says quietly.

"For what?" I ask.

"Changing the subject," he replies.

"You noticed." I smile.

"When it comes to you, there's not much I don't," he says.

His confession injects a shot of awareness throughout my body. I feel my breaths—shallow and fast, in sync with my pulse. I think about looking away, but I don't. Our eyes lock, until Lyric's stupid comment interrupts our shared energy.

"Guess you're not dressed for the fun and games today, Tilda?" Lyric says.

"We're not the ones on trial," Kiran snaps. "Remember, we're mere mortals who can still be hacked. Case in point: Cai. You twelve EPs hold the keys to the kingdom. Hope you know how to unlock the door."

A tremor travels up and down my back as my focus shifts from Darren's eyes to Kiran's warning. As if we don't already know the significance of the Project.

"Don't let him or anybody else push you into a fear state, clerics," a voice to my right exhorts. Phoebe smiles, wearing a colorful version of our formfitting outfits. With her hair pulled back, she looks even ten years younger than she did yesterday.

"On behalf of the Senior Board of Clerics—welcome to the Abyss," Phoebe pronounces. "Speaking of the board, our thoughts and prayers go out to Cai and to you, Aryedne."

I'm sure Phoebe meant it to be encouraging, but the stares from the clerics in the other cohorts give me a serious dose of discomfort.

"My husband, André, passes on his regrets for missing our first day in the Abyss. He and another Senior Board member, Chevon, needed to devote their attention to last night's hacking. Right now they're meeting with the League of Nations and presenting a plan to beef up security and plug any further leaks SWARM may seek to exploit."

Tilda steps forward, interrupting Phoebe. "I hope each of you clerics realize what's at stake. SWARM's recent actions prove they're scared. If ELIXIR Project succeeds, then SWARM's eradication is inevitable. But if you fail, then our personal nightmares will soon become the reality for all humankind."

"Thank you for that epic pressure and for the interruption," Phoebe says. "They already know the cost of failing. I'm told your unresolved grief at the Name Change ceremony made that abundantly clear."

"Perhaps now would be a good time to begin the orientation?" Edge suggests.

"Actually, I wasn't quite finished—" Tilda starts to say.

"Brilliant idea," Phoebe says. "You have my permission, Edge."

"Then I hope you don't mind getting wet," he says. "Our natatorium has over one million gallons of water. Follow me."

CHAPTER
TWENTY-FIVE

EDGE LEADS US single file down a staircase, into a smaller-sized room known as the wet room. Although I've never been inside it before, one of my friends on the swim team never shuts up about it.

I can't see how swimming or underwater video technology has anything to do with eradicating SWARM.

"Grab a seat, clerics," Tilda orders. "And make sure you buckle yourself in."

"After you, Chloe," Nick says, offering his girlfriend an open seat to his right.

Chloe moves gracefully past his thick frame. A second later, Nick belts out a freakish yell. Several chairs around him slide and snap under his massive weight. He falls to the floor in a heap, facedown. His body convulses in a series of seizure-like movements. Chloe drops to her knees, calling his name over and over again. She tries flipping him over without success. I rush to help her.

"He needs air," she yells.

A deep belly laugh emerges from the corner of the room. "Kiran, did you see…" McNultey doubles over laughing. "Did you see the way he fell? Didn't even see it coming."

"You had to shoot him this early?" Tilda complains. "Before the orientation even started?"

"You heard what André said," McNultey says in defense. "Our orders were clear. No more clerics' given names."

"Reverse the effects now!" Phoebe commands loudly.

The seasoned soldier flips a switch on his pistol-like weapon. He points the barrel at Nick and presses the trigger. A second later, Nick's convulsing ceases and he lets out a sickened grunt. With lethargic, uncoordinated movements, he scoots his knees under his body. Chloe assists him enough so he can sit up. He blinks, squints, and then massages his temple with his thumb and middle finger.

"Gonna feel that for a while," Kiran says. "But that's the beauty of these new EMF guns. You never know that it hit you until after it's hit you."

Kiran and McNultey continue finding humor in a situation the rest of us find disturbing. If saying the names *Darren*, *Chloe*, or *Nick* means getting shot with an EMF gun, then I think I'll pass. I guess it's *Damon*,

Karme, and *Phoenix* until this Project is all over. I'd hate to see what effects McNultey's gun has on someone half the size of Phoenix.

"Sorry you had to see that," Phoebe apologizes. "Rest assured, Phoenix, there's no permanent damage. Only repeated exposure threatens our ability to bring people back."

Damon, Karme, and I help Phoenix stand up. He shuffles slowly over to one of the chairs, leaning on us as he moves. We struggle to hold him up. I hope he regains use of his limbs soon, because we're going to need him at full strength if we want to beat the other cohorts and get our Boons.

Somebody's future may be in jeopardy if we lose. Then again, if Cai's warning in my dream was real, then somebody's future may be in jeopardy if we win.

CHAPTER
TWENTY-SIX

"Look around the room, clerics. Notice something similar? Anyone want to guess?"

"All our chairs have the same type of weird footrest and seat belt," Erida says. Ophion and Metis laugh at their fellow cleric.

"True. But I'm referring to something else," Tilda says. "Your age. You're all young adults. We think it somehow contributes to your unhackability. Latest studies in neuroscience reveal your prefrontal cortex isn't fully developed until at least the age of twenty-five. This means your brain is still forming and that you're highly unaware of your own capabilities."

"What, like we don't know our own strength?" Pallas says.

"Not strength—superpowers," Kiran says, correcting him. "Let's do a quick test. Raise your hands if this is true for you. Do you see things others don't see or hear things others don't hear? Maybe you feel like you're connected to a different frequency? Or that you can sense what's going to happen next?"

Every hand in the room goes up, including mine.

I think back to last night's Unveiling. I could feel Cai's warning on the tower without his saying a word. And I sensed evil right before SWARM hacked the live stream.

"Here's another," Kiran says. "Have you become so engrossed in a project or conversation that you've lost track of time itself? A time when six hours felt like six minutes?"

I experience this sensation when I write. Sometimes it comes during a journal entry, but most often when I'm writing a chapter in one of my novels.

Again, every hand in the room goes up. I notice Kiran gleefully beaming in the corner. Although he tries to stay seated, he's totally amped, like someone who just downed a six-pack of energy drinks.

"Good. What about times when everything else around you disappeared, including distractions, and even your sense of self? You didn't edit or judge, and your brain's inner critic shut up long enough to achieve higher performance. Maybe you felt significant advances cognitively, physically, and emotionally?"

Sounds like sometimes when I work out and achieve

a personal record. Again, we all raise our hands.

"Is this just coincidence?" Tilda asks. "Or does someone, *besides Kiran,* have a logical explanation?"

As expected in a room full of teens still getting comfortable with one another, nobody stirs. "I'll give it a try," says Lelantos. He uncrosses his right leg and then pauses before speaking. "I don't know. They say we only use, what, ten percent of our brains? Maybe, we clerics just use a higher percentage somehow? Like twenty percent?"

"Decent guess," Tilda replies. "Anybody else want to take a shot?"

After a few seconds of silence, Tilda throws Kiran a bone. "Kiran?"

"It's actually the complete opposite. By monitoring you, we've observed a unique phenomenon. Rather than working harder and faster, you've tapped into some kind of talent for slowing down and deactivating entire cognitive functions."

"It's called bullet time," Phoebe explains. "Like for seasoned athletes, for you twelve clerics, the game could slow down long enough so you can influence the outcome. While the rest of the population simply reacts to life, you have a way to steer it."

"Sounds advantageous," Styx says. "So what's the bad news?"

"Without a fully developed prefrontal cortex, you're

unstable," Kiran says. "Some moments you might be brilliant and others moments a serious liability to yourselves and others."

"Edge, the goggles please?" Tilda asks.

The large proxy saunters over to the corner of the room and removes a rectangular white sheet of fabric, revealing a small steel cart underneath. From the top of the cart, he distributes a mirrored case to each cohort. He hands amrita's case to Ophion, soma's case to Lyric, and ichor's case to me.

The sleek metal box feels cool in my hands, but I can't locate any handles, locks, or levers.

"When your entire cohort touches the case simultaneously, the internal lock opens. Reads your biometric data."

Click. Click. Click.

Each case snaps open, revealing four pairs of black silicone straps attached to mirrored lenses. Ours have a greenish tint to them.

"Think of them as something similar to virtual reality goggles," Tilda says. "You'll use them for the Verdicts."

"Verdicts?" Damon asks. "Who's on trial?"

"Why, truth, of course." Tilda smiles. "Clerics, please strap yourself in—then put on your goggles."

I can't remember the last time I felt goggles snug against my head—must have been back in swimming lessons as a little kid. Cai hated waking me up those summer mornings, and I hated jumping into the freezing water.

"I got visuals on all twelve, dearie," I hear Kiran say. I can't see anything clearly through these goggles.

"When's the show going to start?" a cleric behind me asks.

Edge replies, "In three, two, one."

"Heck yeah!" a cleric on my right roars. "Here it comes."

And quite honestly, that's the last sane memory I think before the kaleidoscope of colors inject into my awareness.

My subconscious mind tells me my body is propelling through the air. Ten thousand pins prick against my skin, but not deep enough to be uncomfortable. They engage my outer layer, exfoliating doubt, fear, and disbelief.

I reach down to scratch my arm, but it's not there. Neither is my stomach, or my knees or my toes, for that matter. Like a glass of liquid spilled on a table, my soul crawls across the surface, limitless. There are no edges, borders, or boundaries. How can there be when you're integrated into everything else? The past loses its power; the future, its promise. All I know is the Deep Now.

I open my eyes. I sit stiffly on a wooden bench. Karme sits next to me. Damon and Phoenix sit farther down on the same bench.

To my right sit the four clerics from amrita: Ophion,

Ares, Erida, and Metis. And to my left are the four clerics from soma: Lyric, Pallas, Lelantos, and Styx.

In front of me, on a raised wooden platform inside a domed wooden archway, rest three large thrones. It looks like I'm inside some sort of courtroom.

On the center throne, an unfamiliar, attractive man with raven-black hair sits, relaxed, both hands leaning on the armrests. He wears a dark coat with matching pants and a crisp white shirt. Confidence flows effortlessly from his high position.

"Greetings, clerics. My name is André," he says smoothly. "I apologize for the bumpy ride. You underwent a process called Purging." He smiles before continuing.

"To maximize your time here inside the Abyss, we needed to first remove your obsolete neural patterns. Even though your brains are still young, you've lost a significant amount of plasticity. We needed to prepare your brains for Instantaneous Skill Acquisition download. We call it ISA for short."

"One more time, boss?" Metis asks.

"He can't hear you," Tilda says. "And you can't see us. Your minds are inside a simulation program called Apparition. You'll appreciate ISA soon enough."

Although I believe Tilda, the images I see seem so real. I count the tiles in the floor below me. I feel the grooves in the bench beneath me. And I admire the craftsmanship in the crown molding above me.

"We're monitoring you from inside the wet room," Tilda explains. "Just listen to André's programmed orientation and save your questions for the end.

"Clerics, you'll gather in the Apparition prior to each Verdict," André continues.

"We'll download the skills you need for the Verdict you're about to face. You'll wake back up inside the Abyss, where you'll compete for a Boon point. And at the conclusion of all three Verdicts, the cohort with the most points receives their Boons. The two other surviving cohorts are awarded with their lives."

André's image disappears, and we're left alone to deal with the impact of his words. "We're highly confident a clear winner will emerge," Phoebe reassures us. "But if there's a tie, we'll simply enter into sudden death."

Call me crazy, but I think there might be a double meaning for the term *sudden death*.

"I know you're all motivated to win your Boon, but remember the stakes are much higher. SWARM is playing for keeps, and the only way we can defeat them is to discover why you're unhackable. If we do, then we can create the ELIXIR vaccine, a permanent solution to prevent a collective hack of the human race. Our preliminary research indicates your unhackability revolves around three specific elements, each highlighted within the three Verdicts."

"Skills download successful," a voice says.

"Great. Bring them back to the Abyss. It's time for their first Verdict," another voice says.

CHAPTER
TWENTY-SEVEN

I REMOVE MY goggles and recognize the wet room. The tug around my waist reminds me I'm still restrained and can't stand up. Keeping us immobilized makes sense, especially when they're downloading skills into our brains. Funny how your mind can travel to a new world without your body even moving an inch.

Tilda grabs a remote. "When our orientation concludes, you will enter the pool wherever you want—north, south, east, or west. Doesn't matter." She uses the laser to point to the various entrances.

"The pool is comprised of ninety-nine percent water, just like the cerebrospinal fluid surrounding your brain. The other one percent mimics the remaining properties of cerebrospinal fluid, or CSF."

"We're going to swim in brain fluid?" Metis says. "That's gross."

"She said it's ninety-nine percent water, you idiot," Ophion says.

"Why CSF?" Lelantos asks.

"We refer to the first Verdict as Idea Verdict and for good reason," Kiran explains. "There are many things we don't know about ideas yet, but some things we do—like the fact that flawless ideas do exist. A phenomenon called idea anatomy proves this."

I'm confused by Kiran's jargon, and judging by the expressions on the other clerics' faces, I'm not alone. Tilda jumps in and breaks it down into layman's terms.

"Look, clerics, ideas don't change the world—*perfect* ideas do. Although everyone inherently knows not all ideas are created equal, nobody understands the specific conditions or components that make up flawless ideas. Whoever discovers this first—SWARM or ELIXIR— scores a significant advantage.

"Imagine: What if we could dissect the perfect idea, identify those components, master those mechanics, reverse engineer the process, and then leverage those results? We'd crack the code and discover the truth—that anything is possible."

"Hold on," Karme says to Tilda. "You think by us jumping into that pool of brain fluid that somehow you're going to 'crack the code' and discover how to create perfect ideas. Then you're going to leverage those ideas to beat SWARM?"

All the clerics direct their attention to Tilda. But Phoebe responds for her. "We don't *think* it will work, Karme. We *know* it will. Remember, Idea Verdict is only the first of three. If we want to beat SWARM, we need to achieve all of them."

"I still don't understand," Styx says. "Why is idea anatomy so critical? And what does it have to do with ELIXIR Project?"

Tilda's demeanor changes. I sense impatience, but she composes herself before continuing. "As we've heard, ideas are a dime a dozen. Although ideas proliferate in our minds, the majority of people die with these ideas still inside them. Why is that?"

Nobody offers an answer.

Tilda pushes further. "Should humanity, the pinnacle of creation, exist as an idea factory that never experiences the implementation of those ideas?"

Again, none of us speaks on this topic that feels so foreign.

"Let me reference an ancient book to help you understand," Tilda says. "God said, 'Let there be light,' and there was light. See it? From the beginning of time, a formula existed—beneath the surface and under the radar. It knew no gap between ideation and implementation. Translation? Thoughts became experience. Beliefs became reality. But then, suddenly and without warning, something hacked the system. Simply put, something hacked us. Throughout history, we cursed this widening gap, redefining it as resistance, self-sabotage, and other less noble terms. Today we know our enemy by its true name: SWARM."

"So you're saying we're going to become gods?" Phoenix asks sarcastically.

"No. I'm saying we're *supposed* to be gods—just like the ancient book says, created in God's image, to co-create. It's our divine destiny. So in Idea Verdict, you'll outwit your opposing cohorts in a war of ideas inside the pool. You'll eliminate that gap between ideation and implementation. And by observation and analysis, we'll be able to deconstruct flawless ideas inside the Verdict and then replicate it in the real world."

"That explanation doesn't make it any clearer," Karme says. "I still don't understand."

"You will when you jump in the pool," Kiran laughs.

"But why now? Ideas have existed as long as time itself," argues Phoenix, ignoring Kiran's comment. "Surely other people have had flawless ideas in the past."

"True in one sense," Tilda replies, "but false in another. We've never had the technology required to do such analysis. You'll be wearing IR goggles—short for 'Imagined Reality.' And you'll be swimming in a sea of potential—literally. Once you pop into the pool with those goggles, fresh off your ISA download, let's just say your ideas should manifest in real time."

"So we swim in a pool and you observe us. Big deal," Lyric says, seething. "If my Boon is on the line, I want to know how to win. What are the rules and what's the penalty for breaking those rules?"

"Does she plan on cheating?" Karme whispers, loud enough for me to hear. I wonder the same thing.

"The pool is merely a tool," Phoebe explains. "It's neutral and unbiased. It won't ruin you; it simply reveals you. And you won't know the rules until you jump in—just like in life. You can sit on the side and speculate all you want. But your first step is to leap—the saying goes, 'Build your wings on the way down.' Besides, even if we wanted to, we can't tell you the exact point of the Verdict—because, honestly, we don't know yet ourselves."

Her explanation is far from clear. And if Cai's taught me anything about business and presenting your point, it's that clarity attracts and confusion repels. There are so many unknowns swirling in my head, including Cai's health. But sitting in the Abyss, worrying, isn't helping anyone, especially Cai. The faster I achieve these Verdicts, the faster I can see him. Sounds like the board gave us everything we need to take the first step—in this case, plunging into the pool.

The other clerics sit in their chairs, fear plastered on their faces. But I'm not about to let fear hack my brain, especially after SWARM hacked Cai's heart. My uncle lies in ICU while SWARM roams freely. I think it's time to win this first Verdict.

"Well then, what are we waiting for?" I find myself saying out loud. "Time to get wet."

CHAPTER
TWENTY-EIGHT

"Edge, make sure you give them their elixir-gills, too," Tilda says. "I don't want any oxygen-deprived clerics out there."

Edge hands me four green pairs, and I distribute them to Karme, Phoenix, and Damon.

"Make sure you put them on correctly like this," Edge says, demonstrating. "Thinking underwater requires breathing underwater."

"Clerics, your goggles enable you to experience whatever you imagine," Tilda explains. "Use this creativity to your advantage. If you remove your goggles while in the pool, your entire cohort is automatically disqualified from the Idea Verdict. Lastly, remember to work together and communicate."

"Underwater? How?" Karme asks.

"You'll communicate with each other through your thoughts."

"*Excuse me?*" Karme says.

"Is it that difficult to comprehend?" Tilda says. "I assumed your studies in quantum physics would have tipped you off."

"Yeah, that isn't my best subject. I might be switching majors soon."

Tilda ignores Karme's confession and goes right on talking. "If you choose to work independently, you'll overstress your fellow clerics and inject an unhealthy amount of cortisol into the cerebrospinal fluid in your area. This error will create a cloud of orange fluid and send you to the surface in a mild state of cardiogenic shock—the fastest path to losing this Verdict."

"I don't care about losing," Lyric says. "I want to know how to win."

"Easy, Lyric," Tilda says. "The underwater scoreboard tells you who wins. Whichever cohort achieves a flawless idea makes it onto the scoreboard. Look for your color—soma, yellow; amrita, blue; and ichor, green. If you can sustain your flawless idea for thirty seconds, the Verdict ends and the Boon point is awarded."

"Put fifteen minutes on the scoreboard," McNultey says. "And start the countdown timer. If your cohort isn't in the pool when the buzzer sounds, my EMF gun will make you wish you were."

I walk with Phoenix, Damon, and Karme to the west

side of the pool. We huddle together in the middle of the walkway.

"Okay, guys, what's the plan?" Phoenix whispers.

"Got anything, Aryedne?" Damon asks. "Edge handed you the silver case for a reason. He must think you're the leader, and I tend to agree."

Though I'm flattered, I'm also intimidated at the thought of picking our strategy. Part of me wants my Boon as much as the other clerics and another part of me is still worried about Cai's warning in my dream and what happens if we don't lose. "I have some ideas, but they're only ideas."

"It's better than what I've got," Phoenix says.

"Yeah, we're listening, roomie." I love the way Karme's such an encourager. Her confidence gives me confidence.

"Okay, I think I understand the part about communicating with our thoughts. Uncle Cai often brings home new gadgets to show off. Some of these devices you control with your brain. They call the technology auto-elixir. Headsets to play video games, interfaces to drive your car, prosthetic limbs to make movement easier, and even speakers that let you select your favorite songs by merely thinking about them."

"Makes sense," Phoenix says. "For decades, EEGs have recorded the electrical activity inside our brains. We're constantly sending and receiving signals. Why couldn't we transmit our thoughts to one another?"

"Okay, five minutes left. Let me give the quantum physics piece a try," Damon says. "In class, we've been studying the famous double-slit experiment and how matter can be in two places at one time. So why wouldn't this be true with ideas, too? Ideas are thoughts, and thoughts are electrical energy. This means they have electrons, and we know electrons can exist in two places at once."

"So ideas exist in two places at once, too," Damon and I both say in unison.

"Okay, that was freaky," Karme jokes.

I see where Damon is going now and jump in to get us there faster. "Ideas manifest in the mind of the person imagining the thought," I say. "And that same idea exists somewhere else in the universe simultaneously."

Phoenix smiles and adds to the energy of the conversation. "Just like this athletic center. The architect imagined it. When he did it, he created it in his mind the first time. Years later, when the final brick was laid, he created the idea a second time. Ideation and implementation. First creation and second creation."

"Does that mean if you think it, you can do it?" Karme asks.

"Even crazier," Damon says. "It means if you think it, you've already done it."

"Great…but how about cutting the philosophy and coming up with a strategy?" Karme asks.

"Sixty seconds!" McNultey shouts.

My pulse races. I press my palm against my chest and feel it. Still tucked next to my heart, against my skin, is the small, flat disk Cai handed me on the roof—husheye! Cai said it jammed their signal. Whoever *they* he was referring to.

With all that underwater surveillance there's no way I can risk turning it on with my hand. Hopefully, Cai created husheye with auto-elixir capabilities. Turning it on with my thoughts is still a risk, but one I might need to take. There is a chance I will need to block someone from listening in on our thoughts.

"Idea Verdict begins in three, two, one…," Edge shouts.

I catch McNultey out of the corner of my eye. He stands across the water with his EMF gun drawn and pointed in our direction.

I grab Damon's hand and throw my weight forward. I feel time freeze as we hang, suspended in the air. The water beneath us dances in slow motion. I can only imagine what awaits me in a pool called ideation.

And with an imagination like mine, I know I should be deeply concerned.

CHAPTER
TWENTY-NINE

I STEP TOWARD a small crowd of people. Their backs face me. Although the room is dim, the mood feels happy—almost joyous. They gather around something—or someone. They're too tall for me to see—either that or I'm too short.

I see streamers and balloons throughout the room. I hear muted voices and laughter. The pace of the images and voices around me feels sluggish, like it's ten times too slow. My thoughts are the complete opposite—they dart and spin, trying to make sense of my surroundings.

The entire group starts singing, but I can't make out the melody. I push my way to the center for a better view. They surround someone sitting at a table. The little red-haired girl claps her hands in slow motion, smiling at all the people. Now I can see people easier. Some faces look familiar, but a different, younger version of themselves.

Uncle Cai stands next to a taller man with the same color eyes and the same color hair—a few inches, the only distinction between these two. The taller one holds the hand of the most beautiful woman I've ever seen. She leans in and kisses his cheek, then tucks her auburn-colored hair behind her ears.

They gaze into each other's eyes and then back at the little girl just in front of them. She sucks in a massive mouthful of air when the voices complete their freeze-framed song. With a flurry of energy, she unleashes her breath upon the three yellow candles on the cake in front of her.

A profound urge pushes me even closer to the table. I need to read the elegant script on the cake, written with vibrant pink icing. I see five letters.

SWARM

The room grows darker and colder. Fog leaks up from the floor and down from the ceiling.

I want to run. Expressions in the circle shift from lighthearted smiles to stern glares. A dark hooded figure walks around the perimeter of the circle. In the small gaps between the heads of the people, I notice him holding something.

As he makes his way around the circle, I realize he cradles a small body in his arms, clothed only in a torn, soiled blanket. A brown-and-white cowboy hat prevents me from seeing the face. *William!*

The circle of people breaks, allowing the hooded figure to step through. He moves closer to me. The little red-haired girl in pigtails starts screaming and reaches out to the couple standing near her, the one holding each other's hands. Instead of comforting the little girl, the woman picks up a present from the pile and gives it to the birthday girl.

"Aletheia," the woman says indolently in a digitized masculine voice.

The little girl reaches for the gift. She rips the yellow wrapping paper from one side of the box. The couple smile deviously at each other.

Before she tears off the final side of the yellow wrapping paper, I hear Damon yell, "Wake up, Aryedne. It's a trap!"

CHAPTER THIRTY

"Lyric is after you," I hear Karme say in my thoughts. "She just tried to get you to open that gift."

I turn my head and spot four black bodies off in the distance, swimming away from us. Yellow lights encircle their wrists and ankles. Soma.

"What was inside the box?"

"I couldn't tell. We all saw the scene unfolding, except you. Lyric must have had you in some kind of trance—until Damon woke you out of it."

"Why do you say it was Lyric?"

"The yellow candles and yellow wrapping paper gave a hint. But mainly because she's the only one wicked enough to imagine an idea like that."

"I don't understand," I say.

"She saw your family photograph at the Unveiling, right? Maybe she used your Boon against you and preyed on an emotionally charged memory. You know…trying to sideline you inside the Verdict."

"Well, it almost worked. Phoebe warned us it was a war of ideas," I tell Karme in my thoughts. "Where are the guys?"

"They're holding off amrita on the north side of the pool," she thinks back.

"We'd better join them. You heard Tilda's warning about working independently."

"I bet working in pairs is the only reason we're swimming and not floating from cardiogenic shock." She emerges from a sunken ship just to my right. I follow close behind her.

We move through the water and away from soma at an incredible speed. New swim strokes and techniques feel like second nature to me. I could get used to these Instantaneous Skill Acquisition programs.

Ahead of us, green lights slash the water. Must be Phoenix and Damon. I swim closer and see red tentacles wrapped around their torsos and legs, trying to pull them into some kind of dark cave.

"This squid is trying to rip us apart!" Phoenix yells inside our heads. "The eyes are flashing blue. It's got to be amrita's idea. Get rid of them or this squid—quick."

"On it, baby," Karme replies.

Then I spot a dark, murky fish emerging from inside

the giant cave. I scream when I see the menacing dorsal fin. "Shark!"

Even with our ISA download, there's no way the other cohorts can outswim it. A violent spray of bubbles shoots from several clerics. Amrita must have imagined underwater jet packs. Four black bodies with blue lights whiz past, leaving soma cohort in their wake, exposed and easy shark food.

Panic sets in.

I watch the large shark with green flashing eyes sink its teeth into the squid's skin. Wispy clouds of red pour out of the holes where the teeth bit down. The bright billows grow in mass and density. Phoenix and Damon swim away from the lifeless tentacles.

The shark turns from the carcass and heads straight for soma. I know Karme doesn't intend to kill Lyric and the rest of her cohort with the great white shark. Still, Tilda never told us what happens if we die inside Imagined Reality. I'm all for winning, but not at the expense of my fellow clerics being torn apart by razor-sharp teeth.

I imagine an idea. Each soma cleric is locked in a shark cage at a different side of the pool—north, south, east, and west. Five seconds later, I watch each cleric float up in an orange cloud of cortisol. Proxies dive into the water and retrieve the four clerics, who are convulsing in shock.

Only two cohorts remain now—amrita and us. The first Boon point is within our reach. Phoenix and Damon join us. We circle up to strategize our next move.

"Amrita will be back any moment with their next round of attacks," Phoenix thinks. "Anyone have another idea?"

"I say we go on the offense. Take them out while they're scrambling," Karme replies.

Even underwater, I sense Damon waiting for my response. I know he respects me, but I want him to know I feel the same way about his ideas.

"I know you have something, Damon," I think. "What is it?"

"Let Phoenix and Karme work on our offensive strategy," he replies. "But rather than accessing another stored image—like squids or sharks—this time imagine something entirely new. This will confuse the amrita clerics, and they won't know how to respond."

I smile—although breathing through my mouthpiece doesn't make curling my lips easy. The more I know Damon's mind, the more I love it.

Before I have time to respond, I notice Phoenix shaking his finger at me. Perplexed by his gesture, I turn. Four giant moray eels with blue eyes are swimming directly at us. Time dilates long enough for me to see the rows of razor-sharp teeth in each eel's mouth.

I lift my forearm up to shield my head. Although I

protect my neck and face, I feel agonizing pressure clamp down on my arm. Hundreds of tiny knives pierce my flesh, biting down deep into the muscle and ligaments. Even underwater I hear bones snap in two.

I struggle to keep from passing out. Losing consciousness underwater could be the last mistake I make. Bright red blood pours into my ears, nose, and mouth. I try to formulate a new idea before I float away into my forever darkness.

CHAPTER
THIRTY-ONE

My cheeks and shoulders soak up warmth. The sun hangs dead center in a perfect light blue sky shining down on a massive sea of humanity.

I sit in the second row on the sports field itself, just a few feet from center stage in a maximum-capacity outdoor arena. An old lady on my right reeks of cheap perfume.

Jumbotrons positioned throughout the stadium project the dignitaries seated on the raised platform in front of us. The audience in the upper and lower grandstands enjoys a 360-degree view of the action. Damon sits to my left. Karme and Phoenix are beside him. Karme and I wear dresses; the guys wear suits.

Children adorned in multicolored ceremonial costumes pour onto the field from all directions. About fifty of them run single file up the stairs and onto the stage.

The other costumed children stand at their assigned position on the field itself. Musical instruments begin playing the national anthem of a South American country.

Beneath a Jumbotron but just above the scoreboard, the English translation scrolls so the global audience watching via live stream can understand. When the final note ends, the children perform a brief dance and then exit.

Guns salute, fireworks ignite, and voices cheer.

A government official slowly limps to the podium. He lifts his hand, and the crowd goes quiet. The English captions translate that he's honored to announce his older daughter as the new president and to share this special day with his wife, younger daughter Sofia, and the entire country.

When the new president rises from her chair, the whole stadium erupts in a standing ovation. My three friends and I stand and share in the elation. The rows of chairs press snugly against my body in front and behind. A slight wave of anxiety passes over me. I feel boxed in by this many people in such a tight space.

The new president approaches the podium, beaming with excitement. I now recognize her—Lyric from the soma cohort.

On the Jumbotrons in bright green numbers, a thirty-second countdown timer begins. Lyric starts her inaugural speech. I glance at Damon, Karme, and Phoenix.

Instead of looking into their eyes, I see my own reflection in their green-mirrored goggles. Perplexed, I reach up and feel a silicone strap, snug against my face. The countdown timer shows twenty seconds now. Reality sets in as I realize where we are—inside a flawless idea!

The events around me screech to a halt. I look back up at the stage and see Uncle Cai standing behind Lyric. I feel the alarm in his eyes and remember his warning. I know what I need to do, and I don't have time to second-guess. I use my thoughts to turn on the husheye device inside my dress. It vibrates and then engages, jamming the signal. I can communicate freely to anyone within a fifteen-foot radius without fear of others listening in.

Sixteen seconds.

"We can't win this Verdict," I tell Damon.

"Why not?" he says.

"Cai said if we do, we die—all of us. He came back to warn us. He's on the stage now."

Thirteen seconds.

I imagine the idea of a lone bumblebee buzzing around my head.

"Fake a fall and rip off my goggles," I tell Damon.

"What?" he asks.

"You have to trust me."

Nine seconds.

"Amrita wants you to forfeit so they win the Boon point," Karme yells. "They've planted the idea inside your head, Aryedne!"

Five seconds.

The bee lands on my shoulder.

"Do it, Damon!" I scream. "If you don't, we're all dead."

Damon smacks the bee and in the process loses his balance. Because of the tight rows, my feet can't move to adjust for his momentum. I notice my body falling toward the old lady.

He wraps his right arm around me, tucking my head—protecting me from the impact with the chairs. The fingers on his left hand slink toward me, and the silicone strap rips from my face. Hard plastic snaps back, stinging my cheeks. We tumble on top of each other in a careless, crumpled pile.

A loud voice broadcasts through the speakers, "Ichor cohort disqualified. Idea Verdict achieved."

CHAPTER THIRTY-TWO

THE SKY ABOVE my head sparkles and shimmers. My body feels weightless, like I'm floating through air. Without even trying, I glide toward the light.

My head breaks through the surface, and I take in familiar sights and sounds. I realize where I am—back inside the natatorium.

I remove the elixir-gills from my mouth and suck in a deep breath of air. Although the device did its job, nothing beats fresh oxygen swirling inside my lungs.

I peer down into the pool, and next to my foot I spot a pair of mirrored green goggles with a broken strap, swaying effortlessly in the water. I glance up at the scoreboard and notice four green numerals—00:01—plastered on the timer. Although I'm usually furious when I don't win, in this case I've never been more relieved to lose.

I'm startled by the black cap on my left breaking the surface of the water—or brain fluid, as Metis called it. But if Cai is right, then there's no more Metis.

Two other black caps pop up around me. It's my three friends. Still no sign of amrita. Maybe they're still underwater?

"What are you? *Stupid?*" Karme spews out while removing her breathing device and goggles. I knew she might be upset, but the tone of her voice sounds so foreign I'm not even sure she's talking to me.

"W-what do you mean?" I ask, fighting back the tears starting to collect in the corners of my eyes.

The guys pull off their goggles. "What the heck were you thinking, Damon?" Phoenix says. "I can't believe you got us disqualified."

I turn to Damon, hoping he'll defend me. But he doesn't say anything.

"Amrita better be dead, or our friendship will be," Karme threatens me. "If you want to blow your own chances of winning the Boon, then be my guest. But don't screw mine. Amy's life is on the line, in case you forgot."

She hops out of the pool, and Phoenix follows, equally furious. They walk back to the wet room, squeaking on the hard floor with each step they take.

I don't want to examine my forearm, but I must. Nope—no moray eel tooth marks or broken bones.

Yet my right cheek still feels tender from the goggles snapping against my face. I didn't imagine the part about the strap breaking.

"Ten minutes until debrief," McNultey yells across the pool. "Soma's gonna need every second to recover from shock."

A painful silence fills the space between Damon and me. Although he stands less than two feet away, the distance separating us feels like galaxies. I know he took a risk—trusting me. Hope he doesn't think I screwed his chances of getting his Boon, too. "I'm so sorry, Damon. I didn't have time to explain myself in there."

Finally, he breaks the silence. "Look, if there's even a slim chance Cai's right, then I didn't want to gamble with your life," he says.

"Thanks," I say.

"Besides, with a guilty conscience like mine, there's no damage if we lose the Boon," he confesses. "Aryedne, I've already been dead for years, and I doubt there's a chance for my redemption anyway."

His words weigh on me. "I don't believe it. Nothing you could have done is *that* horrible."

"I'm not who you think I am," he says. "Maybe someday I'll tell you about it."

He pulls himself out of the pool. Water rolls off his hair and onto the floor. The sleek black fabric hugs his skin, highlighting every inch of his body. He grabs a towel from a nearby table, removes his cap, and pats down his face. Then he walks toward the wet room without turning back to acknowledge me.

Great. I lose my entire cohort's loyalty because of one single choice—and one I made to save their lives. Filled with frustration, I press my chest to turn off husheye. With nowhere else to go, I exit the pool on autopilot and make my way to join the others for the debrief. Maybe if I beg them they'll forgive me?

"Aryedne," a voice calls from behind me. "Hold on. I'll walk with you."

I turn to see Phoebe exiting the pool. Was she in there the whole time?

"Very impressive," she says, drying herself off with a towel.

"Seriously?"

"Absolutely. The Verdict went as predicted in the beginning. But then, in the midst of the eel attack, you had the presence of mind to shift the energy from fear and negativity to gratitude and positivity. How did you know to do that?"

"Not sure." I shrug. "I knew I needed an idea, and that's the first one that came to mind."

"Idea replacement, that's how," she says. "I don't know how the board missed it. We kept focusing on resisting. And then you come along and show us the power of replacement."

I smile, momentarily forgetting about my own cohort's disapproval.

"There are so many brilliant components you integrated: Lyric's dream for the presidency, her desire to be reunited with Sofia, her father's introduction, but even the fact that you used Lyric in the first place? Not taking revenge on someone who hurt you, but instead believing the best for her? Aryedne, you gave ELIXIR a master-level education—not to mention a serious upgrade in our chances of eradicating SWARM."

I try not to be embarrassed, but it's too difficult to hide my appreciation for her approval. Under the present circumstances, a compliment goes a long way.

I spot Tilda fixated on her glass tablet ahead of us. She looks up and waits for us to reach her.

"Aryedne, great work in there," Tilda says. "I'm sure the board will take time to unpack it all since we recorded the footage. We'll replay it over and over again."

But then she stops. "There's something I can't quite figure out, though."

Her voice has an edge to it, the same edge I feel every time I engage with her. A significant contrast to Phoebe's warm demeanor.

"The audio went dead beginning at the last twenty seconds of the countdown timer."

She waits for a response. When I don't give one, she continues, "Kiran took agonizing steps to ensure clear, continual audio and video surveillance. He had backups and then backups for those backups. What happened?"

I weigh my words before deciding on using humor to diffuse the situation. "Uncle Cai always says, technology and Murphy's Law go together like peanut butter and jelly." I chuckle.

Phoebe smiles at my joke, but Tilda has only a flat affect.

"From our end, you were so close to winning," Tilda observes. "You had the Idea Verdict in the bag—until the last four seconds."

"I know, and I wanted that Boon point so badly." I try switching tactics and go for the emotional angle instead.

Beads of sweat form along the top of my forehead. One drips down my face. Good thing she'll never know if that drop was sweat from stress or water from the pool.

"I already can't stand bumblebees. But now I hate them even more," I say, grasping for whatever words pop into my mind. "If that stupid bumblebee wasn't there, I would have never tripped and been disqualified."

"But that's just it, Aryedne....You're the one who imagined everything," Tilda points out. "That entire scene was completely your idea, including the bumblebee."

I'm caught and I didn't even see the setup. My heart pumps fast and loud. I worry the skintight material will reveal the outline of the husheye stashed inside my suit.

Instead of replying, I stare into Tilda's eyes, and she

stares back. Does she suspect the truth? We both read each other, mining for a tell. But on this day, in this game, neither of us breaks under the pressure.

"One thing is for sure," Phoebe interjects. "Damon wanted to protect you. Keep an eye on that one, Aryedne. He's a nice boy, and if you ask me, I think he likes you."

This time I don't fight back blushing. Maybe it will satisfy their curiosity?

In the remaining steps to the wet room, I know I should rehearse Tilda's interrogation of my performance inside the Idea Verdict. But no matter how hard I try, Phoebe's observation keeps distracting me. What if she's right?

What if Damon does like me?

CHAPTER THIRTY-THREE

"WELL, LOOKY HERE. The loser has enough guts to show her face in public," Lyric says from a prone position inside the wet room.

Normally, I don't retaliate, but I still owe her for shoving me last night. "Not going to lie. Losing hurts, Lyric. But I'm sure losing by going into cardiogenic shock hurts even worse." She turns her head the other way—too sore for a verbal spar.

"You have no idea," Styx moans. "Did you have to imagine us in separate shark cages?"

"Better than being eaten by one," Damon says, reminding Styx of the context.

I don't need to explain my motives to soma. I thank Damon with a smile. Then I look to find an empty chair. Damon motions to one near him. I stroll past Lelantos and Pallas in the same position as Styx and Lyric—facedown.

Still no sign of amrita. *Maybe Cai was right about the danger of winning the Verdict?*

"You sure you want to sit next to me after what I just told you?" Damon asks.

"My feelings haven't changed," I say.

Toward the front of the room, Phoebe, Tilda, and Kiran huddle, whispering and tapping their tablets. I wish I knew what they were saying. Hopefully, the footage doesn't tip them off about husheye.

A dozen soldiers dressed in black enter the wet room, each carrying one of those long sticks at their side, the weapons that cast a pulsating orange glow. The proxies stand motionless along the perimeter.

I stretch my neck past Damon, hoping to make eye contact with Karme. If I can catch her expression, I'll know if she still needs time to cool off. Unfortunately, Phoenix's immense shoulders block me from seeing her.

"Please join me in welcoming our Idea Verdict victors," Tilda announces. "Those of you strong enough to stand, let's show our support." Kiran hops up and down, then high-fives Ares, Erida, Metis, and Ophion as they enter the room.

The four amrita clerics saunter in, their pride and confidence growing with each step. The applause doesn't stop until they do, in front of the four open chairs closest to the front.

The soma clerics aren't in any shape for standing. And

yet the effects of the shock seem to be waning. Everyone but Lyric sits up in their chairs. She still lies facedown.

Karme decides to make eye contact now, causing me to feel worse than I already do. But with amrita alive and well, I now know Cai was wrong. That or I imagined the warning. He *is* in a coma, after all, and I don't think he could've infiltrated my dream last night.

"Please sit," Tilda says. "Our proxies will be taking your dinner orders. Request whatever you want. They'll start with amrita."

"To the victors belong the spoils," Nick mutters.

Tilda remains standing. "When André and Phoebe invited me to be part of the Project, I couldn't fathom how SWARM could ever be stopped. But based upon your performances today, I don't know how SWARM could ever win."

Kiran belts out a deafening war cry. No one else joins in, making the awkwardness even more palpable.

"Thank you, Tilda, for sharing your excitement," Phoebe says. "André and I are elated with the results, too. However, I wouldn't get overconfident...."

"Not overconfident, Phoebe, only thrilled that William's perpetrators will finally be brought to justice and—"

"Thank you, Tilda. Please be seated...now!" Phoebe says. "André asked *me* to share his thoughts about the Verdict."

"Why, yes, of course." Color flushes into Tilda's cheeks. She straightens her jacket before moving to an open seat in the middle of the room.

"Clerics, I share in Tilda's enthusiasm—we all do. I'll read André and Chevon's message.

"'We are beyond pleased with the clerics for their performance inside the Idea Verdict. A cursory read of the initial report gives us enough data to begin experimenting with idea replacement immediately.

"'All twelve clerics achieved a zero-second gap between ideation and implementation, and the result was a seamless integration between thinking and doing. We've already initiated a continual feedback loop to deconstruct the conditions and components.

"'We'll use the data to reconstruct it in real time. We've got a long way to go, and we're fighting a formidable enemy. But, God willing, we'll eradicate SWARM swiftly. Our future survival as a species depends upon it.'"

Their final warning drops like a pile of boulders. There's no clapping, no cheering, and no celebrating. Although our Project achieved the first Verdict, we still have two more to go. And if sharks, eels, and squids defined the first one, I have no inkling what the next two will bring.

"Tilda, please unpack the Project Paradigm with the clerics," Phoebe instructs. "It's getting late and the

clerics need their rest before the next Verdict tomorrow."
With the weight of our mission reestablished, Phoebe
hands the reins back over to the ELIXIR spokesperson.

The proxies make their way to our cohort. Phoenix
requests chicken, steak, and fish, plus all the sides you
can imagine. One short and stout proxy reads back his
order to ensure he got it all down correctly.

"Nothing for me," I say. "I'm not hungry."

Half the proxies leave the room equipped with food
orders. The other half stand at attention holding their
weapon—though I'm not sure why. With the Senior
Board's initiative of plugging any security leaks from
last night's hack, I highly doubt SWARM would be
successful again.

"If you look at the screen, you'll notice our Project
Paradigm," Tilda says.

"Each arrow represents a Verdict. We need to
achieve all three Verdicts to unlock how you twelve are

unhackable. We'll utilize that knowledge to develop the ELIXIR vaccine. Through a global network of 3-D printers we'll mass-produce the vaccine and then distribute it via drones. At most, seventy-two hours after we achieve the third Verdict, all humanity will be vaccinated, ensuring permanent immunity from all things SWARM.

"In the subsequent days, we'll launch our own series of attacks and by week's end, SWARM will be a distant memory."

"When all three Verdicts are achieved, the winning cohort will be awarded their prize at the Boon Ceremony inside St. Paul's. We'll broadcast the entire ceremony via live stream. Unlike SWARM, you twelve clerics will be remembered forever."

Lyric perks up, sliding her body into a seated position. Anybody watching can discern the delusions of grandeur swimming inside her mind.

"It's that simple?" Lelantos asks. "We just win points and then get the Boon? End of story?"

"Your Boon will be distributed after one of the winning clerics gives a victory speech at the ceremony," Tilda explains.

Lyric gives a sly smile—mentally rehearsing her speech, I'm sure. "But today, victory goes to amrita," Tilda announces while advancing the next slide in her presentation.

"Don't despair, soma or ichor. Tomorrow is a new day and a new Verdict. You'll each have the opportunity to score the next point," Tilda says, consoling the losing cohorts. "And now we'll dismiss you to your dinner, down the hall. You'll be eating with your own cohort tonight. Use the time to strategize or, for some of you, to strengthen bonds."

She glances over at Karme and I. Maybe my

roommate's anger is more obvious than I thought?

Phoebe gives the final words before dismissal. "We'll be collecting your rings now. Although we've stepped up our security, the hack by SWARM at the Unveiling proves if you're connected to anything online, you're susceptible. We should have known better, but we're taking every precaution to protect you and make this the safest place on the planet. We've locked down the physical campus and we have video surveillance inside and outside of every building. Our proxies will continue patrolling these grounds twenty-four seven until the last drone has delivered the final dose of ELIXIR vaccine.

"On your way out the door, please turn in your phones, rings, and any other device you may have. If you're caught online, you'll be eliminated. We can't jeopardize the entire Project over one obstinate cleric."

Grunts and groans reverberate throughout the wet room about being completely disconnected from the world. Knowing ELIXIR, they'll be perpetually checking our online accounts, monitoring for any activity.

"Be back at six a.m. sharp to begin the second Verdict. Soma, we have a proxy with a cart waiting out front," Phoebe explains. "When you're done with dinner, he'll drive you back to your sleeping quarters. Obviously, you're not up to par yet. But by morning you'll be fine."

I stand up from my chair and remove my ring.

"Hey, aren't you going to give us some kind of hint

about tomorrow?" Ophion asks. "It's easier to strategize when we know details."

"Any hints, McNultey?" Tilda asks.

"Certainly." The officer grins, grabbing one of the long glowing weapons from a proxy near him. "One word: skylatis."

CHAPTER
THIRTY-FOUR

"We're not leaving this room until you two talk it out," Phoenix says.

"I'm with you," Damon agrees. "There's no way we can win the Boon with you girls divided."

"Well, there's no way we can win if you keep getting us disqualified!" Karme shouts.

Her words sting. "It's *my* fault—okay, Karme? Damon didn't have anything to do with it. I went with my gut."

"Don't take all the blame," Damon interrupts. "You said Cai warned you, so he's partly responsible."

As much as I would love to spread the blame, I value the truth too much. "Cai didn't *exactly* warn me," I hedge.

"What do you mean, *exactly*?" Karme presses.

"I had a dream last night about Cai warning me. He said if we won inside the Abyss we'd be killed."

"You gave up a point—maybe even our chance at

the Boon—*because of a stupid dream?*" Karme spews out.

"There's nothing we can do about it now," Damon says. "Let's focus on what we can control—like how we show up at tomorrow's Verdict."

Damon's suggestion hangs like a thick fog in our private dining room. I've seen other students use the room we're in for aerobics, yoga, martial arts, and dance classes. The maple sprung floor, mirrored walls, and glass windows and doors typically give this space a warm, optimistic feel. But tonight, on the receiving side of Karme's rage, nothing inside these four walls feels warm or optimistic.

She looks at me and glares disapprovingly.

"Can you forgive me, friend?" I ask.

After a few seconds, her stern expression breaks. "Ah, what's the use? How can I stay angry at my roomie? You're the only one who listens to all my endless rants. What was I going to do? Give you the silent treatment back in our room tonight? Everyone knows I can't shut up for eight minutes—not to mention eight hours."

I smile because she's right. She could never keep quiet that long.

"Now, get over here and give me a hug before I start crying," Karme says. We break into a stint of laughter. I think everyone is emotional from the Verdict. The thought of kicking back, laughing, and eating—knowing nobody's monitoring our conversation through our

Cortex rings—is a freeing thought indeed.

It feels good to hug my roommate. I sure wasn't looking forward to being on the other side of someone with such a sharp tongue.

"So no more dissention in the ranks?" Damon asks.

"Nope," Karme says.

"Not here," I echo.

"Well, then shall we dig into this fantastic spread?" Phoenix asks.

"Sounds good," I chuckle. He would be the one to initiate eating. "Guess my appetite returned now that Karme isn't ticked any longer."

"Who said I'm sharing any of my food with you?" Phoenix teases.

"Haven't you learned your lesson yet?" Karme scolds. "Never get between a hungry woman and her food."

I pile some of the hors d'oeuvres onto a fancy plate and then pour myself a glass of ice water from the pitcher.

"By the sound of McNultey's clue, we're all going to need our strength to fight with the skylatis tomorrow," Damon says. "I guess it's *quite* the weapon. I overheard him talking about it in the wet room. Something about how it's designed to wound the mind and then cause subsequent trauma to the body."

"Sounds delightful," Karme says sarcastically. "But I'm up for anything if it means getting Amy back."

"I'm just hoping they give us an ISA download so we know how to use it," Phoenix says.

"I'll second that," Damon agrees.

"Hey, since we have a moment to finally breathe, either of you guys care to explain?" Karme asks.

"Explain what?" Phoenix mumbles in between his bites of food.

"Tilda seemed to think getting your Boon would help protect your reputation?" Karme asks. "Does that have anything to do with McNultey's reference back at the airport? Something about an organization you contacted at the age of sixteen?"

Phoenix's face goes pale. He chews his food slowly—weighing his options.

"You're my boyfriend and I don't believe in secrets—at least secrets like this. Besides, if we can't trust each other, who can we trust?"

Phoenix breathes deeply before saying anything. For a guy who's usually rock solid, in this moment he seems...*fragile.* He begins slowly. "Two years ago I contacted SWARM."

"You what?" Karme interrupts.

"Listen, if you want me to share, you're going to have to suspend judgment. Okay?"

She nods and grabs his hand hesitantly.

"My older brother got killed in Cleveland while visiting some friends. A gang leader shot him—mistook him for someone else." He struggles getting his next words out.

"So you were angry and contacted SWARM?" I ask, trying to make it easier for him to share his story.

"My brother, James, was my hero—the father I never had. And when they killed him, they killed me, too. I tried to move on, but I couldn't. I obsessed over ways to get even, to take revenge, to make his killers suffer—the same way they made James suffer."

Phoenix pulls his hand from Karme and tucks it underneath his arms. He stares at the ground before continuing. "The police and court systems weren't going to do anything about his murder, so I took the injustice upon myself and reached out to the strongest source I knew."

"*SWARM?*" Karme asks.

"Not exactly. A friend of mine—who's good with computers—helped me get onto the dark web. He created an anonymous profile for me, and we started looking for someone to do the hit. When it came time to talk about money, the guy said he'd do it for free in exchange for me working for his boss. When I discovered his boss was a lieutenant in SWARM, I backed out immediately. I think they wanted me for my size and athletic ability."

Phoenix sips from his glass of water and swallows hard. "Some days I hate myself, guys.…One decision, that's all it takes. I almost became a murderer and joined SWARM in a moment of weakness."

"But you didn't. You were hurt and you didn't know what to do. Nobody can fault you for that," Karme says, wrapping her thin arm around his immense shoulders.

"It feels good to get it off my chest. God knows I've been carrying it so long—hiding it from you and everybody else." Karme embraces Phoenix, making me suddenly aware of Damon's silence during the entire confession.

"My Boon isn't to get James back—he's dead," Phoenix admits. "But my friend turned on me when I got a full scholarship for football. Jealousy, maybe? He's contacted me a few times, threatening to go public with the story. Evidently, he saved the messages I sent on the dark web, and the higher I go with my football career the more I fear a full-out blackmail."

"Your Boon is for those messages to be destroyed so you can move out from under this cloud?" Karme guesses.

"You got it," Phoenix sighs.

With the way his shoulders slump, you'd think Damon's chest weighs five thousand pounds. I want to take his pain. I want to heal him. My eyes invite him to come clean with his story.

"Sorry, Aryedne," he says, loud enough for only me to hear. "Not ready yet."

As much as my heart aches, I understand pushing him won't help. If I do, he'll retreat faster. "That's okay," I say. "I'll be here when you're ready."

"I know," he says, lifting my hand and lacing his fingers between mine.

May 11

Chloe—or should I say Karme?—went to bed a few minutes ago. (I'm never going to get used to calling my roommate by her new name.) At least they can't hack a leather journal.

From what little Cai told me on the roof, it's impossible to tell who "they" are. SWARM? Tilda? McNultey? I'll watch my back regardless.

I want to see Cai. I hate competing in the Verdicts while he's in some hospital room alone. It's not right. Taking care of me all those years. Now no one's there to help him when he needs it most.

Cai's not the only one who needs me now. Damon does, too.

The more Damon pushes me away, the more I want to unwrap him. To get inside his mind. To know what he's thinking. Six months ago I might have ran or maybe even six days ago for that matter.

But when the world can end at any moment and when SWARM can hack any human, I guess it brings perspective. Life is short—too short. And with limited time, I don't want to keep agonizing over every decision.

I want Damon. There, I said it—even if only on paper. Nothing about his past scares me because I want him to be part of my future.

Finally feeling tired now. But trying to sleep with skylatis on the brain is probably a bad idea. I'll let you know how it goes—later.

—Sienna (Aryedne)

P.S. This new name is growing on me. I kind of like the person I'm becoming. So maybe I did get it wrong with the whole "Cai warning" thing. But Karme forgave me, and more important I forgave myself, too. Perfectionism is overrated. Plus I'm learning to trust my gut. And the byproduct called confidence? I'll admit...it's an addicting feeling.

CHAPTER
THIRTY-FIVE

KARME AND I push through the glass doors to the athletic center, the place I now know as the Abyss. The red digital clock to the right of the entrance reads 5:58 a.m.

I'm still getting used to the clothes the proxies picked out for us. When we arrived back at our dorms late last night, we each found an outfit folded on our bed. Formfitting black suits, this time with neon-green iridescent accents spread across sections of the back, chest, arms, and legs. They look like some kind of futuristic military uniform.

We walk over to Phoenix and Damon. "Hey, guys, what's up?" I ask.

"Indigestion," Phoenix says. "I ate way too much last night."

"I told you you'd regret it," Karme laughs.

"He's covering up his anxiety," Damon says. "We've both been snooping around, trying to prep for the Verdict."

"Any luck with that?" I ask.

"Nope," Damon says. "Hey, you must really like the color green."

"Didn't know you paid so much attention to my wardrobe," I reply.

"Well...we better get moving." Damon smiles back.

When I cross the threshold to the wet room, I know something is wrong. Lyric rests her cheek on Pallas's shoulder. He strokes her hair with his fingers. Styx buries her head in Lelantos's chest, sobbing and sniffling.

Tilda looks up from a discussion in the far corner. After acknowledging our arrival, she continues chatting with Phoebe and Kiran. McNultey paces back and forth, mumbling under his breath.

No sign of amrita anywhere. I turn to my cohort, but they look back at me with the same puzzled expression. Edge walks in from the corridor behind us. His thick arms push us to a group of chairs in the front.

"Please sit, ichor," he orders. "We'll begin the next Verdict momentarily."

"It's amrita, isn't it?" Karme says, panicking. "SWARM got them?"

Edge hesitates. "Amrita? Yes. SWARM? No. Hang tight."

We sit down and do what I absolutely hate doing—waiting. My mind riffles through a litany of possible explanations.

"Thank you for arriving promptly," Phoebe says after a couple of minutes. "Clerics, in a way you're opponents, competing against each other for the Boon. But in another sense, you're also teammates. The board even considers you family. This is why it saddens me to announce the passing of the amrita cohort."

I've been on the receiving end of news like this before—the first time when I was three years old. Some people think children are too young to process pain, but I disagree. They know death is final. And they experience finality on a regular basis in other areas of life.

Children *feel* the final days of summer before autumn blows in its blustery air. They *see* the final leaves of a tree turn from fiery red to brittle brown. And *taste* the final bite of an ice-cream cone when only tiny cone flecks remain.

But summer days, autumn leaves, and ice-cream cones always come back again. People don't.

The truth of my parents' deaths made its way into my child's brain relatively quickly. And—from what Cai tells me—when the idea finally took hold, I was never the same. My pictures changed. I went from drawing rainbows to making rain clouds. My prayers changed. I went from thanking God for my blessings to asking

God why he took them. Cai said I didn't stop playing with one particular birthday present—a ballerina music box. I wound that box dozens of times a day.

"What do you mean?" Karme demands.

The board members look at each other and then back at us, unable—or unwilling—to speak. Phoebe breaks the silence. "They committed suicide…every single one of them."

CHAPTER
THIRTY-SIX

"Impossible!" I blurt out. "Clerics with a Boon point would never kill themselves. Why would they, knowing their deepest desire was within their grasp." *Unless Cai was right and his warning was real.*

"How can you be sure, Tilda?" Damon asks. "Did they leave a note?"

"They made a video last night," Tilda explains. "Some of our staff saw the event unfolding in the surveillance room back in the older part of campus. They dispatched the closest proxies to stop them, but they couldn't get to them in time. We didn't believe it, either, until we saw the video ourselves."

On the screen in front of us, I watch Ophion, Metis, Ares, and Erida. It feels a bit surreal, knowing they're gone now.

They sit casually, straddling large white steel

tubes—so young and full of life. Arms wrap around these triangular steel trusses, which look familiar.

"Hello, mates, this is Ares. I know someone's got to be filming us somewhere, so let me give you a proper welcome to our death note—or, in this case, our death video."

Laughs flow freely out of their mouths.

"We were just having our strategy session over dinner, and I thought of a fantastic idea," Erida says. "Ready for it? Drumroll please…" The other three clerics let go of the trusses and pound their hands against their thighs. "A suicide pact!" she exclaims.

"Brilliant idea, my friend. And we're not even drunk or high," Metis says. "Actually, we're quite sane."

"But before we go for good, we felt the board deserves the rationale for our little act of defiance. After all, it's not every day you end your life," Ophion explains.

"Absolutely," Ares says. "We figured, rather than failing the Project, not to mention all of humanity, we'd choose to opt out instead. Why win *or* lose when you can forfeit and get an automatic upgrade to the afterlife instead?"

"Sounds even better when you say it out loud," Metis jokes.

"And so, we wish our fellow clerics the best," Ophion says. "We know you'll perform wonderfully in Verdicts two and three. We've already done our part by winning the first Boon point. Now, go beat SWARM."

Erida is the first to stand. "Ready, amrita? On the count of three." Her fellow clerics stand up, join hands, and exclaim in unison, "One, two, three...*Aletheia!*"

The video pans out. I watch in horror. Somehow, amrita had climbed to the highest point in the field house, more than eighty feet in the air. The video switches to slow motion and captures four bodies dressed in black, diving headfirst toward the solid track below.

I know I should look away. I'm sure the others in the room choose this honorable option. But something inside forces me to keep staring.

Maybe I want to know how it ended—*or that it ended?* Maybe I'm hoping for some weird type of closure? Whatever the reason, I sit, transfixed.

A few feet before impact, their slight bodies flail through the air. And then it comes—the eerie sound of bones crushing.

Necks snap backward.

Arms jut out at awkward angles.

Legs bend in ways never intended.

A twisted pile of potential snuffed out in seconds.

Complete silence fills the indoor field house.

But then I hear it—*shrieking!* One of the clerics didn't die upon impact immediately. In her final moments she cries out, begging for someone to make the pain stop.

Tilda turns off the projector, sparing us from the

amrita's agonizing screams. Silence fills the room—each of us trying to process what we saw.

"All of them were confirmed dead. We dispatched proxies to inform their families today. Tomorrow we'll update the global audience. Naturally, we'll honor these clerics by classifying their deaths as nonbattle casualties."

I don't know what to say or how to feel. In some ways, I don't feel anything at all.

"Video or not, I'm still not convinced," Damon blurts. "Fear of failure might be a powerful motivator, but not enough to kill yourself. None of them looked hopeless. They seemed…almost excited."

I agree with Damon. Their demeanors were weird. And if they were being monitored, why didn't ELIXIR get to the field house faster?

"Yesterday we took you through Purging to create an environment ripe for new mental connections," Kiran explains. "Essentially, we rewired your brain and increased your neuroplasticity potential—five times the norm for your age. Historically, these high levels have only been recorded in babies and young kids.

"Take language, for example. Toddlers master new languages much faster than adults do. But as we're discovering, there are drawbacks to neuroplasticity, too. Because of limited experience, toddlers don't understand danger the same way adults do."

"Is that why kids need to be taught not to trust strangers?" Lelantos asks.

"Precisely," Kiran says. "Or not to run across streets or touch hot stoves. They have no context to convince them otherwise."

Kiran's views don't match my uncle's views. According to Cai, there are no drawbacks for increasing neuroplasticity.

Phoebe grabs a box of tissues and passes it around the circle of clerics. "Achieving the next two Verdicts won't happen without downloading new skills into your brains. But this means exposure to large amounts of neuroplasticity," Phoebe explains. "In their death video, you also saw one of the costs of neuroplasticity paid for in blood. Amrita demonstrated a deep naïveté about the dangers of suicide and threat of heights."

The room goes quiet as we process what she's saying.

"So I imagine you're not going to put us in the Apparition for the other Verdicts," Lyric says. "You said yourself you want to keep us safe. So no more 5X-ing our neuroplasticity?"

We all turn to Kiran. "Abandon neuroplasticity?" Kiran laughs. "Absolutely not. But you're right about one thing. No more increasing your neuroplasticity potential by five. We've cranked it up to ten."

CHAPTER
THIRTY-SEVEN

"Let me clarify," Phoebe interrupts. "Achieving this second Verdict requires a much larger ISA download—that's the only reason we're doubling it. McNultey mentioned last night that you'll be fighting against each other with the skylatis. Receiving an expert rank with this weapon requires years of training. But thanks to the Instantaneous Skill Acquisition, you'll receive yours in about ten minutes. Before I unpack the power of this weapon, Tilda, please describe the second Verdict—the one we call Focus."

Tilda grabs her remote and advances to a new slide.

"In the second Verdict, we need to discover the conditions and components for Deliberate Magnetic Focus."

"Hold on," Styx interrupts. Usually soft-spoken, she wears an expression of deep concern. "For all we know, your carelessness caused their suicides. Do you expect us just to march right back into the next Verdict? How do we know it's safe?"

"It's *not* safe," McNultey replies.

"Please, McNultey," Tilda warns.

"No, I'm serious," says McNultey. "These clerics need to remember we're at war with SWARM. Did they expect it would be a walk in the park? There will be casualties, and we just witnessed some. But these clerics earned my respect for one reason: Although they weren't tough enough, at least they had the guts to let us know. We shouldn't mourn them. We should celebrate their bravery."

Clearly, McNultey's lost all sense of reality. He's either self-deceived or completely irrational.

"Styx, I think what he's trying to say is that our campaign with SWARM is complicated," Phoebe explains. "If we're going to survive as a species, we need the ELIXIR vaccine. We're only two Verdicts away from achieving this critical mission. And don't forget: SWARM made it personal by what they did to your grandma. She needs you to be courageous in this moment because her life is depending on your decisions—on what you do and what you choose not to do."

Styx's demeanor shifts from worry to fiery resolve. "I understand," she replies.

"Good," Phoebe says. "Does anyone else have any reservations? I'd rather hash out your questions and concerns here than inside the Verdict, where you could be seriously injured for matters of fear or reluctance. Anyone?"

"What if we quit?" Lyric asks.

"*Quit?*" Tilda asks, astonished. Is she actually surprised someone would want to quit her precious Project? Especially with our lives on the line. She must truly be delusional.

"Lyric, don't forget two things," Tilda says. "First, if anyone quits, then your Boon is off the table. There's a real chance you'd never see your sister, Sofia, again. But second, why would you quit? Is playing video games back at your parents' house more satisfying than saving the world?"

"It is if we want to live," Lelantos comments.

"Get a clue, clerics," Kiran snaps. "Living in a world where SWARM reigns is hardly living."

Despite his condescending tone, Kiran has a point.

"Now that we have that settled, are you ready to learn about the second Verdict?" Tilda asks. "It centers on something called Deliberate Magnetic Focus."

"How about using words we understand?" Karme says.

I wait for a snide comment from Lyric—how Karme is an idiot for expressing ignorance—but strangely it doesn't come.

"For years, people have casually tossed around sound bites regarding the law of attraction," Phoebe says. "Unfortunately, most of this information has not only been inaccurate, but also incomplete. The law of attraction states that by focusing on positive or negative thoughts, we bring positive or negative experiences into our lives. Proponents believe thoughts are made from pure energy, and like energy attracts like energy."

"My aunt got burned by some guy teaching this stuff," Lelantos says. "She had liver cancer, and a friend told her to read a book about attraction. The book said if she thought about being healthy, she would attract healthy cells into her body. Guess what? After applying those principles for three months, the cancer spread throughout her whole body, and she died."

"Sorry to hear about your aunt's passing," Phoebe says sincerely. "As I said, many people spread inaccurate and incomplete information. But, at ELIXIR, we put our faith in science and technology, not unproven philosophy. Achieving what you want in life isn't about wishing it to be true or willing it into existence. It comes down to focus and, specifically, your RAS filter."

"My what filter?" Pallas asks.

"Try this little experiment, Pallas, and you'll see what I mean," Tilda says. "Have you ever wanted to get a certain make and model of car?"

"Absolutely," Pallas replies.

"And what color was that car?"

"Red, of course."

"Once you made up your mind, how often did you see other red cars just like it?" Tilda asks.

"Every day and everywhere—in magazines, on the Internet, on the road, in parking lots...even in a movie!"

"Let me guess: He was using his special powers to attract the car to him," Karme says.

"Not unless you call his RAS filter a special power." Phoebe smiles. "And considering the fact that every person has one, I wouldn't call it special. Kiran, please explain."

"RAS stands for Reticular Activating System. Your RAS filter is at the base of your brain, and it sifts through all incoming stimuli. It decides what sensory input to address and which to ignore. It ignores more than ninety-nine percent, and the tiny part it focuses on deals with one of four elements: surprise, danger, changes in the environment, or fear."

"Or...?" Tilda pushes.

"Or it focuses on what you tell it to focus on, like in the case of Pallas, the idea of a red car," Kiran says.

"Those red cars were there all along. You didn't see them because you weren't focused on them," Phoebe explains. "We now know the conscious mind processes somewhere between forty and two hundred bits of information per second. However, the unconscious mind processes billions and billions of bits of information in that same amount of time. If there were no filter, your conscious mind would experience information overload and literally go into meltdown mode."

"Does this make sense?" Tilda asks.

"I'm kind of getting it," Pallas replies.

"Think about what you did regarding the red car," Tilda says. "You set your mind on it. And once you consciously made that decision, your unconscious mind did the rest of the work. It sifted through billions and billions of bits of information to find what you told it to look for—in this case, a red car. Some call this phenomenon your mind's eye.

"The main premise is this: Don't focus on attracting into your life what you want. Instead, focus on what's already all around you. Just open your mind's eye and you'll see everything you need to implement your idea."

"Sounds amazing," Phoenix comments. "Any drawbacks?"

"Of course there are always drawbacks," Kiran says arrogantly. "If you believe you're an idiot per se—a fact for most of you—then your RAS filter works overtime finding evidence to back up that belief. It will ignore the billions of reasons why you're brilliant and focus on the few that suggest you're not. Once this happens, you need to reset your mind with the idea that you're brilliant. When you do, then your RAS filter kicks into overdrive, scavenging for all the evidence to support the belief that you're brilliant."

"The mind is powerful," Tilda says. "It shapes what we believe and dictates the version of truth we tell ourselves."

"But I thought truth was absolute and external," Damon observes. "Are you saying it's relative and internal?"

"That's the question we hope to answer in today's Verdict," Tilda says. "Time to hop into your seats. The Apparition awaits."

CHAPTER
THIRTY-EIGHT

I WAKE UP inside the Apparition again. My head feels foggy.

Damon, Karme, and Phoenix sit next to me on the same wooden bench. Like our last visit, Lyric, Pallas, Lelantos, and Styx sit to my left.

I'm not brave enough to look to my right, because I know who's missing. I won't see Metis smirking or Ophion's tattoos. None of Erida's spunk or Ares calling us mate for the twentieth time. I'll never see or hear any of those clerics again. And for all I know, because of them 10X-ing our neuroplasticity, any one of us clerics could be next.

André sits on the center throne again.

My eyes focus on the stained glass behind the three thrones. I'm mesmerized by the vivid blues, reds, and purples.

But this time the letters *T-I-H-A-E-L-E-A* pop out. My mind focuses on the letters, unscrambling them into the word *ALETHEIA*.

Aletheia—the same word iris told me to tell McNultey—the one that made him release Karme in the atrium, moments before the Unveiling. The same word the woman said to the pigtailed girl at the birthday party gone wrong. And the same word the amrita clerics shouted moments before their brutal suicides. Before I have time to unpack the pattern, André speaks.

"In this Verdict, we'll push you to the edge. Brace yourself because you will experience pain."

My body tenses. The image of those eel teeth tearing into my forearm pops back into my mind.

"Skills download successful," a voice from beyond the Apparition says.

"Great. Bring them back to the Abyss. It's time for Verdict number two," another voice says.

CHAPTER
THIRTY-NINE

I OPEN MY eyes and notice a strange pressure on the back of my head. I hope it's not from the increased neuroplasticity levels already taking effect. I remove the restraint around my waist and the goggles around my head. Edge was kind enough to give me a new pair.

"Okay, listen up, clerics," Tilda says, grabbing her remote. "We call this the Focus Verdict, and it doesn't end until somebody wins. We'll meet inside the ten-thousand-square-foot multiactivity court you might have seen when you entered the athletic center.

"Similar to a roller derby, you'll race around a track—the only difference being our track is a square, not a circle. You'll draw straws to see who you're competing against—males against males, females against females. Each cleric will complete four laps and then tag the next cleric in line. Whichever cohort crosses the finish line first wins."

"Sounds pretty straightforward to me," Pallas says.

"Except that we've added a few twists," Tilda explains. "First, please swallow the pill Edge is distributing."

"I'm not swallowing anything unless you tell me what it is," Lyric says.

"No pill, no race," Kiran says, tapping away at his glass tablet, not even bothering to make eye contact.

"It's a chemical designed to enhance the RAS accelerant," Phoebe says. "A RAS accelerant could be surprise, danger, a change in environment, or fear. We'll release one per series of four laps, allowing every cleric to experience an accelerant firsthand."

Edge makes his way around the wet room, distributing a pill and a helmet to each cleric—yellow for soma and green for ichor. "These helmets will measure your focus levels throughout the Verdict," Tilda says. "You'll race on a RAS-board—a cross between a snowboard and a hovercraft. And you'll fight with a skylatis—a cross between a lance and a sword. McNultey, care to explain?"

"My pleasure," he says, spinning a skylatis. He hops off a counter and makes his way forward to the front of the room. "Skylatis was engineered to deactivate your RAS filter. When that happens, billions and billions of bits of information from your subconscious mind flow straight into your conscious mind. A microsecond later, your brain snaps into information overload and you suffer from a colossal mind meltdown.

"We call it an SKO—short for Skylatis Knockout. Pop your opponent in the head with one of these, and they'll experience the sensation of ten thousand bees stinging their brain—and that's just the beginning of their troubles."

"If your cohort crosses the finish line without scoring an SKO, you'll repeat the race again until someone does," Tilda says.

"Hopefully there's no way to get disqualified in this one?" I ask, posing my question as innocently as possible. I need to know all my options because Cai's warning for the first Verdict was dead on—literally.

"Disqualified." Kiran snickers. "Not a chance. In this Verdict, we'll keep repeating the race until a RAS filter get deactivated. The data demands it. Without an SKO, we can't create the vaccine."

"Why do you ask? You preparing to lose again?" Lyric sneers.

"Actually, the exact opposite," I say.

Despite my confident reply to Lyric, I know the choice isn't this simple. Amrita's deaths feels too coincidental to simply ignore Cai's warning, and I'm not about to win a Verdict if it means losing my life.

Losing the first Verdict was only as painful as losing

a Boon point. But based on McNultey's description, losing this second Verdict could mean losing my mind. At the moment, neither option seem too appealing.

CHAPTER FORTY

"W E DRAW STRAWS a little differently around here," McNultey says. "Ladies pick first and race last. Men pick last and race first. I have eight skylatises up here—four yellow and four green. They're grouped in two sections, male and female. Each of your names is on the bottom of one skylatis. I'll start the process."

He reaches into the female group's skylatises and pulls one out.

"Styx! You're first to pick. Reach in and grab a green one. That's who you'll be racing." Styx walks toward the case. "I got Karme." My roommate strolls to the front of the room nonchalantly, but I know better. She always plays with her fingers when she's nervous. Bending and twisting, cracking and picking—the constant movement must set her at ease. She accepts her green skylatis and shakes Styx's hand.

"Lyric, this means you'll be racing Aryedne. Come get your skylatises and shake hands." I grab the skylatis with my left hand and extend my right hand. Lyric clasps my hand and then, with a sudden jerk, yanks me close to her chest.

She whispers under her breath, "Ready to join your uncle in ICU? Look on the bright side: At least you'll die together."

Trash-talking doesn't faze me when I'm the target. But Cai's off limits—especially when he's in a coma.

My reflexes snap into action. I wield the slender stick—twisting and spinning, twirling and slicing—like it's an extension of my hands.

I don't remember thinking *if* I should hit her or *how* I should hit her. All I know is I *did* hit her, over a dozen times in less than three seconds. I would have stopped striking had I thought about it, but that's the problem: *I didn't*. She attacked someone I love and on instinct I defended him.

Lyric lies on the wet room floor moaning, clutching her legs and side—regretting the verbal venom she so carelessly discharged in my direction, I'm sure.

"Nice moves," McNultey says. "Good thing I didn't turn the power on yet or we'd be carrying her out in a stretcher."

"Easy, Aryedne," Phoenix says.

The remnants of adrenaline surge through me—my cheeks still feel hot. I don't know what came over me.

Maybe stress? Or just pure instinct from the skills download program? Whatever it was, a growing twinge of guilt tells me I may have crossed a line. I offer her a hand up off the floor.

"Get away from me!" Lyric screams. Pallas crouches by her side and helps her to her feet. "I'll get my revenge in the race," threatens Lyric.

McNultey chuckles and Kiran joins in the laughter. "Got to love it when women fight," McNultey says. "All right. Time for the men. Pick your opponent, Phoenix."

"I got Lelantos," Phoenix says. The lanky European cleric comes forward and grabs his yellow skylatis. I wish Damon had him. They're more evenly matched in terms of body size.

"Go easy on me, eh, Phoenix?" Lelantos says.

"SWARM's my enemy, not you," Phoenix says reassuringly.

"Aw. Isn't that sweet," the officer says. "Now, grab your skylatises, Damon and Pallas! The Verdict awaits."

We stand like soldiers. Eight clerics dressed in the same black uniforms—only neon colors distinguish us.

"Time to strategize with your cohort," Edge says. "But be in the square in thirty minutes. And remember: To get the Boon point, you must cross the finish line first and have scored a knockout. The order of heats will be Phoenix versus Lelantos, Damon versus Pallas, Karme versus Styx, and finally Aryedne versus Lyric. Best of luck. Fear no one but truth."

CHAPTER
FORTY-ONE

"I'VE GOT A PLAN," Damon says, loud enough so only we can hear.

"Let's duck into one of these rooms," I suggest.

Phoenix waits until the door slams shut before speaking. "Okay, I'll keep track of the clock."

"We need to lose this Verdict," Damon bursts out.

As much as I agree with him, I know what this means for one of us.

"Aryedne was right yesterday," Damon says, "and the only reason we're still breathing is because she trusted her gut."

"I agree," Karme says.

"*You do?*" I reply.

"Yep. As much as I want the Boon, I also want to live. You said Cai warned you about the danger of winning a Verdict, and you were right."

"But how do we know it wasn't a coincidence?" Phoenix says. "That's quite a bet we're making."

"I thought so, too," Damon says, "until I considered our options. Think about it. If we win, we get a Boon point, but we may be dead by morning. That's a huge gamble."

"And if we lose…?" Karme asks.

"Well…then we arrive in the wet room down a point. If the soma cohort is dead by morning, then we made the right choice. Or if soma's still alive, then we focus all our efforts on winning the third and final Verdict."

"You want us to shoot for a tie?" Karme asks.

"Yep. And move into the sudden death round," Damon says. "I know we can beat them there."

"You sound confident," Phoenix points out.

"What other choice do we have?" Damon says. "Either way it's a gamble."

"You forgot one thing," I say. "Losing the Verdict means one of us getting—"

"I know. I'm volunteering to get the SKO," Damon interrupts.

"And have your mind go into meltdown mode? No way!" I push back.

"You're so stubborn, Aryedne. It's incredibly unattractive."

His words hit me like a hand grenade to the face.

"Leave!" I yell. I'm surprised to hear my own voice

speaking. It sounds too confident, too aggressive. I think the pressure of the Verdicts and the uncertainty of Cai's condition are taking their toll.

"Who? Me?" Damon asks.

"No, Karme and Phoenix. Now!"

"But we only have twenty minutes left," Phoenix says.

"Well, give us ten," I say slowly, trying to keep my blood pressure at a manageable level.

"Come on, Phoenix," Karme says. "Let's give them some space."

I do everything I can to wait for the door to close before I start shouting. "Who do you think you are, calling me ugly?"

"What are you talking about? I never said you were ugly. I said you were stubborn."

Damon's clarification removes some of the sting, but somewhere inside, my heart still hurts.

"Besides, how can I call you ugly? You're beautiful... inside and out—and that's why I have to take the SKO. I couldn't live with myself knowing I stood by while you got your RAS filter deactivated. The way they described it, I don't wish it upon anyone."

"And what? I'm supposed to stand by and watch you suffer?"

"Aryedne..." Damon holds out a hand to me. As much as part of me wants to stay standing on my side of the room, another part longs to move toward him.

"I'm not going to hurt you. I…want to hold you."

"*Hold me?* Are you serious right now? Because if you are, then why don't you trust me? You keep pulling back, keeping your secret stuffed inside you," I argue. "You don't need a Boon to clear your conscience. You can start by being honest with me."

He pauses and looks up at the clock. "*Right now?* You want me to tell you fifteen minutes before we need to race?"

"Either of us could die in there—so *yes!* You should tell me."

"Fine. But you're not going to like it," he warns. I maintain eye contact, hoping to give him strength, hoping to make it easier for him. He clears his throat and finally comes clean.

"I used to work for SWARM."

CHAPTER
FORTY-TWO

THEY SAY SOMETIMES you never see the truth coming. In this case, I'm sure any inkling would have softened the blow. But nothing could have prepared me for that bombshell. *SWARM? Seriously?* I feel my body taking a step back, away from him.

"Let me explain," Damon begs.

"Please," I reply.

"A couple summers ago, my parents encouraged me to get a job. I never liked the idea of working for someone else, so I started a business instead—designing apps for people online. Technology always came easy for me, so I set up a profile on one of those sites and started doing a few gigs here and there. In the beginning, the money wasn't great, but I learned a ton."

He pauses and swallows hard.

"Over time one customer kept coming back—

Suedomai. He kept wanting modifications for the app I created for him—a cutting-edge game for kids that integrated with the GPS tracking components from their device.

"He always paid me up front, and soon he wanted to be the only client I served. He sweetened the deal by paying ten times my posted rate, promising me a long-term business relationship. I didn't ask too many questions and socked most of the money away in a college fund.

"Over the next few weeks, I got suspicious and did a little digging. Something in my gut didn't feel right, and his business model seemed a little cryptic. I was just about to back out when the story broke worldwide. The owners of the app were some of SWARM's low-level pawns. They used the app as a tracking program to kidnap kids and then sell them on the dark web. In a sophisticated sting operation, ELIXIR helped law enforcement crack the case."

Like a judge on her bench listening to a confession, I process every word, discerning every intention. Although none of us is completely pure in this life, I weigh his motives, my head and heart trying to reconcile the actions of the boy I keep thinking about.

Damon looks down at the ground and then back into my eyes. "Because of my anonymous profile on that third-party job-posting site, I was never officially linked to the app. And I doubt I'd ever be culpable for creating a simple kids app anyway. But…it's what SWARM did with the app that eats at my soul every day.

"No matter how I try to shake it, I feel responsible for all those kids ripped apart from their families. Without the app, they would still be in their homes, safe and sound at night. I don't want to even imagine the horrors some are experiencing at this exact moment."

I gaze at Damon. He's a tortured soul in need of saving—just like the rest of us. "You don't know that," I say. "They would have found another designer if they didn't use you. In my book, you're innocent and SWARM's the one to blame. SWARM's *always* the one to blame."

I hit a breaking point. The tears come without trying. I wrap my arms around myself because it's too hard to be strong. I can't carry the weight of the world or the weight of the Project any longer. Cai might die at any moment. And we all might be dead by morning.

Damon steps toward me. "Aryedne…" His arms stretch out and his fingertips are now only inches away from me. The walls around my heart have protected me from pain for far too long. I'm not sure I can live without them. Then again, I'm not sure I can live with them, either.

I unwrap my arms from around myself and fling them around his body, burying my head to his chest.

I hear his heart beating. I taste the salt from my tears, and for the first time...I feel connected.

"We can come back later," Karme jokes. She and Phoenix poke their heads in the doorway.

"You know we start in eight minutes," Phoenix says.

I lift my head from inside Damon's arms and fight back a smile.

"Wow, you two should fight more often," Karme laughs.

"I'm going to take the SKO," Damon explains.

"Hey, I never agreed to that," I say.

"Well then, you can volunteer for the third Verdict."

"You think you're going to be sane enough to compete in the third Verdict?" I ask.

"I've got a reason to stay sane now. Don't you think?"

"I'm serious, Damon!"

"I am, too. Trust me. I'll be fine."

"Five minutes!" Phoenix warns.

"The plan?" Karme asks.

"All right, here it is," Damon says. "Phoenix, you'll do the first four laps. Stay away from Lelantos and his skylatis. Besides, it sounds like he's afraid of you. On my third lap, I'll let Pallas hit me with an SKO.

"My RAS deactivation should cause enough distraction that he'll finish his laps, no problem. Then Styx and Lyric can complete their laps and cross the finish line with the required SKO—end of Verdict."

"Three minutes, guys," Phoenix says. "We gotta go." We grab our skylatises and head out the door to the square.

"Don't do anything stupid and die in there," I say to Damon. "Because if you do, I swear I'll find a way to bring you back and kill you again."

He stops and I stare back at him—deep enough to see past the pretenses that come so easy at a time like this.

"And skip out seeing you angry again? I wouldn't miss it for the world."

We walk down the corridor together, about to face untold danger, but in this moment I feel more alive than I can remember.

CHAPTER
FORTY-THREE

"I HAD MY EMF gun ready to come find you," McNultey shouts to us.

"They were probably just strategizing a little—that's all," Phoebe says. "Your Boon is a strong motivator, right, Aryedne?"

"Absolutely." I smile.

"Oh, I forgot to tell you, and I know you've been asking the proxies about Cai's condition incessantly. I got a message from André early this morning. He said Cai went into surgery. The doctors are fixing him up as we speak. It looks like he's starting to make a turnaround. After you complete these next two Verdicts, maybe I can pull a few strings and get you a special transport to go see him."

"That would be amazing," I say. "No pressure, right?"

"I'm not worried. You've got a fiery spirit. Reminds

me so much of myself when I was your age. Maybe your mom and I were related in another life?" She smiles. The way she speaks about my deceased mother makes me feel uneasy.

"I'll take that as a compliment," I say, verbalizing the first thing that came into my mind. She reaches out and squeezes my hand. I squeeze back.

"I swear you and Kore would have passed as sisters."

I rack my brain. "Kore?" I ask. *Should I know that name?* I don't want to embarrass myself by asking. "Um, sorry. Who's that?"

"Our daughter," Phoebe says. "I thought I told you about her?"

"Oh, of course, in my room before the Name Change. I was so nervous that night. I forgot her name."

"Your cohort will do fine in there. Remember to trust yourself. We downloaded all the skills you need—so lean into them. And don't focus on the RAS accelerants. They're designed to distract you."

A loud horn interrupts us.

"I'll be watching and monitoring from up there in the observatory—with the rest of the board."

Above us, I notice a balcony surrounding the entire square. Although one small section is enclosed in glass—the observatory, I presume—the rest is exposed. A waist-high metal barricade prevents observers from falling off the open sections.

"All clerics, please come down in front," Edge says. "We'll strap the guys into your boards first. The rest of you can watch through the glass by the staging area, where our proxies will strap you in, too. Remember, this is a race. You'll enter the square when the cleric before you is on their final lap. They'll tag you, and you'll complete your four laps, then tag the next cleric in line."

"Marvelous!" Kiran shouts. "I'll kill the overhead lights. And now—I've always wanted to say this—let there be *black* lights!"

I spin around and see my fellow clerics. The yellow and green accents on our bodies shimmer under the black lights.

Dozens of proxies pour onto the balcony from both directions as mind-numbing music cuts in, reverberating off the metal walls. The neon-orange accents on their bodies cast a menacing halo above us.

Intense purple, red, orange, blue, and yellow lights shoot down from the ceiling, transforming the square into a multisensory experience rivaling any headliner, except for one small distinction. This isn't a concert where everybody goes home unscathed, raving about the show. This is a Verdict, where people may never go home—at least in their right minds.

Bubbles of panic start bursting inside my gut. I want to vomit, but I close my eyes instead, hoping to shut out the pounding music.

When I open them back up, I see Tilda, McNultey, Phoebe, and Kiran shuffle into the observatory. They stand against the glass and peer down, waiting for the race to begin.

Phoenix and Lelantos descend a step and enter the square. Several proxies help them activate their RAS-boards and skylatises. Phoenix outweighs Lelantos by at least seventy pounds.

"Clerics, to your marks," Edge instructs them. "Get set. Go!"

CHAPTER
FORTY-FOUR

PHOENIX MAKES IT look easy. Despite his massive body, he's a natural on the RAS-board. Maybe it's a good thing they 10X-ed our neuroplasticity.

Both racers complete the first lap without much effort. Sure, there's pulsating music, disrupting lights, and the threat of your brain going into meltdown mode from getting smacked in the head by a skylatis. But all things considered, the guys cruise around fairly carefree.

Then it happens on lap three—the first RAS accelerant. From the southeast corner, a patch of darkness flitters onto the track. At first, I'm not sure what the blackness is, but then—even above the music—I hear them. High-pitched squeaks—thousands of them, maybe even tens of thousands of them. Bats!

The furry, flying creatures dive-bomb Phoenix's and

Lelantos's heads, causing them to swerve like intoxicated drivers.

Lelantos takes advantage of the change in environment. He winds up for a baseball bat swing and aims at Phoenix's head. A split second before the bat connects, Phoenix spots the streak of neon yellow slicing toward his forehead. He flinches—wrenching his elbow up and neck down. His reflexes deflect the attack, and Phoenix comes back with his own counterswing, taking out Lelantos's legs.

Lelantos lands with a thud, his butt on the board— but then loses his balance and falls off.

"That jerk played the scared-little-boy act perfectly," Karme shouts.

"Guess he wants his Boon back," Damon says. "Still bitter about SWARM stealing his intellectual property."

Phoenix enters the final lap crouching low on his board, dodging the bats above. Lelantos hops back on his board and chases after him, gaining with each passing second.

I turn away from the race and spot Damon prepping, waiting for Phoenix to cross the line and tag him. I wish I could think of something intelligent to say, but I don't want to distract him.

I need to face the truth, though. Sometime in the next four laps, his brain might go into meltdown mode. Maybe Phoenix was right. Maybe the amrita clerics' deaths were just a coincidence. Maybe he doesn't need to get hit with a skylatis.

But as Damon said, either way it's a gamble. I sure hope for his sake we made the correct one.

Three more seconds pass. I can't sit here and watch when the guy I want to be with is minutes away from getting bashed in the head. What should I tell him? *Good luck?*

I dash over to him. He veers off any awkwardness by speaking first. "Smile. I'll be fine. Besides, I got an idea."

"Oh yeah? What's that?" I reply.

"I figured out a way to avoid the surge of billions of bits of information rushing into my conscious mind all at once."

"Now I'm curious," I say.

"Right before I get hit with his skylatis, I'm going to focus on one thing," Damon says. "You know...tell my conscious mind to lock onto something. Want to know what it is?"

"Dying to know," I say, as playfully as I can pretend.

But before he has time to reply, I hear the whoosh of Phoenix's RAS-board. He tags Damon, and on instinct Damon bolts off the starting line, not even saying good-bye.

Then he's gone—I only hope his mind won't be gone.

CHAPTER
FORTY-FIVE

As PLANNED, DAMON SLOWS. Pallas closes the gap by the second lap, his dreadlocks flapping in the wind behind him. He grips his skylatis and cuts the corner, preparing to strike. *I can only imagine what a mind meltdown might look like.*

But then over the music I hear a deafening roar. "Damon!" I scream.

He glances over his shoulder, teeters, and then falls onto his board. A lion with black tufts of fur around his mouth and jagged frosty teeth leaps over his head, missing him by mere inches.

Pallas cruises past.

From where I stand, the simulated images appear so lifelike. The enhancers we swallowed work against us, playing tricks on our minds.

Several other male lions swoop from numerous

angles, causing the guys to dip and sway on their boards. By accident—an unintentional swipe of his weapon—Pallas figures out his skylatis doubles as a lion killer. He uses that awareness to plow ahead, making it impossible for Damon to catch him.

By the time Damon finishes his fourth lap, Styx is already out on the floor.

Flustered, he tags Karme.

Damon smacks his hand against the glass wall in disgust. "Those enhancers mess with your head! I knew the lions weren't real, but my subconscious wouldn't let me stand up."

"It's not like you could help it," I say. "Let me get hit on my turn."

"Not a chance," he argues. "Phoebe said we repeat the race if no one crosses the finish line without scoring an SKO. I'll take the hit on my second heat."

I wonder what RAS accelerant they'll use next. With bats for surprise and lions for danger, that leaves change in condition and fear. And if they're going in order, then I'll get fear in my heat. Lucky me.

"Look!" Phoenix shouts. "The whole square is transforming."

The track morphs into a series of blades, tunnels, traps, and flames. Both nimble and small in stature, Styx and Karme make a race out of it. They chase each other through the changes in elevation and temperature, avoiding the flames and hopping the hurdles.

On the last turn, Karme leaps off her board, avoiding a simulated blade about knee level. While airborne, Styx hits the brakes and, in one continuous motion, slashes her skylatis upward and to the side—connecting with Karme's face.

The awkward angle of the strike sends her flying in the direction she was already headed—forward.

Her eyes roll to the back of her head. Knocked out cold, she has no way to brace herself. She skims past the finish line, then slams into the acrylic glass wall at full speed, her helmet taking the brunt of the impact.

Our entire cohort gasps, still unsure what happened. Styx lets out a whoop and slides into the finish line, tagging Lyric as she arrives. Lyric takes off like a thoroughbred shooting out of the starting gate.

My instinct is to go check on my friend. Is she still breathing?

But a proxy yanks me in another direction. I resist, but then, with her own skylatis, she pushes me. Evidently, crossing the finish line unconscious still counts as a tag.

I take off after Lyric.

In the heat of the moment, after I witnessed Styx's attack on my roommate, my adrenaline takes over my better judgment. If I can't take back what she did to Karme, at least I can make her cohort pay.

CHAPTER
FORTY-SIX

I ENTER THE square more than half a lap behind Lyric. Lucky for me, her long limbs don't favor the RAS-board. She flies around the curves with exaggerated patterns, offering me plenty of opportunities to catch up. Halfway through the second lap, I'm just a couple of yards behind her—close enough to see her neon-yellow accents glowing under the black lights above.

I know the final RAS accelerant is around the corner—literally. And the anticipation is nerve-racking. I wish fear would stop hiding and show its ugly face. But then it does—in the form of the same dark hooded figure I saw at the Unveiling and the birthday party.

Though I'm traveling around the track at an implausible pace, the enhancer produces an unexpected result. My subconscious slows long enough for me to process every bit of information, every thought, every idea, one by one, like single grains of sand passing through an hourglass.

Still, my board is going too fast and my reaction time is too slow. I head straight toward the hooded figure cradling a toddler in his arms, the same way a mother rocks a child to sleep. I'm ten feet away now but moving closer. The toddler isn't a boy with a cowboy hat, but a girl—with red pigtails.

It's the same girl from the birthday party gone wrong. And the same girl from the photograph, the one memory I have of my family. I'm five feet away now, near enough to see the fear in her eyes. She begins to cry. I notice the necklace she wears. It's a name in fancy script. It's *my* name: *Sienna*. That little girl is me.

My focus narrows and my instincts take over.

I grip my skylatis with two hands, crouching low on my RAS-board. I rotate my weight and spin. With each revolution, I build up more and more knockout power, circling and twirling, until I decide to strike.

The hooded figure absorbs the full effect of my swing, letting out a bloodcurdling growl. The force knocks him off his feet, sending the little girl sailing. I think about catching her, but then the toddler vanishes in the air.

I turn my head and see the hooded figure hurling toward the large acrylic panels. When he smacks the glass wall, neon-yellow accents appear all over his body.

Reality hits me. I didn't attack a hooded figure, but my fellow cleric—Lyric.

The fear I confronted wasn't even real, but a simulated image sent to distract me.

The facts emerge with crystal clarity: Damon missed his chance at getting hit. Karme suffered an SKO at the hands of Styx. And Lyric suffered one because of my own misjudgment.

The truth is, I feel destined to cross the finish line, win the race, and score the Boon point. But I still can't shake Cai's warning or the amrita cohort's deaths. I feel claustrophobic in my own thoughts, backed into a tight corner.

I close my eyes to focus and shut out the noise. An option emerges—one I never even saw before. I move toward Lyric's broken body, now knowing what I must do.

CHAPTER FORTY-SEVEN

Glistening liquid drips from her face, forming a small but growing pool of blood alongside her cheek. I flip her over. Even in the dark lighting, I can tell her wounds are significant.

As cruel as Lyric's heart might be, nobody deserves this type of assault. A sickening feeling passes over me. If she dies, I'll never forgive myself, even if the accelerant and ISA download are partly to blame.

I move my RAS-board next to her and drag her on top of it. Her weight would normally make the dragging part difficult, but the epinephrine coursing through my body gives me uncharacteristic strength. I use as few jarring movements as possible because if any bones are fractured, I don't want to make them worse.

Once stabilized, I hover through the air across the finish line—me standing, Lyric lying down. When I do, the music stops and the overhead lights turn back on. Phoebe, Kiran, McNultey, and Tilda exit the glass observatory onto the balcony.

Phoebe begins clapping. The other board members echo her applause. Soon the entire circle of proxies on the balcony join in the ovation. "Impressive!" Phoebe says. "And unexpected. You discovered a way to share the win and tie the Verdict."

The reality of Phoebe's words hits me. There's no way both of our cohorts can lose our lives for winning the Verdict. Killing all eight of us clerics would destroy the Project and mean failure for ELIXIR and victory for SWARM.

"The power of focus and your RAS filter," Tilda says. "Amazing what the mind's eye can see when it knows what it's looking for."

"And what was I looking for?" I ask.

"We'll review the data," Tilda replies. "But your fear was exclusively created from your own subconscious. We provided the space, and your thoughts decided how to fill that space."

"Medic proxies, down on the square now!" Phoebe orders. "Transport Karme and Lyric to the health center immediately." Half a dozen proxies with a thin white band on their right arms rush over to the wounded clerics. A few others wheel in two black stretchers and begin stabilizing the clerics for transport.

"Lyric's wounds are much worse," Phoebe continues. "Be sure Dr. Christopher sees her. Karme can receive care from any of the other ELIXIR docs."

"Will they be all right?" Phoenix asks.

"Your girlfriend will be, dearie," Kiran answers. "Styx used a clean shot on her. But Lyric? Well…that's anybody's guess. Aryedne used excessive force, so we won't know until the doctor examines her."

I used excessive force? Anyone can tell the simulation deceived me.

"We'll send this data to André and Chevon," Phoebe says. "Our Senior Board of Clerics will discuss the results. After that, we'll prep for tomorrow's third and final Verdict."

The medic proxies push both stretchers through the exit doors.

"Are you going to give us any hints?" Styx asks.

"Why? So you can land the first hit again?" Phoenix replies.

"Shut up, ichor!" Pallas threatens. "You're not the only one with a girlfriend down. Redhead here may have killed mine—accident or not."

"I only hit Karme because I want my grandmother to live," Styx says defensively. "If I don't get that Boon, then she doesn't get a healthy kidney."

"Quiet!" Damon says. "Aryedne has her own pain, in case you forgot. Her uncle's heart got hacked and he nearly died, remember? SWARM's the real enemy here. How about we work together for once and achieve the third Verdict? Then maybe we can all go back to our normal lives."

His words silence the squabbling, at least temporarily. Life as normal would be a welcome change.

"Thank you, Damon. When we're in pain, it's easy to blame others," Phoebe says. "To answer your original question, Styx, no, we can't give you any hints, but Tilda can give you a schedule of events."

Tilda pulls up her glass tablet and begins scanning. "The rest of the day is yours, clerics. Use the time to recover. Focus on eating, sleeping, and resting because you'll need your strength. Flow Verdict begins tomorrow at six a.m."

Flow? A dozen or more times over the past few years during dinner discussions, Cai has ranted and raved about the newest breakthroughs in Flow.

"But this is different," Cai told me. "Flow is optimal human performance. In Flow states, we're five hundred percent more productive. We can shut out distraction, gather more information, and experience enhanced pattern recognition. Flow gives us the ability to make faster connections between ideas."

My heart feels heavy. He may never be well enough—physically or mentally—to share the latest breakthroughs with me over dinner discussions again.

Tilda locates another note on her tablet. "Flow Verdict will conclude midmorning. By that time, we'll have all the data we need. Our teams will combine the results from all three Verdicts to create the ELIXIR vaccine." She hands her tablet to Edge. "Any questions?"

Lelantos removes his helmet. "When do we receive our Boon?" We all turn to Tilda, who seems to have glossed over that important detail.

"Of course that slipped my mind. Tomorrow night the winning cohort will be awarded their Boon at the ceremony inside St. Paul's."

"You mean to tell me you're going to be able to locate our Boon and then transport that Boon all in the span of a few hours—the time between when the final Verdict ends and the ceremony begins?" Damon asks.

"I'll answer the questions that pertain to my role, and Phoebe can answer hers," Tilda says. "I'm responsible for the Boon Ceremony itself. My teams have already been dispatched to take care of the technological needs for the live stream. I have another team devoted to managing media relations. The global audience has been glued to its screens for days, salivating over hourly updates of your progress. You've been *the* trending topic on all social media platforms since the start of the Unveiling.

"Kiran and McNultey, I know in Cai's absence you've been monitoring our security. Any updates?" Tilda asks.

"Sure. There's been no sign of SWARM anywhere

since André and Chevon met with the League of Nations," Kiran explains. "We're all clear on our end."

"Our security on campus is quite strong—impenetrable, even," McNultey says. "However, under no conditions should the clerics go outside the two-mile radius surrounding our campus. SWARM may have suspended their activity temporarily, but our experience proves they're relentless. They'd love nothing more than to harm our clerics and compromise the entire Project."

"Noted," Tilda says. "And now, Phoebe, would you care to address the lingering question?"

Phoebe smiles and puts her arms behind her back. "We've made all the necessary preparations to locate and transport the winning cohort's Boons at a moment's notice. Remember, clerics, ELIXIR has an endless supply of money, power, and connections. We will make good on our promise. Our reputation with you and the live global audience is on the line."

Her explanation sounds plausible. ELIXIR does have so much at stake tomorrow night, and if they don't deliver, they'll lose a ton of credibility.

"Clerics, as we dismiss today, I want to reiterate our deep appreciation," Phoebe says. "I know it's been difficult for each of you in different ways. But history reveals this is always the pattern when warring against an arduous opponent. Take courage. By week's end, SWARM will be a distant memory, all thanks to you."

Proxies come around and collect our helmets. Phoebe's right about one thing: the war imagery. It's an accurate description of the Project. And in war there are injuries, betrayals, and even deaths.

For Karme's and Lyric's sake, I hope these doctors know what they're doing. The fact that they're on ELIXIR's payroll gives me some peace of mind.

Damon, Phoenix, and I push through the exit doors and leave the Abyss, at least for today. I'll probably never be able to enter this athletic center quite the same way after the Project is over. I used to think of it as the place I stretched, ran, and lifted. But now I remember it as the place where my roommate got injured, my fellow clerics committed suicide, and perhaps where I killed Lyric.

Who knows? Tomorrow night could be a major step toward life becoming normal again. Or if Cai's warning was wrong and if I'm lucky enough to win the Boon, my life might be abnormal forever and in the best way possible.

May 12

In an hour, Damon, Phoenix, and I are going to check on Karme at the health center. Without her here, our dorm room is quiet for the first time in a long time.

We'll check on Lyric while we're there, too. For as much grief she caused me, if I've seriously injured her, I'll never forgive myself.

The amrita cohort's suicides still don't stack up. Feels like Tilda's hiding something. I've heard Cai talk about neuroplasticity enough to know there are no side effects like the ones the Senior Board tried to spin.

Speaking of Cai, Phoebe said I might be able to see him soon. I want to give my uncle a great, big bear hug. I miss him. Looking back over our last few interactions, I feel so foolish now. He never stopped protecting me and yet I kept pushing him away—doubting his intentions.

One good thing. Damon finally opened up and trusted me with the truth. It felt amazing, him holding me in his arms and no longer a big secret between us.

We all know the Boon we're after. Karme wants to rescue Amy from one of SWARM's trafficking rings. Phoenix wants to protect his reputation by eliminating potential blackmail. And Damon wants to clear his conscience by removing any ties to the app he created unknowingly for SWARM. And who knows? Maybe even rescue the children who were taken as a result.

Then there's me.

The Boon I want doesn't seem possible. And yet why would they flash a picture of my family up on the screen? To torture me? I doubt it. So I'll end this entry clinging to the small shred of faith I still have swimming somewhere deep inside my heart.

With ELIXIR's technology on our side, who knows what's possible? Maybe they've found a way to bring back the dead. But then again maybe my Boon is something completely different.

Either way, I know this for sure. I'm hungry for the truth.

—Aryedne (Sienna)

CHAPTER
FORTY-EIGHT

"Karme, can you please pass the salt?" Damon asks.

"Oh, you're really going to make me move my arm?" she says. "Here, take it."

"I'm sorry. I forgot you're still sore. You look so much better."

"Hey, watch it. She's my girlfriend." Phoenix smiles, then leans over and kisses her on the cheek. "He's got a point, though. You *do* look much better."

"I'm just glad the doctor said the strike wasn't significant," I say. "And look on the bright side. He discharged you in time for dinner, even if it is a late one."

"I'd like to know if Styx turned it off intentionally," Phoenix says.

"Or was it a malfunction?" I ask. "She doesn't strike me as the violent type."

"Yeah, but as we've seen, competing for the Boon does weird things to you," Karme says.

"Think they'll make you compete in the Verdict tomorrow?" Phoenix asks Karme.

"Knowing Tilda's temperament? The short answer is yes," I say.

"I think you're right," Karme replies. "I swear that woman has a death wish to take down SWARM. It's like she's blind to anything else."

"Revenge is a powerful motivator," Damon says, cutting his salad. "But you can't blame her, the way they took William."

"I can't imagine what she feels," I say, reaching for my glass of water. "So are we going to talk strategy for the Flow Verdict tomorrow?"

"Anxious to get our Boon, are we?" Damon teases.

"Well, aren't you?" I reply.

"See, that's the problem, though," Damon says between bites. "Everything doesn't make sense. For example, how does ELIXIR know our deepest desire?"

"Um, maybe because they've been inside our minds for who knows how long?" Karme says with a bit of sarcasm. "And before monitoring us through our rings, they hacked our phones. You can tell a lot about a person by stalking them."

"Can you?" Damon says, setting down his fork and knife.

"What do you mean?" Phoenix asks.

"I mean our *deepest desire*? I'm not sure most people

even know what they truly want. It's not like we pick up our phones and say to our friends, 'You know, the other day I was thinking about my deepest desire.'"

"Yeah, well, they've had access to our e-mails and social media accounts, too," Karme says in defense. "They've been with us for months. Everything we saw, they saw. Everywhere we went, they went."

"I hear you, but something still doesn't add up. I've been grinding on all this—trying to make it fit in my mind."

"And it's not?" I ask.

"Well, here's something puzzling. How can they promise to deliver our Boon to us tomorrow? They're not going to even find out who wins until midmorning. What then? They just create our Boon out of thin air? They make it sound like they're God or something."

"Have you ever heard André in an interview?" Phoenix asks. "Sounds like becoming God is literally on his bucket list."

"He has enough money, power, and connections to rival God," Karme jokes.

"No, I'm serious," Damon pushes. "Think about it. What's the only thing stopping André from being God?"

"SWARM," I say.

"Exactly," says Damon. "Now, I know I've never met the guy...except for his simulated self inside the Apparition. Have you ever met him, Aryedne?"

"No. Cai hasn't even met him. He says André always

meets virtually for their board meetings."

"Sounds suspicious to me," Karme says.

"So what are you saying, Damon?" Phoenix asks.

"I don't know what I'm saying," he admits. "I'm only asking questions. But here's another thing. Take your Boon, for example, Aryedne. At the Unveiling, Tilda flashed a photograph of your family when you were a little girl."

Heat rises from my neck up to my cheeks the moment he brings up my family. I set down my sandwich and sip some more water rather than speak. My breaths become shorter and faster.

"No disrespect, but your parents are dead. And they have been for a long time."

"Damon, I don't really want to talk about my parents now, especially here."

Karme reaches across the table and wraps her fingers around my right hand. "Normally, I'd tell Damon to shut up if you don't want to go there, but this kind of relates to SWARM, ELIXIR, and the fate of the world. He's not trying to hurt you."

I hate it when she's right. I know Karme's coming from a good place, and Damon, too, for that matter. Sometimes I don't mind a truth teller, but times like now I could do without one.

"Aryedne," she says, clasping my hand tighter. "We care about you."

"I know you do," I say, staring at the other half of the sandwich on my plate, intentionally distracting myself so I don't start crying. "And I know you want what's best for me. It's just a tough topic."

"That's why I didn't want to bring it up," Damon says, putting his hand on top of my other hand. "But I don't want any one of us stepping into tomorrow's Verdict or the Boon Ceremony believing a lie. We both know the truth sets us free."

"But sometimes lies are easier," I say.

"Easier—not better," Phoenix replies.

"What? All three of you are ganging up on me now?" I say.

"You must feel really loved," Karme says.

"Okay, okay. You win. I'm willing to be honest. So what was the question, Damon?"

"About your Boon," Phoenix says. "Why would the board show you that photograph?"

"Right…and the answer to that is I don't know why. A small part of me hopes they're still alive. I know it's probably impossible, but hope is all I have." I reach for my napkin and wipe away a tear. I hate looking weak in front of others. "If we lose hope, then we lose one of the things that make us human, right?" I let out a deep breath and then take another sip of water. It feels good to verbalize what I've been stuffing inside the past few days.

"You mentioned Cai. How is he?" Phoenix asks.

"Phoebe made it sound like he's doing better," I explain. "But besides his immediate health, he seems troubled lately—about a number of things."

"What do you mean, *troubled*?" Karme asks.

"Well...remember on the night of the Unveiling, during the break, when you guys went outside?"

"Yeah, why?" says Damon.

"Cai asked me to meet him on the roof. He was worried."

"About what?" Karme asks.

"He said things like: 'Things aren't always what they seem' and 'Don't believe what you think; believe what you know.'"

"What else did he say?" asks Damon.

"Not much except 'They're watching us.'"

"That's cryptic," Karme says.

"That's what I told him. But then Tilda's text interrupted us. She asked to meet with him about the script that evening. Then we went back to the Unveiling, and SWARM crashed the party."

"You think Cai let SWARM hack the Unveiling intentionally?" Phoenix asks.

"And nearly die in the process? No, not a chance. That was a real hack and a real heart attack."

"So what are you saying, roomie?" Karme asks.

"I don't know. I'm in the same boat as Damon. I have no idea what to think."

"Then do what Cai told you to do," Damon says. "Don't focus on what you think, focus on what you know instead."

"You want to know what I know?"

"I…do," Damon says.

"We all do," Karme agrees.

"Okay, but you might not like what I'm going to say." I reflect on a few of the glaring gaps I've observed the past few days. I lean forward to share them, but then I hear the chime on the door. McNultey and a dozen other proxies dressed in black fatigues enter the café, heading toward our table.

"There's been a security breach," McNultey barks. "Come with us—now!" I notice his left hand trembling.

"What are you talking about?" Karme argues.

McNultey rips a skylatis out of a proxy's hands and flips it on. The weapon hums to life, buzzing and crackling. "It's soma," he says. "We gave one simple request: Don't leave the two-mile radius. And what do they do? They put the whole Project in jeopardy."

"Why did they leave?" Phoenix asks.

"Because Pallas wanted steak and potatoes. I don't know. Your guess is as good as mine. Now, come with us." The proxies grab our arms and twist them behind our backs—forcing our wrists into some type of restraint.

"Are we prisoners now?" I ask.

"Tracker cuffs," McNultey replies. "They serve a dual

purpose—restraining and monitoring. Thanks to soma's stunt, we can't take any more chances.

"SWARM may have apprehended them for all I know. And Lyric is still in critical condition. This means you four EPs are all we've got for the final Verdict, so we're keeping you inside the Abyss until tomorrow. We'll remove your cuffs once we take you to your detainment facilities."

"You mean prison cells," Karme says. "What? Are we dangerous now?"

"No time for attitude, young lady," McNultey snarls. "You're not dangerous; SWARM is. And if you don't achieve the Flow Verdict, then there's no ELIXIR vaccine. Think about someone besides yourself for a second."

He doubles over in pain, bracing himself with a hand on the café table.

"You all right, sir?" a proxy asks.

"Want me to call a medic?" another suggests.

"I'll be fine. But if these arrogant clerics would co-operate, I'd be even better."

"Okay, okay, we're going," Karme says.

"Guess we'll just finish our strategy session back at the Abyss," I say.

The officer spins to face me. "You misunderstood. You're going to be *alone*. There's no more strategizing, collaborating, or whatever it is you were planning on doing. You'll wake up tomorrow and go straight into the wet room at six a.m."

He pushes us forward and out the door. With the long night ahead of us—imprisoned in a solitary confinement of sorts—there's only one person left to tell what I know. Unfortunately, that's me…and based on what I have to say, it's not something even I want to hear.

CHAPTER FORTY-NINE

I'M NOT SURE how they expect us to sleep in here. For one thing, there's an echo. If I cough, sneeze, or clear my throat, I hear the sound reverberate at least half a dozen times off the twenty-foot-high walls on all four sides.

I don't need anyone to tell me that the modifications they made to these racquetball courts make it clear this renovation Project wasn't a spur-of-the-moment decision. That's not a comforting thought.

I overheard Edge talking with the other proxies—something about how on the morning of the Unveiling, Tilda, the ultra planner herself, snapped into an episode of paranoia. All over campus, she initiated contingency plans in case something went awry with the Project. For this particular initiative, she commissioned several squads of proxies to work around the clock constructing what they now affectionately refer to as "the tank."

It's a temporary holding place designed to keep anyone from going out or coming in. Lying on the raised platform, staring at the ceiling above me, I'd vote it's serving its purpose quite effectively.

I try to get comfortable—untying my shoes and placing them next to my feet. The platform has enough space for me to sprawl out, but that's about it. I'm guessing it's six feet long, three feet wide, and twelve feet off the ground. There isn't much else to do in the middle of the night except speculate about the dimensions of your own prison cell.

Although the proxies left two water bottles and a couple of protein bars on the platform, I have no desire to eat. Damon, Karme, and Phoenix were placed in their own cells, with their own raised platforms. Phoenix probably wolfed down his protein bars within a couple of minutes.

Seven proxies stand next to each other just outside my cell. The orange glow from their skylatises leaks onto the otherwise pitch-black court. I find the ambience it creates comforting—in a strange sort of way.

Tilda informed us there would be no bathroom breaks until morning. And if we do try to leave the raised platform, by jumping or climbing, the electrified floor below will engage and make us wish we stayed put.

My mind has been working on overdrive ever since Damon urged me to focus on what I know.

So what do I know? Good question.

I know I have some ideas about the Project, SWARM, and the vaccine. A few ideas might even be correct, but I can't verbalize them because they're tickling the edges of my brain.

One thing is for sure: I know more today than I did yesterday. The Focus Verdict taught me that much. My mind's eye is open and my RAS filter is set. The moment I focused on finding answers, the pieces started appearing. But I still lack the ability to see how they fit together. If only I knew how to recognize the pattern.

My foot accidentally kicks one of my shoes off the platform. A flash of orange illuminates the entire court. A moment later, I hear the remaining part of my shoe sizzling. The smell of burning rubber permeates the air.

"Quiet in there," one of the proxies warns.

I close my eyes, hoping that will make the smell of the singed shoe more bearable. A thought comes rushing back again. *If only I knew how to recognize the pattern.* Something stuffed way down in my subconscious rips back up into my awareness. I recall the conversation Cai and I had during one of our table talks about Flow.

In Flow states, we can experience enhanced pattern recognition. Flow allows us the ability to make faster connection between ideas.

Maybe that's the answer I've been looking for— Flow? Maybe tomorrow's Verdict will help me put all these random pieces together into one complete puzzle.

Who knows for sure?

It's probably a long shot, but something about that idea gives me peace of mind. And tonight, as I lie helpless, all alone, and in the dark—I could desperately use some more of that.

CHAPTER
FIFTY

My MIND TELLS my eyelids to open, but they prefer a different response.

Yuck, what's that smell? Burnt bacon? Reminds me of the Saturday morning Cai tried reading a science journal and cooking at the same time. The screaming smoke alarm woke him back to his culinary responsibilities.

I will my eyes into submission, and this time they obey. Nothing looks familiar. I'm not lying down in my room and Cai's not in the kitchen cooking. I roll over to look at the digital clock on the nightstand beside my bed, but it's not there. Twelve feet below me, the wood floor spins. I grip the sides of the platform to catch myself from falling. An image of twisted limbs flashes into my mind—this time not any of the amrita cohort's, but my own.

Where am I?

I rub my eyes. A flurry of images hijack my mind. The dark hooded figure. A sick uncle. Lyric's broken body. Damon's warm embrace. A lingering Verdict. An uncertain Boon.

A door opens. "Time to go, Aryedne," a voice from below instructs.

I feel my body descending, until the platform under me stops with an abrupt jolt. A hand reaches down to help me up. I pull against it, stand up, and brush myself off. By my foot I observe the remnants of the scorched shoe, still smoldering from the night before. "I think I'm going to need another pair of shoes."

A female proxy laughs. "I can arrange that."

I follow the others out the door, up the stairs, and into the wet room. Karme sits next to Phoenix—looking as ragged as I feel. Damon stretches out his legs and crosses them at the ankles. He senses my presence, looks up, and smiles. "How did you sleep, Aryedne?"

"Probably about as good as you," I say.

Edge walks over to us with four proxies accompanying him.

"Morning, clerics," he says. "They'll take your breakfast order. If you want my suggestion, get lots of protein: eggs, ham, avocados…and try the smoothies. They're delicious. After the Verdict, you'll have plenty of time to freshen up before the Boon Ceremony tonight."

"If we succeed," I say, with more apprehension than intended.

"Trust me, Aryedne. You will," he replies matter-of-factly. "The board will be here shortly. They ended late last night and started back up early this morning."

"Soma's disappearance kept them up, no doubt?" Karme asks.

Edge refuses to respond and attends to other matters at the front of the room. After a couple minutes, I walk over and engage him in some chitchat. He's always been kind to me for Cai's sake and I've got nothing else to do until the board shows up.

I ask him how he's doing, and he tells me he was quite shaken up about amrita's suicides. I'm surprised because he looks bulletproof, like nothing could penetrate his tough outer shell.

He says the video reminded him about his twins—a son and a daughter. They were about the same age as us clerics.

Years ago, he worked as a florist and his wife worked as a translator for ELIXIR at one of the international labs. Evidently, ELIXIR wanted him to work alongside his wife. He declined their repeated offers because of his love for flowers in his day job.

Months later, on an ordinary day, his kids didn't come home from school. He and his wife received a package in the mail that same day—two dead flowers.

The card in the package was signed *SWARM*.

A week later, the authorities discovered his kids' bodies with gunshot wounds to their heads. Edge was devastated and sold his floral business to begin working for ELIXIR, too. It gave him satisfaction to know his talents were being used to take down the organization that murdered his kids.

The next year his wife passed in a car accident, and the rest is history. He moved up through the ranks to where he presently serves—as Tilda's personal assistant. He wakes up every day excited, knowing that today might be the day SWARM is eradicated.

His story touches me and I tell him so. It's rather ironic how pain unites the entire world against a shared enemy.

Midway through our makeshift breakfast, the board members enter, and Tilda is the first to speak. "Thanks for your understanding about the tank. It was for your safety."

"For future reference, a blanket and pillow would be nice," Karme says.

"If you want someone to blame, start with soma," McNultey barks. He seems even more on edge than usual this morning.

"Did they give a reason for going off campus?" Phoenix asks.

"Yeah, they texted us all those details on their imaginary

phones right before they disobeyed orders and snuck off," Kiran says, sarcastically.

"Lelantos is the one responsible," Phoebe says. "Yesterday afternoon we became suspicious when one of our teams discovered he snuck into the computer lab and logged into some of his online accounts. We put a watch on him, and in a matter of minutes he crossed into the dark web. Once inside, he used an alias and contacted SWARM."

Why would he disobey such clear instructions? I wonder.

"I don't believe it," Damon says, arms folded across his chest. "Why would he contact the very people who stole his intellectual property from him?"

Phoebe is the first to enlighten us. "Simple. First, yesterday's Verdict ended in a tie—thanks to Aryedne. Second, Lyric was too injured to continue in today's Verdict. Those two outcomes made him nervous. You saw him yourself yesterday. He was losing his grip and getting desperate, even manipulating Phoenix by pretending to be scared."

"What are you saying?" Karme asks.

"Lelantos sold you out…all of you. When he thought he couldn't win the Boon, he made a deal with SWARM. He manipulated his fellow clerics, guaranteeing them their Boon. He promised Styx a perfect kidney for her grandmother and Pallas a brother returned home safely."

Damon doesn't budge.

"You scared him, ichor," Tilda says. "When he saw what you were capable of in the other Verdicts, he knew he couldn't win. He thought betrayal was the only way to secure his Boon."

"For all we know, it's just another lie you've spun together. I want proof," Damon demands.

"No need to get snippy," Phoebe says. "Kiran, please show Damon the *proof* he so righteously demands."

Kiran clicks away on this tablet and cues up some video footage.

"Once we found him online—an infringement in and of itself—a team of proxies initiated a series of hacks to watch him," Kiran explains. "A simple keylogger and we were good to go. After we had access to his log-in credentials and passwords, we scanned past messages, posts, and e-mails. Finally, we commandeered his webcam and initiated real-time screen surveillance."

The video on the screen reveals Lelantos logging into the dark web and chatting with SWARM. Sweat drips down his head as they discuss terms. They agree on a pickup time and location and then end the conversation abruptly.

Footage shifts to the campus. Three figures walk down one of the paths that split the campus in half. On a road near St. Paul's, a dark vehicle approaches. The camera closes in on the faces before they open the door. Without a doubt, it's Styx, Pallas, and Lelantos.

"If you caught all this in real time, even hacked his

computer, then why didn't you stop them?" Karme asks.

"We knew following them would lead us straight to a nearby SWARM sleeper cell," McNultey says. "A sting like that only comes around once in a person's career. Apprehending this sleeper cell would save many lives in the long run."

Tilda weighs in. "We wanted Lelantos and company to feel confident they left campus unnoticed. Once they drove away we dispatched a vehicle to track them."

"Brilliant," Damon says, laying the sarcasm on thick. "And with ELIXIR's unlimited money, power, and connections, I'm sure you tracked them down, infiltrated the sleeper cell, and brought the hacktivists to justice."

"They're dead, Damon," Tilda says plainly. "Within three minutes of boarding the vehicle, SWARM already double-crossed them. We followed them and spotted three round objects ejected from their vehicle. When our driver got closer, he saw the last head rolling off the road and into a ditch. Our team recovered the remains of the third cleric late last night using flashlights and dogs. We can show you those body parts, too, if you still doubt our intentions, Damon."

The room grows uncomfortably quiet as we process the news—three more clerics dead, their lives snuffed out by another SWARM attack.

"Okay," Damon says.

"Okay what?" Tilda replies.

"Okay, I'll see them," Damon says.

"What are you...sick?" Tilda replies, shocked by his gruesome request.

"I want to identify the clerics," he says. "And verify your story."

"Come on, Damon, just trust them," I say. "Let's get this Verdict over with. The sooner we start, the sooner we can complete the Project."

"Let him! If you want to see your friends' severed heads, then be my guest," Phoebe commands. "While the rest of you finish breakfast, Damon, you can follow McNultey."

The past five minutes offend me beyond words. It's all wrong for so many reasons.

Lelantos's decision to choose fortune over friendship.

ELIXIR's decision to let the clerics walk into a trap.

SWARM's decision to decapitate my fellow clerics.

And Damon's decision to validate Tilda's story.

We eat our breakfast in silence. After a few minutes Damon walks back into the room with McNultey. I've seen movies with ghosts that have more color than on their faces.

"Satisfied?" Phoebe asks.

"Sorry—for doubting," Damon says somberly.

"May we continue now?"

"Yes," he says emphatically. "SWARM will pay for their sins."

CHAPTER
FIFTY-ONE

"Congratulations, clerics, you've made it to this third and final Verdict—Flow," André says.

A quick scan around the courtroom reveals empty benches. Twelve of us were so full of life. Twelve of us believed we could receive our Boon. Twelve of us felt like we could change the fate of the world. But today, only four of us remain.

"Flow is the area I've invested most of my personal time in," André says. "It's also the area where I've made most of my personal wealth. I may know more about Flow than most, but you clerics are the ones hardwired to become the masters of it.

"Flow is the final element needed to create the ELIXIR vaccine. Once in our possession, neither height nor depth—not even SWARM itself—will be able to separate us from what we set our minds to do."

The way André speaks is unsettling, though I'm not sure

why. I think it's not what he says, but rather how he says it.

"You'll see the Project Paradigm on the screen to my right. Notice how all three Verdicts integrate. Idea. Focus. Flow."

"Our research proves unhackability begins with Flawless Idea Anatomy. From there it moves into Deliberate Magnetic Focus and then concludes with Optimal Human Performance. This ELIXIR of the gods will vaccinate us all from the stain of SWARM."

Now I'm definitely uncomfortable with his speech.

"Inside this Verdict, your performance, creativity, and problem-solving skills will increase by five hundred percent. Remember, clerics, fear no one but truth."

And then André's image disappears.

"Skills download successful," a voice from beyond the Apparition says.

"Bring them back to the Abyss. It's time for their final Verdict," says another voice.

CHAPTER
FIFTY-TWO

PHOENIX JUMPS IN immediately. "How is that even possible? We've reached moments of Flow in game-time situations, but sustaining five hundred percent sounds like science fiction."

"Correction, dearie—*science fact*," Kiran says. "In Flow, your brain releases five of the most potent neurochemicals on the planet: norepinephrine, dopamine, endorphins, anandamide, and serotonin. Each plays a critical role. Norepinephrine increases heart rate, attention, and emotional control. Dopamine blends nicely with your RAS filter, allowing you superhuman focus that leads to pattern recognition and skill-enhancing abilities. Endorphins increase your threshold for withstanding physical, emotional, and mental discomfort."

"We're not talking about a little pain, either," McNultey says.

No doubt, McNultey will be the one inflicting it. I've warned Cai so many times that there's a cost for playing God. Sounds like he never passed the memo on to ELIXIR.

"Most people have experienced Flow without even knowing it," Phoebe says. "Long-distance runners call it runner's high. Musicians call it playing in the pocket. Football players call it being in the zone."

Kiran continues to unpack the final two neurochemicals. "Anandamide elevates mood, relieves pain, and augments lateral thinking—your ability to link contrasting ideas together."

That's what I need. The ability to recognize how all these pieces fit together.

"And serotonin is the fifth and final one," Kiran explains. "It helps you stick with a task in spite of pain."

"Sounds powerful. So what's ELIXIR's role, then?" Damon asks.

"By monitoring your brains, we've discovered that part of what makes you four clerics unhackable is your propensity for Flow," Kiran says. "Although the general population has varying levels of Flow potential, yours is limitless."

"What are you saying?" I ask.

"That we've never seen anything like it before," Phoebe clarifies. "It's quite simply herculean—and if it can be harnessed and reproduced, you'll be the very definition of Optimal Human Performance. We're going to punch the pedal to see what you're made of."

"Lucky us," Karme says sarcastically.

"Time will tell that," McNultey laughs.

"But helmets will help," Tilda says. "We'll use them to monitor your Flow state inside the Verdict."

I wonder what new skills they shot into our psyche this time. Then again, based on the other two Verdicts, maybe I don't want to know.

"Clerics, when you're in a Flow state you experience near-perfect decision-making—absorbing information, synthesizing it, and then integrating it," Tilda says. "You're so focused in the moment you're not even aware of yourself or your limitations. Your inner critic goes silent and you no longer self-edit."

I can't imagine a time where I no longer self-edit. My life is one constant judgment. *How do I look? How do I sound? What do they think? Is this right?*

"There's a dark side to Flow, though," Tilda cautions. "There's a chance you won't want to come back."

I lean in, worried.

"Don't underestimate these five neurochemicals. Ask any addict," Tilda continues. "And don't get so caught up in the Deep Now you forget the true reason we sent you in. You're in there because we need the ELIXIR vaccine."

Her words snap me back to reality. If we fail—or *if*

we fail to come back, humanity pays the ultimate price.

"So when do we start?" Damon asks.

With elation plastered across his face, Kiran replies, "There's no time like the present."

A female proxy distributes helmets. Others roam around collecting the remaining breakfast dishes. Edge bends to pick up some silverware near me and places something inside my hand. Then he curls my fingers shut and I feel it—silky smooth.

"Petals from a fire lily—the twins' favorite flower. When you're in there today, Aryedne, you'll be in my heart and my prayers. And remember—Aletheia."

Then he stands back up discreetly so no one notices. Before I can thank him, he moves on, giving another proxy some instructions. I open my fingers and see them—two spiraled fire-orange petals.

I grab an unused napkin from my breakfast, wrap it around the petals, and place it inside one of my pockets. We all follow Tilda into the field house.

The space is massive and features a two-hundred-yard track, complete with pole vault boxes, and sandpits. I'm fully aware of my small stature compared to the soaring glass walls. I stand there, neck craned, mouth gaping, looking at the massive arched ceiling. I move my feet, turning to get a 360-degree view. Halfway through my spin, my helmet strap passes through my fingers and falls to the ground. I bend down to pick it off the track, and notice it.

The bright red stain, soaked into the tawny-colored track.

Amrita!

I gaze above me—and spot the steel white trusses high in the air. That's where they jumped and this is where they landed. I want to cry or gag—or maybe both. More than that I want to finish this Project and visit Cai.

"Welcome to Flow Ball," Tilda says. "If you look just below the trusses on the track floor, you'll notice four gigantic HVAC units. Each one has air ducts that dump fresh air into this space. Study these units. Memorize their position in relation to the steel trusses above us. You'll begin on the east side, where a lift will raise you up to the steel truss. Your goal is to climb from that point all the way to the west side. Once there, you'll ring a bell to signal you've completed the climb."

"No problem," Phoenix boasts.

Tilda doesn't acknowledge his confidence, but continues on with her explanation. "The arched roof is three hundred feet wide and eighty feet high in the center. We've modified each air duct to shoot baseball-sized Flow Balls at you while you're making your climb. Each ball travels at ninety miles per hour and carries three hundred joules of electrical shock. This is more than ten times the power of your conventional electrical fence. A direct hit from a Flow Ball disrupts your nervous system, causing you to experience temporary paralysis.

Naturally, you'll lose all motor control and fall from the steel trusses."

"Are you crazy?" Karme says. "Didn't you see enough blood when amrita fell?"

"There will be a net to catch you," Tilda says. "There are four units on both the east and west side of the field house and six air ducts on each unit. One unit begins firing seven seconds into your climb. Then every seven seconds later another unit will join in. At the fifty-six-second mark, all forty-eight air ducts will be firing for the remainder of your climb, releasing a new Flow Ball every second."

"Still not a problem?" I ask Phoenix. He forces a nervous laugh and shrugs his shoulders.

"You'll be given five climbs and each cleric must perform one of these climbs," Tilda explains. "Your cohort can decide which one of you will do the fifth one."

"What if we make it on our first try?" Phoenix asks.

"The first four climbs are practice—for you to get better and to discover how to get into Flow. But the Flow Verdict can only be achieved on the fifth climb because it's different in two ways. Number one, you must make that climb in sixty seconds or less. And number two, you must do it without a net."

"*No net?*" Damon says, the exact words I'm thinking. "With forty-eight Flow Balls firing from all directions? Isn't that a bit extreme?"

Kiran huffs. "I've run the formulas dozens of times. The climb is difficult, but not impossible. To achieve a deep Flow state, you must experience a real chance of failing."

"And if the cleric falls on the fifth climb, then what?" I ask.

"Then we have three other clerics to do the sixth, seventh, and eighth climbs," McNultey laughs.

The fact that Phoebe doesn't correct him is troubling, to say the least.

"Well then, let's get started," Tilda says. "Clerics, please head over to the east side of the field house. Our proxies will ready the net and prep the first cleric."

CHAPTER
FIFTY-THREE

"I'LL GO FIRST," Karme says, snapping on her helmet. "I'd rather just get it over with."

"You got this," I say, trying to calm the frightened eyes I see through her face shield. "Remember, you got a net under you."

"Thanks. Just watch me and you'll learn what *not* to do," she says anxiously.

A lift elevates Karme up to the first steel truss. The thick white tubes dwarf her. Kiran turns on the two scoreboards located at both ends of the field house.

Edge announces, "Cleric, on your mark...get set... go!"

At the loud *bang* from his starting pistol, she springs into action. Like a startled squirrel hopping from branch to branch, she maneuvers through the twisted metal suspended in space. The skills download worked well, judging by the way her body moves in and out. Arms and legs, hands and feet, she repositions herself—utilizing momentum to advance down the beam.

Then they come—the orange Flow Balls, zipping through the air at dizzying speed. Getting beaned by a baseball at ninety miles an hour is bad enough. But knowing each ball carries with it enough shock to knock us out of the air or maybe even out of our minds is a troubling thought.

Karme dodges the first Flow Ball without a struggle. The next one hits the white tube, near her leg. Every seven seconds a new unit begins firing off another six Flow Balls. The assault of orange on Karme is maddening from where we stand below. I can't imagine what it feels like from way up there.

Before I have time to imagine, I hear it—a piercing scream. Then I see it—a falling body. The black net sinks down and springs back up. We rush over to see if she's hurt.

Karme lies motionless. No grunting or groaning. No twisting or turning. Several proxies descend upon the net. They pass her body to the side of the net we're on. Phoenix fights his way near her and lifts up his arms. Without any effort, he single-handedly lowers her gently to the ground.

Several proxies with thin white bands around their right arms use wires and devices to measure her four vital signs:

body temperature, blood pressure, pulse, and breathing rate. "All signs are within range," one male proxy says. "I'm giving her the antidote now. It should lessen the effects."

After a few seconds, she coughs, sits up, and then rubs her head. "My shoulder kills," she moans.

"That's where the Flow Ball hit," Kiran says. "And you were just getting into a Flow state, too."

"How far did I get?"

"About thirty feet."

"What? Only ten percent of the beam?"

"You're going to have to do better than that," Tilda says. "You were pitiful."

"Give her some credit," Phoenix says, defending her. "At least she got up there."

"Get up th…"—Tilda tries finding her words—"Get up—there? Do you realize what's at stake? If you don't figure out how to get into deep Flow, then that's it. Might as well hand SWARM the keys to the planet. And you say at least she got up there!"

"Calm down," Phoebe intervenes. "They have at least four more tries to get it. And according to Kiran's data, there's a chance they can achieve it."

"A chance?" Damon asks. "You're betting on beating SWARM and our survival as a species on chance?"

"No," Phoebe replies calmly. "We're betting it on you. And I believe in you, clerics, otherwise you wouldn't be here. Now, who's next?"

None of us budges. If Tilda meant to scare us, it worked.

"I'll go," Damon says.

"Good, because I'm staying right here with Karme until the next climb," Phoenix says.

Damon snaps his helmet on and squeezes my hand. I walk with him over to the lift. "Hey, you never finished telling me something."

"What's that?" he says.

"If I knew, I wouldn't ask," I say, jabbing him with my elbow playfully.

"You mean when I was about to race in the square?" he says, stepping onto the lift. "Oh, I remember. I was going to tell you the one thing I was going to focus on to help me get through the race." The lift ascends slowly to the steel truss.

"And that was…"

"The same thing I'm focusing on to get through this one."

"Do I even get a hint?"

The lift reaches its full height, now several stories in the air. Damon puts both hands on the railing and peers down from the lift above, like he's going to speak.

Edge breaks in, "Cleric, on your mark…get set…go!"

A *bang* fills the space—the space that was supposed to be for me. I look up toward Damon, expecting to see him looking back down at me—but he's already gone.

CHAPTER FIFTY-FOUR

DAMON ISN'T AS small as Karme, but he's definitely faster. By watching her go first, he must have used that as a type of feedback loop and adjusted his strategy. Instead of weaving in between the tubes with his arms and legs, Damon maneuvers outside of them. He hugs the beams with his body and uses his feet to prop himself up. After the first five feet, he almost runs across the beam, using his limbs to balance his rapid movements.

But then the Flow Balls start flying. He bobs and curls, ducks and crouches, never pausing. An orange ball sails toward his left hand, the one gripping the white tube and sustaining his weight. A microsecond before the ball's impact, he releases his hand, causing his body to flip. He hangs upside down—held in place merely by one leg, which twists around a different white tube.

After a few more balls whiz by his head, he swings

back up to the main steel truss, allowing his feet to dangle. Then he advances farther down the beam with both hands and no feet.

"He's doing it!" Kiran says, looking at his tablet.

"Doing what?" McNultey asks.

"Entering into a Flow state, you idiot."

My mind drifts back to our interaction a couple minutes ago. I'm surprised Damon started his climb so relaxed—holding my hand, even flirting. It's almost as if he wasn't focused on the climb.

"He missed the tube!" Kiran yells.

I snap out of my daydream just in time to see Damon smack the net and pop back up. "Was he hit?" I ask.

"Nope. Must have slipped," Phoenix says, holding Karme's hand. She sips on a water bottle with her other hand, looking much more like herself.

I hurry over to the net and am greeted by a big grin. "What a rush!" Damon says. "I can't believe I fell, though."

"What happened?" Tilda asks. "You were covering so much ground."

"I stopped to think, that's what," he says, somersaulting over the edge of the net while still maintaining his grip. He lowers himself to the ground—like circus performers do.

"Up until the point my hands slipped, I didn't even think about the beams, or the balls, for that matter. I didn't think about anything—really. I kept moving and the steel bars kept coming."

"Your numbers prove that," Kiran says.

"How far did I get and what was my time?" Damon asks.

"Fifty percent and almost three minutes."

"Seriously? We need to shave off two minutes and go twice as far?"

"Minus the net," McNultey adds.

"Thanks for the reminder," he says, wincing.

"My turn," Phoenix says, pushing through us and heading over to the lift. "Watch and learn."

Someone who doesn't know him might think he's cocky. But I've sat with Karme during enough of his games on blustery Saturday afternoons to realize what he's doing. He's talking himself into a frenzy.

The lift raises him to the third steel truss. After the *bang*, Phoenix begins where Damon left off, manhandling the white steel tubes with a monkey bars approach.

Because of his upper-body strength, he makes quick progress. But three hundred feet is the length of a football field. Advancing your body weight down a beam while being pelted with forty-eight Flow Balls every second—each supercharged with three hundred joules a pop—is difficult for anybody.

The first ball hits him on his left ankle. His

subsequent scream removes any doubt that the jolt found its mark. Miraculously, he wills himself farther down the beam. Maybe his body weight diffused the shock somehow?

But at this point it's obvious something is wrong. His attention shifted from subconscious Flow to conscious fear. The sting of the first ball distracts him from the task at hand. His mind gives up before his body does, and on the way down, two more balls bean him—one on his back and the other straight onto his helmet, cracking it upon impact.

The net swallows him up, absorbing a fraction of his downward force. It takes six large proxies to move him from the center to the edge and another six to lower him to the floor.

"This one sits for the remainder of the Verdict," Phoebe says. "Give him an antidote and assign two medics to monitor him outside the field house. We can't afford any distractions during the remaining climbs." The proxies lift Phoenix onto a stretcher. Karme holds his hand and consoles him.

"Aryedne, you're up next," Tilda says. "After your climb, your cohort may meet for fifteen minutes. You can strategize and choose the cleric for the fifth climb."

I nod. "Got any tips, Mr. Flow?" I ask Damon on the way to the lift.

"Yeah, don't get hit by a ball," he teases.

"I think I got that part already. Phoenix and Karme made that pretty clear."

He stops walking. Then he turns and faces me, grabbing both of my hands. "I've got a crazy idea."

"Why am I not surprised?" I say.

"I'll ignore your abundant enthusiasm," he says sarcastically. "When you're up there on the beam, just enjoy yourself."

"You weren't joking. That *is* crazy."

"No, I'm serious," he says. "If you're focused on getting hit, making time, or saving the world, then you'll struggle. But if you're unattached to the outcome, it's easier to relax. Let your subconscious mind take over. Remember, billions of bits of information versus two hundred bits—which one do you think will help you more up there?"

The lift raises me up to the steel truss.

"Unattached to the outcome," I repeat, looking down over the railing, watching him get smaller. But the higher I go, the more anxiety I feel.

"Enjoy yourself," he says, nodding.

"Got it."

"And buckle your helmet."

"Cleric, on your mark...get set...*go!*"

CHAPTER
FIFTY-FIVE

IF THE *BANG* went off, I never heard it. Before I even decide to move, my body is already ten feet across the beam, moving through the obstacles. What did they download inside us—some kind of parkour program?

I make it up as I go, free-running down the truss. My fingers wrap around the cool steel, not once second-guessing myself. With preprogrammed movements, I tic tac through the crossbars—at times precision jumping, other times gap jumping. A pop vault here and a reverse underbar there. The beams can't come fast enough.

My stomach lifts up into my chest, reminding me of the sensation I experienced on the makeshift playground Uncle Cai created in the backyard.

While most kids had swings, slides, and trampolines, Uncle Cai designed a kinesthetic complex of ramps, bars, and something the neighbor kids called the "spider's web." We'd play on that web for hours—a combination of ropes and tires suspended a couple feet off the ground.

I insisted on being the spider most of the time because I loved chasing the other kids, who pretended to be flies. My friend Kale was the only other person allowed to be a spider. She was fast, too, but as a "fly," I could outclimb her.

I pretend these white steel beams are thick white ropes. And I'm not a fly being chased; I'm the spider—chasing Kale. And in my imagination, Cai isn't incoherent, lying in a hospital bed. He's lying on a lounge chair, engaged in his book.

Kale?

That name is significant, but I'm not sure why. Perhaps it's a piece of the puzzle? If only I knew the image of the completed puzzle I'm trying to solve.

Time slows enough for me to see the dimples on each Flow Ball, bearing straight toward me. With effortless sidesteps, every single ball glides past. I remain connected to the joy of the moment and the rush of neurochemicals coursing through my body.

I know my heart must be racing, but I'm aware enough to feel each beat. My lungs must burn for oxygen, but I'm conscious of each measured breath.

Energy without borders.

Risk without hesitation.

Attention without distraction.

I am the essence of Flow.

For the first time in my climb, I look backward. Halfway between east and west, I hear a whisper of fear beckoning me, longing to confuse and overwhelm me with self-doubt.

I hear my name—or at least my new one—from somewhere below. I redirect my focus and see tiny figures eight stories under me. My vision spins. My arms shake—enough for me to notice them wobble. An uncomfortable tingle begins in my fingers, traveling down my toes and up through my spine. I'm suddenly aware of the Flow Balls, the cost of failing, and the dizzying track below.

I shake my head. *Are my eyes playing tricks?* From this high up, I notice Damon and Karme encircled in blood. I must be on the exact truss—in the exact spot—where the amrita cohort made their life-altering decision and fell to their deaths.

A Flow Ball strikes the beam three inches in front of me, almost grazing my hand—close enough for me to feel the shifting air. Panic rips through me. I see myself falling from the beam just like Erida, plummeting to the hard track.

Acrophobia.

Where have I heard that word before?

In a movie? A song? A book, perhaps? It's right there, but I can't grasp it. I have to finish this climb for

Cai, for Erida, and even for Lyric. The pang of guilt for striking her with my skylatis distracts me even further.

Self-limiting beliefs come rushing into my mind: *You're too slow. The beam is too high. You're going to fail.*

An orange ball dings the white beam, next to my knee. Everything in me wants to hunker down, cling to the truss, and give up, right here. The net looks so inviting. I could fake a slip, and no one would know the difference.

But then the truth smacks me with the same velocity of a Flow Ball. *Acrophobia! Kale!* I'm so close to unlocking the pattern.

My choices become clear: I can stay frozen and visit with this familiar friend named fear, or I can go deeper into Flow and solve this mental puzzle.

I know what I must do: Rise up, reestablish my mental state, and make up lost ground. I take off toward my intended target, the west truss. Fifty feet into my free run, the dopamine rockets me into another gear, and for the first time I experience invincibility.

I reach out, ring the bell, and smile.

I conquered the climb.

CHAPTER FIFTY-SIX

I REMOVE MY helmet and try not to revel too much in my victory. The lift on the west side lowers me down to the track. The tops of their heads appear in order from tallest to shortest—Damon, Tilda, Phoebe, Edge, Karme, and Kiran. Phoenix must still be outside the field house.

"According to my data, you're looking at Ms. Serotonin herself," Kiran announces.

"Way to go, Aryedne," Damon says. "You were awesome."

"That's my roomie," Karme says, grinning. "We're so proud of you."

"Thanks," I say.

"Well…how did it feel up there?" Phoebe asks.

"Um…amazing…brilliant…otherworldly."

"Those are good adjectives," Phoebe replies.

"Her levels weren't high enough," Tilda barks.

"Couldn't she enjoy her victory for ten seconds?" Phoebe complains.

"She failed. Did you see the timer?"

I look and see 1:59. My heart sinks, but I'm not about to let it show. "I can do better," I say. "You saw me—up there in the middle of the beam. I wasted at least thirty seconds."

"Yeah, want to share what you were thinking?" Tilda asks. "The scan shows you started coming out of the Flow state, but then somehow you reentered it, going even deeper. How did you do that?"

"I guess I just let myself go and stopped trying to fight it."

"'Let yourself go'?" McNultey says. Well, isn't that nice and scientific. We can reproduce that in the lab, can't we, Kiran? 'I just let myself go' will do wonders for the ELIXIR vaccine, no doubt."

"Aryedne, we need a Flow state about twice as deep to complete the final Verdict," Phoebe says. "Ringing the bell in sixty seconds or less will get you there. You think you can do it?"

"Absolutely!"

"*Without a net?*" Damon objects.

"We already explained; that part is nonnegotiable," Tilda says. "She needs to experience the potential for failure."

"But with her own life?" he snaps.

"You've got ten minutes before the fifth climb begins," Tilda replies. "Trust me, clerics. SWARM isn't waiting around for us to figure this out."

We start walking to get away from Tilda and her endless supply of negativity. "I think you should be the climber, Aryedne," Karme says, not even bothering to wait before giving her opinion.

"Thanks for your vote of confidence in *my* abilities, Karme," Damon says. "I know I could do better, too."

"Uh, we had a deal in case you forgot," I say, bending down to retie my shoelaces tighter.

"What deal? I never agreed to anything," he says.

"That's where you're wrong. I specifically remember you saying if I let you take the SKO in the second Verdict, then you'd let me volunteer for the third Verdict. Remember?"

"But I never got hit with a skylatis."

"And whose fault is that?" I point out.

"She's got you there," Karme says.

"Outnumbered by the ladies." Damon smirks. "Where's Phoenix when I need him?"

"He'll be fine. But it's time to face the music. Aryedne was better than you up there."

"I agree. But no net?" Damon asks.

"Look we can fight for the next five minutes about gender, size, strength, speed, or any other reason why one of us is more qualified," I say.

"Or?" Damon says.

"Or you can listen to my theory."

"All ears," Damon says.

"Okay, remember last night?"

"Getting locked in a racquetball court, forced to sleep on a narrow platform and eat disgusting-tasting protein bars?" Karme complains. "Yeah, I'm still trying to forget it."

"Before that. I meant at the café, when Damon was asking all kinds of questions."

They both nod.

"Each one of those questions is like a little piece of truth. Separately, they're insignificant, or at least they don't make sense. But when put together, they form a complete picture."

"*Okay?*" Karme says, waiting for some kind of punch line.

"Five minutes till climb time!" Edge announces.

"Last night I couldn't sleep, and I had my own set of questions rolling around in my head, too, about the Boon, my parents, Cai, the Project. Here's the point: When I was up on that steel beam just now—climbing and getting into Flow, those little pieces of truth started to make sense."

"What are you saying?" Damon asks.

"I'm saying, according to Kiran, the guy who

understands this stuff, Flow helps our ability to link contrasting ideas together. I felt it—the beginning of it, anyway. The clues were coming."

"Why did they stop?" Karme asks.

"You heard Tilda. I needed to go deeper."

"Can you?" Damon asks, the one question I can't answer.

"I know with everything on the line I can go twice as fast. The truth about how all those pieces fit together will come."

"But we're talking about your life, roomie."

"It's bigger than that," I say. "We're talking about Cai and Lyric and SWARM, too."

"Might as well throw in there the fate of the world," Damon says sarcastically.

"Might as well." I smile.

"Well...I for one want to hear your victory speech at the Boon Ceremony," Damon says.

"Two minutes till climb time!" Edge announces. "Head over to the lift, please."

I look at the friend I've come to know and the guy I'm beginning to fall for. "Well, I guess this is it." I extend a hand to each one of them. "Don't start crying on me now, Karme." The tears roll down her cheeks. "Here, I've got a tissue." I pull out the napkin from my pocket and spill the two fire lily petals onto the floor.

"You always carry dead flowers in your pocket?"

Damon asks.

"Edge gave them to me. I think he's on our side."

"Are there people here who *aren't* on our side?" Damon says.

"Time to find out, right?" I say. "Here, hold them when I'm up there."

Damon takes the petals, his hand lingering on mine. My chest aches every time he touches me. I want to step toward him and eliminate the space between us.

But this time I don't have to keep aching or longing or wanting. This time he leans in close enough for me to feel his breath against my lips.

I've never had a boy kiss me. And for that matter, I've never kissed one, either. There's a difference. You can simply be kissed—end of story. Or you can kiss back—and, well, create your own new story.

Since this is my first time, I decide to close my eyes and be kissed. The electrical shock generated from our mouths touching sends a shiver through every atom in my body. My right hand moves to the back of his head, and my fingers dance throughout his soft brown hair. Unlike in the vehicle transport from the airport a few days ago, this time he's aware enough to feel it. Aware enough to know how I feel about him.

"Cleric, to your mark," Edge instructs.

I wish I could ignore his warning. I don't want to stop kissing—or start climbing. I don't want to *do* anything or *go* anywhere. Our kiss makes me forget about everything, even for just a moment. I force myself to pull away.

"See you in sixty seconds, once you ring that bell," Damon says encouragingly.

I smile back, and as I step onto the lift, a thought tiptoes into my mind: *Maybe that's why we need relationships. Maybe they're meant to help us forget we're alone.*

The lift keeps rising and I keep staring. I inch closer to the railing, wishing I were still sharing the same air as Damon. The gap between us grows each second until the jolt at the top reminds me why I'm here.

"Get set. Go!"

BANG!

CHAPTER
FIFTY-SEVEN

I DON'T REMEMBER how I got here or where I'm going. For that matter, I don't even remember what I'm doing.

I hear giggling and realize I'm in my backyard, playing on a gigantic version of the "spider's web." The white ropes surround us and protect us from falling. I look around the web and smile back at the faces. Each person wears a cone-shaped hat with an image of a birthday cake and three candles on the front.

The party guests represent different seasons of my life—childhood friends, clerics, and family members alike. I see my childhood friend Kale, my uncle Cai, and a beautiful couple who look strikingly similar to my parents in the photograph.

Lyric and Erida enjoy eating their birthday cake on festive paper plates with pink plastic forks. A twin boy and girl sit next to their father, Edge, each clinging to one of his gigantic tattooed arms. We bounce on the ropes and laugh together.

I see Phoebe to my left. She hands me a card, one of those that plays music when you open it. On the front it reads *Happy Birthday, Ballerina* in big, sparkling letters.

I open it up and hear a song I only remember from a dream. On the inside of the card, I read the word *ALETHEIA* written across a music box. Below the box it says:

To Sienna
From André and Phoebe

The music box reminds me of the one I played with when my parents passed. I turn to thank Phoebe, but she's on the other side of the web, serving my parents a glass of punch. They look beautiful—full of life and joy.

I want to speak to them and tell them I love them. I want to hug them and ask them questions—big and small ones. Like, what's their favorite color? How did they fall in love, and what makes them afraid? They sip their punch and smile back at me.

I glance down at my hands, but when I look back up, the sky behind them grows dark. An evil shadow comes over their faces, shifting their color from bright to pale, causing them to cough and shake. Dark tar oozes from their mouths, leaking down their cheeks. Their grip around the rope loosens and they slink off the web and into blackness.

Panic surges through me, and screams erupt from my lungs. No one hears me. I spin to Phoebe to elicit her help, but she's holding a sleek black pistol with a bright orange stripe. Two bolts of fire rip from the barrel as her hands recoil from the blasts. The bullets find their mark on the twins. Although Edge tries to prop them up, their limp bodies slide out of his arms and into the darkness below.

I shout to warn the others, but they're too distracted to notice, still enjoying their birthday cake. With a dark hood over her head, Phoebe creeps toward Cai and presses her hand against his chest. He hunches over and clutches his heart, his face a yellowish-green color. Moments later he, too, drops into the thick fog.

With panic-filled faces, Lyric and Erida toss their plates and stand up, suddenly aware of Cai's plunge. They scan their surroundings, seeking a way of escape. Too late—Phoebe is in midair, leaping toward Erida, her black robe flowing behind her.

She lands with palpable force, smashing into Erida and sending her flying twenty feet off the ropes. Lyric scrambles to get away. Her foot slips, her legs dangle, and she looks back just in time to see Phoebe's skylatis coming down hard on her face. Knocked unconscious, Lyric skids off the side and joins the fate of the others.

I'm Phoebe's next target. She whips her head around and wipes the saliva dripping from her mouth. Her eyes of fire make it abundantly clear she won't rest until she consumes me. With all four limbs spread out like a spider's, she scurries toward me in a Z pattern.

Propelled by adrenaline, instinct, and the will to survive, I sprint across the white ropes, evading her attack. With every plant of my hands and feet, I notice orange spheres being shot at me from behind.

The oddity of the moment hits me. *Orange spheres intended to kill? Climbing on a web of steel?* Like a busted dam barreling down a dry mountain bed, answers wash over me.

I remember how I got here—Flow Verdict.

I remember where I'm going—the west truss.

I remember what I'm doing—the fifth climb in under sixty seconds.

I feel the spider bearing down on me. I hear her legs chasing and swarming, longing to throw me into the darkness below. On instinct, I lunge out in front of me, smacking my right hand into nothingness. But then I hear it—the welcome ding of the bell. My lungs burn. My eyes water. And my heart nearly cracks through my rib cage.

I look behind me—no spider on the truss.

I look beside me—fifty-nine seconds on the scoreboard.

I look within me—clear answers.

The sudden surge of relief can only mean one thing— Verdict three achieved!

May 13

It's amazing how three days can change your view of everything.

About an hour ago, I looked in the mirror after Phoebe's team worked their magic. I didn't even recognize myself, and not in a good way, either—at least not completely.

No updates about Lyric yet. I entered the Name Change as an innocent girl. I'd never even been in a fight before. But for all I know, now I'm a murderer.

In the past seventy-two hours, I've witnessed more death, betrayal, and violence than in my first eighteen years of life combined.

I'm discovering that growing up isn't without wounds. And yet I feel alive in ways I didn't think possible.

I haven't stopped thinking about Damon since our kiss ended. I feel myself getting stronger. I always wanted permission to be brave. Guess I needed to be backed into a corner for it to come out.

The Boon Ceremony is just one more opportunity. If I tell the truth when the whole world's listening—who knows? That scared little girl inside may run away forever.

I thought the truth would set me free—or at least make me feel lighter. But now I'm aware of a brand-new question—one that scares me even more. Who else besides me knows the truth? And why have they been so hell-bent on hiding it?

Still no word on Uncle Cai. But I can't wait for circumstances to change and come my way. Tonight is the one shot I have to create my own future. I wonder if I'm ready to tell the truth...and quite frankly, I wonder if they're ready to hear it.

I'm sure tonight I'll discover answers to those questions and probably one hundred more.

—Aryedne

CHAPTER
FIFTY-EIGHT

"What are you going to say in there?" Karme asks me from the middle row of our six-seater electric cart.

"Not completely sure. The board gave me a script a few hours ago. But I've never been one to stick to a script. Actually, I had planned on chatting with you guys before they separated us."

"I guess it makes sense, though, whisking us away after the final Verdict for a medical evaluation," Karme says. "They probably don't want to present us to the global audience all banged up."

"Yeah, you're probably right. Why? What do you think I should say?" I ask.

"How about the truth?" Phoenix suggests. He still looks sore from the Flow Balls, but the afternoon of rest seems to have done wonders for his mobility.

"I guess I really don't have another choice," I say.

"We always have a choice," Damon says, loud enough for only me to hear.

He has a point.

The proxies pull up to the back of the church and park the cart right next to the Xcraft—the same place we left it three nights ago.

"After you," Damon says. I stand up and exit the cart along with Karme, who looks stunning in her red angle wrap dress. The guys look amazing, too, decked out in their three-piece midnight-blue mohair dinner suits.

Phoebe's team walked into our dorm room a couple hours ago with the navy military gown she'd selected for me. Although I never would have chosen it myself, I'm not complaining. Based on Damon's compliments on the way over, he's not, either.

I muster up the courage and come out with it. "Guys, I'm not sure how it's all going to go down in there."

They turn to me. "What do you mean?" Phoenix says. "Tilda already told us the agenda. She'll give the global audience a welcome, followed up by your victory speech. After that Phoebe receives the first ELIXIR vaccination in real time, and then André distributes our Boon before the closing remarks. Sounded pretty straightforward to me."

"I know what she *said*, but that's not what I meant."

"Didn't think so," Damon says.

I motion with my eyes for us to step away from the

two proxies who drove us over. Karme gets the hint and pushes the guys over toward the tree near the front of the church.

"I need to," I lower my voice, "tell you something. I just didn't know if it was safe." They give me a puzzled look. "When I was on the beam in the fifth climb, everything clicked—the questions *and* the answers. The neurochemicals did what Kiran said they would."

"That's great," Karme says. "We're happy for you."

"Thanks." I shrug, but I know they still don't get it. Telling them beforehand may put us all in danger. Who knows if they bugged one of us during the medical evaluation? I focus on not frowning. "Just do me one favor, okay?"

"For the girl who scored us our Boon?" Karme says. "Anything."

"During my speech, can you listen with your heart, not your ears?"

"Got it. Heart—no ears." Phoenix tries his best to sound serious.

Damon squeezes my hand. "We'll listen."

CHAPTER FIFTY-NINE

When we push the doors open we're greeted by enthusiastic applause. Proxies fill nearly every seat—even in the balcony. I assumed there would be camera flashes and microphones, not soldiers in black military fatigues holding glowing orange skylatises.

"Proxies, please be seated," Edge announces. "Clerics, we have four seats up here for you."

Damon and I walk behind Phoenix and Karme. I step up the orange-carpeted stairs and immediately notice the gold platter from the Name Change ceremony resting on the rectangular altar.

McNultey stands off to the right side of the platform, keeping a watchful eye. Kiran's chair comes first. He reminds me of a spoiled child proud to be seated at the adult table. Tilda's next, and she's dressed in her typical distinguished style—a designer featherweight gray wool jacket with matching gray skirt.

Phoebe sits on the other side of her, in a strapless white chiffon red-carpet-style dress. The side slits add an elegant touch. My skin crawls when I walk by her and the empty seat beside her. If I close my eyes, I can still imagine her chasing me on the white web.

Edge stays standing to give last-minute instructions. Although he wears a light coat and pants, his personality still shines through—sleeves pushed up and top two shirt buttons undone. "Our tech team prepped a three-camera shoot for the live stream," he explains. "The main camera is aimed at this lectern, so, presenters, please make a note of it. You'll speak from here." He points to the ornate wooden oversize podium.

"Aryedne, please sit in this chair closest to the lectern, followed by Damon, Karme, and then Phoenix."

As instructed, we sit in our assigned seats. I turn and notice behind me a wooden arch leading to a hallway. Looks like it might lead to where the priests keep sacred vessels used in Mass, or perhaps a back exit—from my seat I can't tell.

Edge continues speaking, leaning near my chair—his right hand on the kneeling bench just in front of the platform. I spot a black pistol with an orange stripe, secured in a holster that's strapped to his belt. While giving instructions, he catches me eyeing the weapon and gives me a slight wink—subtle enough I almost miss it. Although I'm perplexed, he winks again.

I smile back. The gun looks strikingly similar to the one Phoebe used in my Flow state up on the beam. Maybe he spoke with Cai and was warned? Or maybe Edge somehow discovered the truth on his own?

"How long until we go live?" Tilda asks.

"Five minutes," Edge replies.

"Great. Kiran, do you have any updates on your end?"

"Yes, dearie," Kiran squeals. "We received confirmation from our lab about thirty minutes ago. They completed the very first dose right on schedule. We've achieved our mission and created the very first ELIXIR vaccine!"

The room explodes into a frenzy. Proxies holler. And more than a hundred skylatises pound against the old wooden floor. Phoebe closes her eyes, and a smile of relief spreads across her face. I think I even see a tear leaking down Tilda's cheek.

Kiran stands on his seat and raises his hands to calm down the pandemonium before he continues. "A Special Forces proxy unit is transporting the vaccine to us. As planned, Phoebe will receive the first injection—a gesture of both faith and generosity. Faith—signifying her confidence in the Project. And generosity—signifying our gratitude to her and André for their financial commitment to eradicate SWARM."

Tilda speaks up. "Edge, I'm told you had some

proxies prepare additional security measures?"

"Of course," he replies. "A team installed an electromagnetic force field up here on the platform. We're not taking any chances tonight. If anyone on the platform feels threatened in any way, you may press the orange button on the remote up here on the altar.

"Once pressed, a shield will instantly engage, protecting the clerics, board members, and the vaccine. This defensive strategy will keep everything out: people, proxies, and even programs that SWARM might try to hack."

"Where's André?" Phoebe asks. "He's never late and I didn't received a text telling me otherwise."

"He said to start without him," Tilda explains. "He's finishing up some details with Chevon."

"He texted *you?*" Phoebe snaps. "Why?"

"Because I'm the ELIXIR spokesperson you both recruited?" Tilda replies. "I don't know. Ask him yourself. He's *your* husband."

"Thirty seconds," Edge says. "Places, everyone. Smile. Be confident. And remember, fear no one but truth."

Then he looks at me and gives an encouraging nod before his countdown. "And we are live in three, two, one!"

CHAPTER SIXTY

"Greetings, global citizens, and welcome to the Boon Ceremony. My name is Tilda Tulane, spokesperson for the Senior Board of Clerics, the governing entity for ELIXIR. We share a common enemy—SWARM—and we share a common goal—the eradication of it."

The proxies initiate a rousing applause and the Senior Board members join in. Karme, Phoenix, Damon, and I follow suit. After a few seconds, Tilda raises her hand to quiet the crowd. "Last time we gathered, it was under much different circumstances—reasons of war and not peace. But today—and from this day forward—all this has changed. I give you…the ELIXIR vaccine!"

The doors on the east side of the church slam wide open. A Special Forces unit parades in, each holding a skylatis. The lead proxy carries a small, mirrored silver box and marches up to the lectern. Tilda bows as she receives the box and then holds it above her head—garnering more cheers and roars from the audience.

"Although we rejoice in this victory, the price was not cheap," Tilda says, walking from the lectern to the altar. She places the sliver box on the altar and lifts the golden platter, gazing at the twelve stones.

"Each stone represents a life," she says solemnly. "Not every cleric who began the Project will cross the finish line with us. Please rise and join me in a moment of silence for our fallen clerics. From the amrita cohort: Ares, Erida, Metis, and Ophion."

A painful moment passes.

"And from the soma cohort: Pallas, Styx, Lelantos... and Lyric."

Tilda's words sting my soul. Her moment of silence for Lyric inflicts more torture than I can bear. I choke back emotions, even my own breath, knowing I'm on the verge of imploding right here in front of a global audience. The impact of her words sinks in. *Now I know I'm a murderer.*

"Time to hear from one of our victors—Aryedne."

Is Tilda calling for me? NOW?

"Come on, Aryedne," she says, motioning with her hand. "Naturally, the past few days we weren't able to give our global audience real-time video updates. The potential threat of SWARM prevented us from doing so. However, now that we've created the ELIXIR vaccine, I can provide a brief highlight reel."

With a few swipes on her glass tablet, she starts the video, narrating the images we see on the screen. "In the Idea Verdict, Aryedne achieved Flawless Idea Anatomy in the pool through the use of Imagined Reality. In the Focus Verdict, she demonstrated mastery of Deliberate Magnetic Focus through the race on her RAS-board. And finally, in the Flow Verdict, she achieved a deep Flow state while scaling the steel truss.

"Achieving these three Verdicts provided our team with the necessary tools and knowledge we needed to complete the Project. Let this Project Paradigm burn into your hearts and minds, the image of your salvation!"

I'm glad the lighting is dim, because my cheeks are hot from embarrassment. During the Verdicts, I didn't have time to think about anything but the task in front of me. But now that I'm seeing it in 3-D with cinematic music, it's a bit overwhelming.

"Please welcome from the ichor cohort Ms. Aryedne Lewis. Well done, faithful cleric."

On cue, the white spotlights turn back on and the proxies shower me with praise. They chant, "Ichor! Ichor! Ichor!" I glance to my left and see my three friends clapping wildly, too.

Tilda motions for everyone to sit and then finds her own seat between Phoebe and Kiran. Ready or not, it's my moment of truth.

"Senior Board of Clerics, proxies, and global citizens, it's my honor to address you tonight," I say with as much poise as I can muster. "When I began the Project, I had my doubts about myself, my fellow clerics, and even ELIXIR. But throughout the Verdicts, over these past three days, I discovered the truth.

"Regarding myself, I discovered that fear is a necessary part of life, and that when it counts most, I need to trust my gut—and listen to my heart.

"Regarding my fellow clerics, I discovered we're flawed, each of us. And that being honest bonds us together, when we don't know the right answers—or even the correct questions.

"And finally I discovered the truth about ELIXIR." I swallow hard and look at Edge standing next to McNultey. I give him another wink, and he winks back.

"My uncle Cai said it best. Recently, he warned me.

"He said, 'They're watching us.' I wondered, *Who's watching?*

"He said, 'Things aren't always what they seem.' I wondered, *What things?*

"And finally he said, 'Don't believe what you think; believe what you know.'

"So here I am—invited to tell you what I know."

I take a deep breath. I stare straight at Phoebe, the woman who manipulated me, who tried to fill the hole my deceased mother left inside my heart. I raise my finger and point right at her.

"I know beyond a shadow of a doubt...Phoebe Saradon is SWARM."

CHAPTER
SIXTY-ONE

IN ONE MICROSECOND, all the oxygen in the room is sucked out of the church.

No one breathes. No one speaks. No one moves.

And then it comes, the audible gasps from all corners of the room—proxies, members of the Senior Board of Clerics, and my friends alike.

Edge springs to life. In one fluid motion he moves toward Phoebe, draws his weapon, reaches his giant arm around her neck, and holds the gun to her head.

"Freeze, everyone!" he yells.

McNultey, Kiran, and the proxies back down—rattled to witness this split-second hostage situation unfold. I scan the seats in front of me, hoping to discern the difference between friend and foe—those on the side of truth and those on the side of SWARM. But in this scenario, it's too risky to tell.

Tilda is the first to voice her confusion. "Are you possessed? What is she talking about, Phoebe?"

"Now, hold on, everybody!" Edges shouts. "We've named them Verdicts, so that's what we're going to have—a global jury. Tonight truth is on trial. Aryedne speaks first, followed by Phoebe and then anybody else on the platform. Hear me when I say this: I'm not bluffing. Anybody tries anything—and Phoebe's dead with a bullet in her brain. No questions asked. Got it?"

Nobody responds.

"Got it?" He jabs the barrel hard against her neck.

Heads move up and down.

"Now, go on, Aryedne—like my friend Cai, I've had my own doubts long enough."

I compose myself, knowing this isn't the time to submit to that little girl inside—the one who wants to hide under the covers when she's scared at night. This moment needs someone who isn't afraid to speak the truth.

"Tilda, you're not going to like what you hear—you especially." For the first time, I see fear in her eyes—not the mask of the confident woman she's always forced to wear.

"The couple you know as André and Phoebe have two very different personas," I explain. "One is admirable— global philanthropists and citizens of the world. The other is intolerable—crime lords and masterminds of all things SWARM.

"Tilda, your reputation for penetrating the dark web and demanding radical reform was at most a nuisance."

Tilda sits on the edge of her seat—eyes and mouth wide open, analyzing every detail of the conspiracy that fooled us all.

"But things got personal the day you published the Arete Report. Your mission was to recruit other influential CEOs to read the report and then join forces to institute dark web reform.

"Those words came as a declaration of war to André and Phoebe. If successful, your actions would destroy SWARM and sabotage plans to expand their financial empire and eventual global takeover.

"Under the pretense of philanthropy, they invested their fortune into the independent research and technology company ELIXIR. They knew ELIXIR possessed the brightest minds capable of creating future technology. They told the world they'd infiltrate the dark web, initiate reform, and ultimately eradicate SWARM.

"With their trap set, the only thing left undone was to persuade you to leave your influential post at Arete and come join ELIXIR. But what would motivate you to leave your career and clout as CEO of one of the wealthiest companies in the world?

"They decided to kill your will for Arete by killing

William, then recruited you to ELIXIR. They promised that with ELIXIR's talent and their funding they'd pick up where the Arete Report left off.

"It was a match made in heaven or, in this case, hell. By night SWARM rose to power through a steady stream of global hacktivism that created a pandemic of fear. And by day ELIXIR positioned itself as the world's savior, the one and only answer for immunity to SWARM.

"Dark Day came off without a hitch. Clearly ill-equipped to deal with a human hack, the League of Nations granted ELIXIR autonomous status, empowering them to use whatever force necessary to eradicate SWARM.

"The past few weeks Cai started poking around and asking too many questions. They suspected he might be catching on to their conspiracy. By taking out Cai, they removed the threat, the only one capable of exposing their evil.

"The next day André met with the League of Nations to pitch their plan for beefing up security and plugging any further leaks SWARM may seek to exploit. With panic pumping through their veins, the League of Nations handed over the reins and approved ELIXIR's plan on the spot.

"This new plan dovetailed perfectly with the wii initiative, giving ELIXIR complete control of the world's population. Now they could hack the minds of anyone anytime, anywhere. Of course, they wanted us to believe we were vulnerable and that the wii initiative was only a temporary fix. So they pushed for ELIXIR Project as the long-term solution.

"But in reality they were scared—scared that EPs were unhackable, unaffected by the wii initiative, and immune to their evil. They wanted to eliminate us clerics, but only after discovering our secret and reproducing it for themselves.

"They isolated our supernatural abilities by having us achieve the three Verdicts, and by analyzing our data, they've created what's now in that silver box—the ELIXIR vaccine—humanity's only hope to experience true unhackability."

I look away from the camera and over at my friends.

"Damon, Karme, and Phoenix—there is no Boon and there never was. It was all a setup, from the moment we stepped inside the airport. That blond woman and her colleague were proxy actors. McNultey didn't dispose of them in that control room. This whole time he and Kiran wanted us to believe they were the good guys."

McNultey smirks—not about to deny or confirm my accusation.

"Now SWARM has nothing and no one in their way. They can divide humanity into 'hack camps' and use us however they please."

I stop to consciously breathe for the first time since I started the speech. I don't know how long I've talked or exactly what I said. All I do know is I spoke my truth, even if certain parts of it were no more than a hunch. I trusted my gut and my heart. Before I have time to evaluate the expressions on the faces of the Senior Board of Clerics, the proxies, or my friends, I hear it.

It begins quietly—so quietly I can't discern what *it* is. A cry? Or maybe a cough? But then I feel it, deep in my gut. An ominous laugh.

CHAPTER
SIXTY-TWO

"THAT'S THE MOST fantastic tale I've ever heard," Phoebe says. "Too bad you're dead wrong. Tilda's the mastermind behind SWARM, not me."

"Quiet, Phoebe," Edge warns, jamming the barrel into her temple. A proxy in the front row leans forward like he's going to stand up.

BAM!

Edge fires a bullet straight into his forehead. The force of the impact jerks the proxy off the bench and into a heap on the floor.

"Next time it's Phoebe!" Edge yells. "I'm not bluffing." The proxies in the room sit taller.

"Aryedne said her truth. And now you can have yours."

"Can you loosen your grip around my neck first?" Phoebe asks.

"Not a chance," he says. "I'm sure you'll find a way to speak. Your life depends on it."

"I'll do my best," she says, clearing her throat. "Hear me when I say Tilda is a master manipulator. My husband and I had no idea of these tendencies when we recruited her.

"Make no mistake—SWARM is a formidable enemy. Aryedne is right about that. And Tilda's son was abducted, abused, and killed by SWARM. But where her story breaks down is the accusations about André and I living a dual persona. Do you really believe what you're saying? Us playing both sides of the fence? SWARM *and* ELIXIR? I'm flattered you think I'm brilliant enough to pull off something as sophisticated as deceiving the entire human race.

"Try this for a more plausible explanation. Tilda joined us to take down SWARM, but in the process she got too close. She studied SWARM obsessively, looking for cracks, flaws, and points of entry. Over time she made connections with SWARM to get more intel. But Tilda started bonding with her son's murderers as a way of coping. She developed feelings of trust and affection for SWARM's leader because it gave her an emotional connection to the memory of her son. She justified her actions because it helped her make sense of the chaos in her mind. Classic Stockholm Syndrome combined with several other mental disorders.

"This whole ELIXIR vaccine was her idea—her passion project, she called it. André and I gave her complete oversight and simply followed her lead, trusting her abilities the whole time. The truth is she's now SWARM's puppet, and they're pulling the strings."

CHAPTER
SIXTY-THREE

"TILDA GETS ONE opportunity to defend her reputation," Edge says. "But as her personal assistant for several years, let me say that I can vouch for her unblemished character."

We turn to Tilda. She sits slumped, arms around herself, rocking back and forth, muttering something.

"Tilda," Edge says, trying to communicate with his unresponsive boss. He tries louder. "Tilda, it's your chance to share your truth!"

"And you doubt me?" Phoebe asks. "This woman is clearly mentally ill. And the way Edge protects her makes me suspicious of him, too."

"Or there's another explanation," I reply. "A number of facts don't add up. Perhaps you can enlighten us?"

"Try me," Phoebe says.

"Erida specifically told me she had acrophobia.

Someone deathly afraid of heights would never climb the steel truss in the field house. And yet she claimed the suicide pact was her idea."

"What are you saying?" Phoebe asks.

"I'm saying you found a way to plant that idea in her mind. You killed her and then you tried covering it up. You told us clerics their suicides were a result of 5X-ing our neuroplasticity. And yet science proves there are no drawbacks to neuroplasticity."

"Impossible!" Phoebe screams.

"And what about Lelantos? He knew the penalty for going online. There's no way he'd risk elimination. You baited him by making the initial contact from SWARM. Then you set up the transport and decapitated him, Pallas, and Styx."

"Lies," Phoebe argues. "You have no proof. I've had enough, Edge. Your gun can't handle all these proxies. After the ceremony you'll be tried in court, punished for your insubordination, and probably executed. You can shoot me, but you can't stop all of them."

Her words find their mark. "Phoebe has a point, Aryedne. Do you have absolute proof for your claims?" Edge asks.

"Proof?" I say. "SWARM killed your kids when you refused to work for ELIXIR. Then once you did, your wife dies in a random car accident? Open your eyes, people. This is their MO."

"Proof, Aryedne—we *need* proof!" Edge pleads. He can't hold a gun against her head forever, and Phoebe's right. There are too many proxies for us to fight.

"You want proof?" I shout. "Fine. Two final questions, Phoebe. Would you agree that a mother never forgets the name of her daughter?"

"Of course. But I don't see the relevance of your question."

"What was her name?"

"The name of my daughter? Why?"

"Answer the question, Phoebe," Edge threatens, digging the barrel into her head.

"*Kale*. Her name was Kale."

"I thought you might say that. And that's why no one should trust a word you're saying." I reach inside my dress and pull out husheye. "In Phoebe's own words, I have the proof you need."

"What's that?" Kiran asks.

"A device Cai designed with only two purposes—recording and jamming."

"I never saw you record me," she says.

"Thanks to auto-elixir technology, I turned it on before the Focus Verdict when you made me uneasy by speaking about my deceased mother. In your own words, you told me I reminded you of your daughter *Kore*. You just said it yourself. A mother would never forget the name of her daughter."

"You're bluffing," Phoebe barks. "She's lying, I tell you."

"Why don't I press Play and let the global audience be the judge?"

Phoebe panics and starts speaking without thinking.

"You could have twisted my words. You could have hacked my phone or my computer. Everything can be hacked—"

"Even the truth." I finish her sentence for her.

She closes her lips tightly before a wave of fury comes over her face. I stare at her defiantly, not about to back down. Her eyes shift to fire. And just like the spider from the Flow Verdict, I know she won't stop until she devours me.

Tilda makes the first move. From the seated position in her chair, she uses the nearest weapon she can find— her tablet. With both hands, she winds up and smacks it across Kiran's face, shattering the glass and breaking his nose. Red blood spurts everywhere.

McNultey doesn't waste a second. He draws his gun and shoots three bullets into Tilda's chest.

Startled by the blast, Edge's finger trips his trigger, sending a bullet through Phoebe's brain. Her body flops off her chair and onto the floor.

Time morphs into a series of freeze-framed scenes. Damon jumps from his seat and dives toward the altar, slamming his fist onto the orange button on the remote.

The electromagnetic force field engages instantly, separating those of us on the platform from all the proxies.

"Freeze! And drop your weapon," McNultey says with his gun drawn and pointed in our direction. Edge hesitates. "Too bad those pistols only hold two bullets." The senior officer smirks. "Looks like you're out. Move and you're dead—all of you." Edge's gun slams to the hardwood floor. "You've served your purpose by creating the vaccine," McNultey says, "but now you're a liability."

My mind races. *This can't be the end.* We need an exit, but the front of the platform is sealed off by the force field separating all of us from a hundred furious proxies and their glowing skylatises. Our only chance is this hallway behind me.

If we die here, so does the hope of humanity. We gave SWARM the final piece they needed. With the ELIXIR vaccine in their possession, they're unhackable and so is their plan for world domination.

Edges glances at McNultey's gun, then back at me. His look tells me all I need to know.

McNultey doesn't realize what Edge is doing until he's already on him. I yank Damon's hand. He pulls Karme and Phoenix with him, and we all spill into the back hallway. I turn my head in time to see Edge's final act—a demonstration of love. Using his body as a human shield, he absorbs the rest of McNultey's clip from point-blank range.

I bite my lip and stumble trying to run and watch Edge's final moments at the same time. He falls onto the altar, then slides to the floor, his red blood streaking across the white linen tablecloth. Damon reaches down and drags me back to my feet. We scramble out the back door, knowing the proxies will be on us in seconds.

Adrenaline surges through my body, helping me forget everything else but escaping. We spot the Xcraft and run toward it, fully aware that our survival depends on starting it.

CHAPTER
SIXTY-FOUR

"It's asking for a security code!" Damon yells from the driver's seat.

"Hurry," Karme cries. "They'll be here any second."

"Just start punching in a bunch of numbers," Phoenix says.

"Don't!" I exclaim. "Enter an incorrect code twice and the entire vehicle shifts over to safe mode. Then it won't start at all."

"Okay then, we've got two tries," Damon says. "Any ideas?"

"ELIXIR," Karme yells.

"Yeah, yeah, try 'ELIXIR'!" Phoenix pressures.

He types in *E-L-I-X-I-R*.

"Incorrect. One try left!" Damon yells.

"They're here!" Karme shrieks.

From both sides of the church, proxies dressed in

black run toward us like a pack of wild dogs, white teeth clenched, poised to kill. "Look!" Phoenix points.

A large mass of soldiers spills onto the field in front of us, waving their skylatises and sprinting toward the Xcraft.

"What code should I try? 'André'? 'SWARM'?"

"No. No!" I say. "Let me try." From the passenger's seat, I type in the letters *A-L-E-T-H-E-I-A* and hold my breath. The engine roars to life.

"Go, go, go!" Phoenix commands.

Slowly, we ascend. A proxy leaps toward us, clinging to the side of the vehicle. Phoenix leans over and cracks him in the jaw. He yelps in pain and lets go.

Another proxy runs up his colleague's back and throws himself at the Xcraft, missing and banging his head. More and more come at us. Several proxies form a human ladder, bridging the gap between soil and sky. A female proxy holding a skylatis scales the bodies and hops onto the back of the Xcraft, towering above us.

Karme cups her ankle with her palm and heaves with all her strength. The proxy smacks the vehicle, dropping her skylatis next to her. Karme stands up in her seat, snatches it, and beats the proxy until she releases her grip and falls below.

The forward thrust finally engages, and we propel away from the proxies and the campus. After about a minute, Phoenix says, "*That*...was close." He uses his hand to wipe the sweat from his head.

"You're not kidding," Damon says. "Where to?"

"Cleveland Clinic. Cai is the one person who can help us—if he's still alive," I say. I reach down to my side. "Shoot! I can't believe I forgot it."

"What? This...?" Karme waves the silver box in the air.

"When did you...?"

"I grabbed it in the commotion. You know—when everyone was getting killed," Karme says.

"Well...aren't you going to open it?"

"No. If anybody deserves to open the box, it's you," she says, handing it to me.

I turn the mirrored box in my hands. Although it weighs a mere pound or two, the weight in my gut is overwhelming. Maybe because this box required the blood of eight of my fellow clerics? Or maybe because SWARM almost got its hands on the vaccine?

I still have so many questions, and my hands won't stop shaking.

"I can't open it," I say. "I—I'm afraid."

Damon reaches for my hands to steady them. "You've been through a lot, Aryedne. We all have. But a beautiful redhead once told me something."

"Oh, yeah? What did she say?"

"She said she joined ELIXIR Project to discover the truth."

"Some good that did," I say sarcastically.

"Well then, can I remind you of something our friend Edge told us?"

"Only if it makes me feel better."

"Fear no one but truth."

"I hate it when you're right," I say, slugging him in the shoulder.

"You don't have to hit me for it," he laughs.

I open the silver box, expecting to find the ELIXIR vaccine. But it's empty—except for a note.

First, congratulations are in order. I knew you'd find a way to escape.

As you now know Tilda fulfilled her purpose by gaining public trust and creating ELIXIR Project. Phoebe fulfilled her purpose by bonding with you throughout the Verdicts. Once they fulfilled their purposes, we did what SWARM does—eliminated them.

The only reason you and your three friends are alive is that you still serve a purpose.

Chevon and I are currently enjoying the benefits of unhackability, thanks to you and the vaccine. We'll take this knowledge and leverage it into world domination. You've done us a deep service by achieving the Verdicts, and for this, SWARM is grateful.

Naturally, we'd never risk sending the vaccine to the Boon Ceremony. By masterminding the events the way we did, we created even more fear in the hearts and minds of the world. Fearful people are foolish people, and SWARM loves to prey on the foolish.

You were wrong about one thing, though. There is still a Boon waiting for you and your friends—IF you're successful. Aryedne—you especially will find your heart's desire well worth the wait. And trust me when I say this: Boons are one thing I never lie about. You've done the work and you'll be compensated if you finish well.

You're probably headed to Cleveland to find Cai and more answers. We'll be waiting for you there.

—André

I set the letter down in my lap.

"How do we know once we've fulfilled our purpose he won't eliminate us, too?" Karme says.

"We don't," I say calmly.

"So why go to Cleveland?" Phoenix asks. "Why not just take this Xcraft and run away somewhere?"

"And what? Go to the beach while the world goes to hell?" Damon snaps.

"Take it easy, man. It was just an idea."

"I know. I know." Damon gazes out the window at the night sky. "It's like he was just a few steps ahead of us the entire time."

"That's an understatement," Karme says. "If Aryedne didn't keep pace, I'd hate to think what would've happened to us back at the ceremony.

"Honestly, I think we haven't even scratched the surface," I reply.

"What do you mean?" Phoenix asks.

"I know it might sound crazy, but I'm telling you, there's something to this whole unhackability thing. That was our first shot at experimenting with the Verdicts, and look at the results. Imagine what might be possible."

"That's what scares me, though," Damon says. "The same potential that's pumping through our veins is now pumping through Chevon's and André's, too."

"You're right," Phoenix moans.

"Sounds like we'll find more answers in Cleveland.

And we can't save the world tonight anyway," Karme says.

Damon and I chat for the next half hour about whatever comes to mind. I think we both need an emotional release from all the stress surrounding the past few days. I laugh at his stories, and he listens to my thoughts. After awhile, when I don't hear anyone talking in the backseat, I turn around. Karme is sleeping with her head on Phoenix's lap.

"I don't know how they can both sleep. My mind is going a million directions after reading a note like that."

"I hear you." Damon smiles. "But I've got a trick. It helped me through the Verdicts. Want to hear my secret?"

"Oh, now you're going to tell me?" I tease.

"You know what they say. Third time's a charm."

"Yeah, and nothing is going to interrupt you this time," I say.

"Well, in that case, here's my big secret. The one thing I focused on to help me get through the Verdicts was…you."

Then he leans down and kisses me. And this time I kiss him back.

I think I'm finally ready to create a new story.

ACKNOWLEDGMENTS

Simply put, this book required every ounce of my being. Without help from these (and others), there would be no *ELIXIR Project*.

SOUL:

- Grace: Inspired by the Father, accomplished through the Son, and distributed by the Spirit. Without you I am nothing....Unending gratitude.

HEART:

- Kelly: Truth teller, wife, and mother extraordinaire. Who knew we'd be here after that first chat in grad school? The wild ride keeps going. You're beautiful.

EMOTION:

- Keegan, Isabel, Addison: My sports buddy, my artist, and my cuddle bug. You're why I keep fighting and showing up, filled up. I believe in you and your dreams.

MIND:

- Mihaly Csikszentmihalyi, Steven Kotler, Jamie Wheal, Marc Goodman, Cal Newport, and many others: Your work planted mental seeds that grew into ELIXIR trees.

BODY:

- Chet Scott and 3P warriors: The acute pain we earn in the basement, paid for by blood and sweat, supplies me with the strength I need to do projects like these.

HANDS:

- David Branderhorst: My talented business partner who's equally as passionate to achieve our moonshot: one million souls ignited by 2020.

EYES:

- Molly O'Neill for showing the way. Julie Scheina, Christine Ma, Joel Kessel, Nannette O'Neal, Monica Coleman, Chris Guyot, and Chris O'Byrne of JETLAUNCH (book interior designer extraordinaire): Your attention to detail made this project even better than I imagined.

EARS:

- Focus@will and Twenty One Pilots: For the lyrical and musical feast that filled my inspirational appetite when I needed it most.

WILL:

- To you: Without your support, there would be no influence or impact. I wake up every day on fire, ready to invest in you.

About the Author

KARY OBERBRUNNER is **Igniting Souls**. Through his writing, speaking, and coaching, he helps individuals and organizations clarify who they are, why they are here, and where they should invest their time and energy.

Kary struggled finding his own distinct voice and passion. As a young man, he suffered from severe stuttering, depression, and self-injury. Today a transformed man, Kary invests his time helping others **experience unhackability** in work and life.

He is the founder of Redeem the Day, which serves the business community, and Igniting Souls, which serves the nonprofit community. He and his wife, Kelly, are blessed with three amazing children and live outside Columbus, Ohio.

About the Publisher

Kary Oberbrunner and David Branderhorst created Author Academy Elite in 2014 rather by accident. Their clients kept asking for a program to help them write, publish, and market their books the right way. After months of resisting, they shared a new publishing paradigm one evening in March on a private call. They had nothing built and knew it would take six months to implement that idea and create a premium experience.

Regardless of the unknowns, twenty-five aspiring authors jumped in immediately, and Author Academy Elite was born. Today Author Academy Elite attracts hundreds of quality authors who share a mutual commitment to create vibrant businesses around their books. Discover more about the model at AuthorAcademyElite.com.

COMMUNITY | CONTENT | CONVERSATION

YOUR UNVEILING AWAITS

ELIXIRPROJECTBOOK.COM

YOU'VE READ THE BOOK.

ARE YOU READY FOR THE EXPERIENCE?

FLAWLESS IDEA ANATOMY
DELIBERATE MAGNETIC FOCUS
OPTIMAL HUMAN PERFORMANCE

IDEA | FOCUS | FLOW

IT'S TIME FOR YOU TO BECOME UNHACKABLE.
ACCESS YOUR FREE TRAINING TODAY.

ElixirProjectExperience.com

CPSIA information can be obtained
at www.ICGtesting.com
Printed in the USA
LVOW04*0048130117
520818LV00005B/30/P